Dec 2012

Martha, the author,
has been my
friend for over 30
years. She's an
excellent writer —
love —
Sharon

The Body
at Cutwater Creek

Martha S. Sargent

QA, Inc.
Bend, Oregon

ISBN-13: 978-0-9825230-3-2
ISBN: 0982523033

Cover photograph by Dennis J. Sargent

ACKNOWLEDGEMENTS

Special thanks to my reviewers (Trish Bradbury, Judy Kafka, and Sharon Ross) for your enthusiasm, advice, helpful suggestions and earnest encouragement. And, to retired Police Chief Ron Devoid, for your insights into police work.

Heartfelt thanks to my husband, Dennis, who has been in on this project since the long car ride when the story was hatched. Thanks for listening, for reviewing my manuscript, for lending me your male perspective, for the cover photograph—and for years of friendship and love, supporting me and my dreams.

This book is dedicated to my mother, Shirley Regan, who told me many times, "Don't just stand back and watch. Join in." And, here I am. Thanks, Mom!

PROLOGUE

The afternoon started out ordinary enough, although far too hot for June. Women shut windows and pulled blinds. Ranchers stroked chestnut horses and checked supplies. Kids tugged on swimsuits as their mothers filled blue plastic pools with tepid water from the garden hose. The Little League coach grimaced as he sorted through bats and balls, swore it'd be the last year he'd sacrifice prime fishing time to hollering at kids, parents hollering at him.

Ordinary folks, doing ordinary things.

On the day the Bakers' dog dug up the body.

The ten-year-old Baker twins trudged through thick gravel along Cutwater Creek, yelling for Rex to quit barking, whistling for him the way their daddy taught them: lips clamped on two fingertips, a deep inhale and expulsion of breath, a satisfied nod at the shrillness. The black Lab paid no mind, yapping and hunkering and circling and pawing the ground in a wide spot twenty yards ahead where spring runoff deposited silt and debris.

"Weather sure is changeable," Annie O'Connor said as she warmed Art Bucknell's coffee and nodded to Pete Morgan, who slouched in a vinyl chair and held a hand over his half-filled ceramic mug.

"Hell," Pete grumbled, "I just shoved my longies in a drawer and here we are like it's middle of August."

"Coffee's the best drink on hot days," Art declared. "Cools you right down."

"So you've told me," Annie said as she set the pot on the burner and peeked at the *Enjoy Coca Cola* wall clock, frowning at the secondhand lazily tick-tocking past Roman numerals, willing three o'clock to hurry, when she could shoo Art and Pete out the door and flip the red and white sign from *Open* to *Closed*. She grabbed a terry dishcloth and wiped the countertop, more for something to do than it needing a polishing, since she'd already cleaned the robin's-egg speckled laminate a dozen times that afternoon. She paused to tuck a long strand of blonde hair behind her ear, another escapee from the knot she'd twisted and ineffectively fastened with a metal clip.

Sarah Montrose entered from the kitchen with short, timid steps; mouth slack, brown eyes wide. Art and Pete did not pause in their debate about the best engine coolant, Sarah's presence no more unusual or interesting than the fly buzzing at the wood-framed picture window stenciled *Bluebell Café*.

Annie waited for Sarah to pivot her way, nodded toward the kitchen. Sarah glanced at the patrons before slipping back through the doorway as Annie focused on the glass refrigerated case hosting remnants of the day's fresh-baked goods: a single piece of peach pie, a half-dozen oatmeal cookies and, as usual, only crumbs on the cinnamon roll tray. She reached under the counter for a spray bottle of window cleaner.

The Baker twins plodded to within ten feet of Rex before Timmy halted and pointed at something protruding from the ground. What's that? he asked. What's what? responded Tommy, wrinkling his nose like he did when sniffing the foul ranch odors where their daddy worked, edging past his brother to peer at the ground Rex pawed.

Kitty Anderson lumbered behind the bar in the Roadside Tavern, breathing hard. She shoved a paper napkin down her flowing purple kaftan to mop perspiration beaded between fleshy breasts, not caring if anyone noticed, age and reputation bestowing the freedom to do as she damn-well pleased. Like refusing to turn on the damned air conditioner and run up her electric bill. "Reminds me of the summer of '75," she said to two ranch hands sipping beer from chilled mugs they occasionally touched against their faces like ice packs. "That was a scorcher. You boys are too young to remember."

The Baker boys darted around shrubby oaks and cottonwood trees, scrambled up the bank to the narrow canyon road where they'd dropped their mountain bikes,

Rex finally leaving his find to race past them. Tommy tripped in his haste, ignored a skinned knee as he mounted his bike. Timmy stood on the pedals and pumped down the road.

Police Chief John Norton adjusted the cheap drugstore reading glasses that were forever slipping down his wide, flat nose and tried to focus on the papers strewn across his desk. Too many lawyers in the world, that's the problem, he thought, and squirmed in his black swivel chair. Got nothing to do but make my life miserable. His phone rang and he peered into the outer office, willing one of his staff to take the call. On the third ring, he sighed and reached for the receiver.

The twins skirted the parking lot of Annie's café, intent on the only destination imaginable: home and their daddy. Bikes clattered to the ground and the boys surged to the front porch where their mother lazed in a creaky rocker that had been in the family for three generations. Hush, she admonished; hadn't she told them time and again their father needed peace and quiet on Saturday afternoons? Tommy flung open the screen door and let it slam behind him.

Art and Pete pushed coffee mugs aside, gathered their ball caps and bid good day to Annie. "Stay cool."

"You do the same." She followed behind them to bolt the door and swivel the sign in the window, even if it was only a quarter to three.

Kent Baker gradually came out of his slumber and focused on his boys, initially unconcerned, knowing their vivid imaginations. But the fear in Timmy's eyes convinced him to rise from the couch, stride to the bedroom and grab the truck keys off the dresser.

Annie counted money from the till, tucked bills into a vinyl bank deposit bag and scribbled the day's take in a ledger.

Kitty Anderson cleared glasses from the bar when the two ranch hands swiveled on their stools, set pointy boots to the wood floor and ambled out the front doorway.

Kent Baker parked where the twins had earlier left their bikes, not totally convinced they'd seen what they thought, but wary nonetheless.

Teens slumped on couches in television trances.

Reverend Kowalski greeted the ladies who'd come to discuss the Fourth of July celebration.

Women surveyed the contents of their refrigerators, wondered what in the world they'd fix for supper without turning on the oven and heating the whole house.

Chief Norton pulled the office door closed and hurried to his truck, intent on responding to the fender-bender report he'd received.

On the day the Bakers' dog dug up the body.

CHAPTER 1

Detective Zack Dalton stared through the windshield of the Ford Fiesta, killed the engine and sat a moment, drumming his fingers on the steering wheel. Three years of drudgery—chasing flimsy leads like cottonwood seed in a swirling breeze, not catching a single break.

Until now.

How ironic. His hope for solving the case had diminished with each exasperating dead end. Now, here he was in Hope, Oregon, with his best chance for success.

He eased his long limbs out of the car, knees complaining of being scrunched on the seven-hour drive, scalp clammy with sweat, blue oxford shirt sticking to his back. He stretched his arms overhead and regarded the low-slung building in front of him. Grey cement blocks supported a red corrugated metal roof, three concrete steps led to a narrow porch and bulky wood door. Built in the post-war expansion era, he guessed, when companies constructed small towns to house mill workers. He twisted to scan the buildings lining the two-laner he'd followed after turning off the main highway. Like the shuttered lumber mills on the outskirts of town, the downtown buildings were dilapidated testimony of more prosperous times.

He squared his shoulders and trudged up the steps, eyes trained on the wooden sign hanging on the wall: *Police Department, Hope, Oregon.* A blast of cold air hit him as he stepped inside.

"Shut the door."

Zack pulled it to behind him, shivering in the abrupt change of temperature.

"Finally got the dang-blamed air conditioner working. No sense letting heat in."

Zack's eyes adjusted to the dim light in the rectangular room and he focused on the portly man standing by a large metal desk. Hairy forearms protruded from the short sleeves of his silver-tan uniform shirt, bushy brows were raised above hooded eyes that regarded Zack like a Great Dane might a yappy poodle—intrigued yet leery. The man crossed his arms across his bulky chest, lips pursed beneath his grey mustache.

Waiting.

A power play, Zack knew, because he'd played it himself. See who blinks first. He set his square jaw and returned the stare with expressionless green eyes.

Finally, the man gestured Zack to follow, walked into an adjacent office and plopped into a black leather chair behind a gunmetal-grey desk, apparently satisfied he'd effectively sent the message of who was in charge.

Round One to the chief.

"Zack Dalton, sir. We spoke on the phone," he said and extended his hand across the desk.

Police Chief John Norton pumped the proffered hand. "I know who you are. Got city written all over you."

Zack shrugged. "This surely isn't San Francisco."

"Thank God for that."

"You have no idea how much I agree."

Norton regarded him a moment, watery blue eyes probing until he sat back and tented his hands. "Shall we get to business?"

Round Two for Zack.

"Your show, sir."

Norton huffed and rolled the chair backwards to grab a manila file from atop a veneered particleboard credenza. "You can drop the 'sir'. Gets no points from me. Chief will do. John, if you're of mind." He returned to the desk, slipped black-rimmed glasses crookedly on his nose before flipping open the file cover and reading from the report within. "Body was found five days ago by two lads at Cutwater Creek. Seems their dog dug until a bloody arm was exposed. Probably haunt those boys many a night. They hustled home to their father, who called it in."

"Body still at the morgue?"

"As requested, Detective Dalton."

"Zack will do, if you're of mind."

A sharp look from the older man before he said, "Don't have an official morgue or a full-time medical examiner. Just Gerald Foster, a local doc who's the coroner when we need him, which isn't often. But, yes, he's got the body in a proper environment over at the funeral home."

"I'll want to examine it."

"Nothing much to see besides what's in the report, but you're welcome to look. Cause of death was gunshot to the upper chest. Severed an artery."

"Other trauma? Signs of a struggle?"

"Nope. Powder burns on the clothing and the nature of the wound indicate the shot was close range. Far as Doc Foster can tell from lividity and insect activity, death occurred ten to twelve hours before the dog found him, which would be four to six o'clock that morning."

"Witnesses?"

"None what's come forward."

"Anybody hear the shot?"

"We're still asking around but nothing yet. Body was a mile up Canyon Road. Little reason to be there. No good campsites. Fishing, maybe, but no signs of gear. Nearest place is the Bluebell Café, which was closed at that hour. Talked with the three people who live on the property. Nothing."

"Did you secure the scene?"

Norton stabbed the air with a thick finger. "What the hell do you think?"

Zack raised both hands in surrender. "Sorry. No offense intended."

"We don't handle many murders in this office, but that don't mean we don't know how."

"My mistake."

"Damn right." Norton leaned over the desk and tapped the folder. "Got everything documented according to Hoyle. It's true I don't have the resources to conduct this investigation alone, but the only reason I haven't turned the case over to the state police is your phone call begging me to wait." He relaxed back in the chair, seemingly satisfied he'd rightfully defended his integrity.

Zack fought to squash impatience. He needed to gain the chief's cooperation, but between his blunders and the man's defensiveness, it was not clear how.

"Called your supervisor."

Zack grimaced and stared at a bulletin board on the wall, overlapping papers haphazardly push-pinned to the cork.

"Sergeant Cory McKesson, San Francisco PD. She said your visit here is not official. Said you're on vacation."

"She stands behind me."

"Said that, too." Norton fiddled with a paperclip he'd released from reports in the file. "Which begs the question of why a big city detective is sitting at my desk unofficially investigating a murder with his supervisor's blessing."

Zack rose and walked to a dusty window, peered past the dried-blood smudge of a swatted insect and frowned at the tuna-can Ford Fiesta baking in the sun.

The time had come to choose his approach with the police chief. He'd imagined many scenarios as he covered the miles to this remote southern Oregon town, wanting to meet the man before deciding whether to lay his cards on the table or hold them close to his chest.

Norton leveled the same haughty stare that had scrutinized Zack when he first entered the office. "Frankly, I don't have much to solve this crime. No weapon, no witnesses or evidence to speak of. 'Cept one thing."

Zack felt a tingle of anticipation. "Yeah?"

"You."

He narrowed his eyes and returned Norton's glare.

The chief's lips curled smugly before he spoke. "Found identification in the dead man's belongings for Edward Freeman and two other names. Ran them all. Zilch. Phony as a Chinese Rolex. So, I had the state boys run the prints. Bingo. Edward Riordan, formerly a resident of San Francisco. Long rap sheet, although nothing in the last five years. No wanteds. Thought I was staring at a dead end. Until you called."

Zack swiped a hand along the sticky cooled sweat on his neck.

Norton spun the paperclip in his fingers. "You didn't drive up here to enjoy my company. I figure you can tell me about Riordan, help me determine who had a reason to shoot him." He smirked and hooked a thumb on the waistband of his trousers. "Don't think I'm some country dumbass awestruck by a big city badge and a cocky attitude. I've been around more blocks than you've seen. You want something. I might be willing and able to help, but this is not a one-way street."

Round Three to the chief.

Zack lowered himself into the scratchy, stiff-backed chair fronting the desk. "You called the department to check on Riordon. The officer you spoke with knew I'd be interested."

"Even though Riordan wasn't wanted on charges?"

"Should've been," Zack snapped, pulse quickening as always when he thought about the fiasco three years earlier; about political and financial influence and a sniveling police chief without the balls to stand by his detectives. "Riordan shot my partner."

***

It had been his first shootout.

Certain details played vividly in Zack's memory: the thump as Lonnie went down, the woman's screams, the back door swinging wide on the speeding van, bullets pinging on metal. Details that haunted; not ones that solved a crime.

Some old-timers on the force enjoyed recounting their first engagement with shots fired. How time elongated yet collapsed, minutes and seconds in a slow-moving haze that exploded in a heartbeat. How obscure details flashed through the chaos—the panic in a gunman's eyes, the shout of a witness, the acrid smell of gunpowder. They spoke of fingers pulling triggers before consciousness registered the consequences, training kicking in before the horror of spilling blood.

Zack had listened, but did not truly understand until the botched ransom drop when Lonnie Wittenberg was shot.

Often, upon waking, he mentally replayed the scene, searching for clues buried deep in his subconscious, willing himself to remember. When nothing new was revealed, he'd rise from bed disgusted, embarrassed he'd missed details he now needed to apprehend the gunmen.

"My partner and I were assigned to a missing person case," he said to Norton. "Not something we typically handled, but the regulars were tied up. The missing woman's sister called it in and was very persistent. The captain wanted her off his back. But before we could do much, the husband said it was all an embarrassing mistake. Claimed she left him."

Norton raised an eyebrow. "You didn't believe him."

"Lonnie didn't. Said the guy made his gut hurt. I was a rookie detective, so I trusted my partner. Lonnie argued that the case smelled, but no one would listen. The husband's a heavy hitter who pulled political strings."

"You were ordered to drop it."

"In no uncertain terms."

"Did you?"

Zack sucked in a big breath. "We were going to. Lonnie was protecting me; said no use making enemies early in my career. So, we drove to the husband's office to return some photos and docs we'd gathered. He was coming out as we arrived and his manner made Lonnie's gut hurt even more. We followed him to his bank. He went in carrying a briefcase, which appeared heavier when he came out."

"You figured payoff."

Zack shrugged. "Or, he'd killed his wife and was skipping. Tailed him to an abandoned industrial site, where he exited his vehicle, briefcase in hand. We parked and approached on foot from behind a warehouse. A white van was the only other vehicle. The back doors opened and two masked men and a woman emerged."

"Your partner had a smart gut."

He shifted in the chair, looked up and scowled at acoustic tiles overhead. If only his gut had been as smart as Lonnie's; or, even smarter. "The kidnappers ordered the husband to place the briefcase on the ground and back off. Things got crazy."

The confrontation had been a collision of split-second decisions; changing any one of them might have altered the final outcome. If the husband hadn't tried to be a hero, hadn't pulled a gun. If the kidnappers hadn't panicked. If Lonnie hadn't run to help the screaming woman.

"Your partner?" Norton imposed upon Zack's silence.

"Walks with a slight limp but he's okay."

"The woman?"

"Fine." Zack closed his eyes a moment. "There was a driver in addition to the two perps we saw. They got clean away."

"And, I have one on ice."

"Never could prove it."

"Which is why no warrants."

Zack's brows knit in anger. "There was a full manhunt at first. You know how it is when an officer is shot. Didn't last long. The husband wanted the case closed. Chief shut us down."

"But you never let it go."

He allowed silence to answer for him.

"You aren't here just to confirm that Riordan is the man you sought and is now quite dead."

Zack sat forward, clenched a fist on the scarred desk. "I want the other two."

"You figure investigating his death may lead you to them."

He braced for another stand-off in their battle of wills. Go ahead, he thought, kiss me off, block me from the investigation. I'll proceed without you.

Norton ran a hand over his bushy moustache before he picked up the reports, tapped them into a neat stack and replaced them in the manila file, which he handed to Zack.

***

Chief Norton was right—his documentation appeared in order. Zack scanned the coroner's report and photos for a detail he hoped to find, exhaled softly as he found it: black spider tattoos on the dead man's left wrist.

At this point, he preferred to hear what the chief had to say; he'd read the reports later. He waited until Norton finished talking with an officer in the outer room and returned to sink into his chair. "Riordan live around here?" Zack asked.

"Nope. Showed up three days earlier."

"Awfully quick to make a stranger mad enough to pull a trigger."

"Can happen," Norton replied.

"You find anyone who knew Riordan before he came to town?"

"No, but maybe they're not owning up, now that he's got himself killed."

"Can happen."

A glare from the older man. "Could've been an accident," Norton said. "Shooter too scared to step forward."

"Someone could have followed him here. Any other strangers in town?'

"Just you."

Zack brushed the answer aside. "He might have come to meet someone."

"That'd be the best scenario for you, wouldn't it?"

He thought of denying the accusation, but decided this was one bluff he shouldn't make. "Frankly, I can't figure much else in this town to attract him."

Norton's head snapped up as he started to speak.

Zack stopped him with outstretched hands. "No offense. Just doesn't match his profile. Riordan was dirty to the core but small-time. He ran numbers and was convicted of theft and embezzlement. Tried countless get-rich-quick schemes, some of them even legal. He liked cities where he could disappear in a crowd."

"You figure he met the other kidnappers?"

"Makes the most sense."

"You don't think they randomly chose Hope."

Zack shook his head.

Norton frowned. "Folks around here are average citizens going about their daily business. Our crime is usually teenagers sowing their oats or older drunks getting too rambunctious. Occasional domestic violence, petty theft, vandalism. Seems a far cry from kidnapping."

"Someone's a murderer."

"Maybe." He chewed his moustache and stared above Zack's head, perhaps running through the citizenry in his mind, searching for someone capable of murder. He finally lowered his gaze. "What's your next step?"

"I'd like to examine the scene."

Norton ran a pudgy hand across his chin and sheepishly ducked his head. "About the crime scene. Kent Baker, the boys' father, called from the canyon to report finding the body. I've got one full-time officer, but he was laid up with the flu, and the part-timer on duty was with me responding to a traffic accident. Told Baker to sit tight, which he did, but seems his wife got worried and called her brother. Word spread until half the town went out to have a look-see. Footprints everywhere. Secured the scene as soon as possible but, mostly, it was too late."

This was the real reason for the man's opening animosity, Zack thought as he fought back an expletive. Couldn't be easy, could it? "Shell? Casing?"

"Bullet fragments found in the autopsy. Nothing usable. No casing, but Officer Jacobs is working a metal detector again as we speak."

"Let's go join him."

Norton pushed back his chair and stood, walked into the main office and selected a set of keys from a wall pegboard. He moved to a rack crammed with baseball caps and parkas and lifted a Stetson before eyeing Zack. "How much you into this thing?"

"I've got three weeks of vacation. I'm not leaving until I get answers."

"Or, hit a dead end."

Not going to happen, Zack vowed. Not this time.

"Being as you're not here officially, you can't flash a badge. You got a cover?"

Keep it simple, Lonnie had advised. "Freelance magazine reporter doing a spread on small-town law enforcement," he replied, as rehearsed.

Norton nodded. "Might work. Folks might open up if they think their name will be in print. You carrying?"

"Not at the moment."

"Last thing I need is more gunfire."

"Not my tendency, Chief, but you've got a killer out there. My weapon will remain secured unless needed."

"One more thing," Norton said as he settled the Stetson on his head and stared hard at Zack. "You were damned right when you said this is my show. Cross me and I'll kick your ass out of town. Clear?"

Zack nodded.

The stare continued until Norton led Zack into the afternoon heat.

CHAPTER 2

Zack stretched his legs in Norton's Ford F-150 as they pulled out of the police station parking lot, frowning again at the tuna-can Fiesta.

He should've driven his own car to Hope.

No way, Lonnie had insisted. You can't blow into a small town in a swanky Mercedes. You'll stick out like a sore thumb. And, why the hell spring for a rental car when I've got an extra vehicle? Here, take my keys.

Typical Lonnie.

Typical that Zack went along with his former partner's twisted logic.

Norton drove past a hodgepodge of crooked wooden structures, dusty and sagging, some with brick or stone facades, doorways sheltered by raggedy, faded blue awnings. Boldly painted signs heralded an attorney's office and a tax preparer and several storefronts for lease. A slender woman and two children emerged from an ice cream parlor, chocolate dribbling as the treat melted faster than the smaller child could lick.

Simple, Zack thought. Hope seemed like a simple town, the antithesis of San Francisco, with its medley of races and beliefs, politics and unending devotion to controversy; its miasma of exhaust and cooking oil and exotic spices, old money chic and new money glitz. Once, he'd found the concoction intoxicating, had explored neighborhoods and restaurants with curiosity and excitement; raised crystal goblets to squint at expensive crimson wines, hailed taxis outside theaters, bought suits perfectly tailored to his long frame and wide shoulders. Once, he'd thought he had everything a man could want. Him, a state college graduate from a middle-class neighborhood. An interloper in the wealthy world. A cop.

Stella Lundgren opened that new world to him; she taught him to scrutinize wine lists, finger fine wools, negotiate with uppity Mercedes dealers. He borrowed her money and her life, playing his role as handsome young husband to one of the city's top attorneys.

Now, dining at expensive restaurants like La Folie had morphed into take-out, theater openings into pay-per-view. He slogged through the city as the outsider he'd been before, deflecting thoughts of escape.

He scowled at the three bars on his cell phone's display. He should check in, see how she was doing; but, she'd been unhappy with his quick departure for Hope. Surely, she'd start in again if he called.

Later.

He powered off the phone and drummed his palm lightly on the armrest, impatient for the chance to finally identify the kidnappers.

They rode west on Main Street, Norton saluting other drivers with two fingers touched to the brim of his Stetson. He played tour guide. "Rexall on the left. Supermarket's up a block on the right. Jim's barber shop. Decent haircut if you stop him talking long enough. Bank's on the corner, county offices down this side street."

Maybe Norton was simply filling silence, or perhaps he was graciously initiating a stranger, although it wouldn't take more than ten minutes to discover every business in town. No, Zack got the feeling that beneath the chief's gruffness dwelled a soft spot for his town.

A half-mile past downtown, Norton slowed, hit the turn signal and nodded at a small one-story building with lap siding painted bright eggshell blue. "Bluebell Café, closest establishment to where Riordan was found."

Zack stared as they turned left on a road that edged by the property. A split-rail fence cordoned the café, a ranch-style house, a metal shed and three log cabins. The fence stretched a hundred yards along the road until halted by deciduous trees and pines climbing a hillside.

"Café's open for breakfast and lunch every day except Sunday. Annie O'Connor keeps those rental cabins, too. Riordan stayed in one of them." Norton steered with his right hand, used his left to point ahead. "This is Canyon Road. Heads south along Cutwater Creek about thirty miles before hooking up with a highway. Winding bugger. Not the quickest way to anywhere."

Black and tan basalt walls hugged the road on the west, while a short but sometimes steep east bank slumped to the creek below. The center line of the neglected asphalt was faded, the surface potholed with craters Norton swung wide to miss. After a downgrade that left them almost at creek level, he slowed and indicated a patrol car parked at a turnout. "Looks like he's still here." He eased the truck to the shoulder and nosed up to the car. "Which reminds me. I'll go along with your cover for all but Doc Foster and Officer Jacobs. They need to know the truth to do their jobs. I trust them both to keep it under their hats."

No use arguing, so Zack nodded. "What about Riordan's vehicle?"

"2005 Buick with Nevada plates, found back at the Bluebell."

"He walked out here?"

"Not much more than a mile."

"You said the coroner believes he died just before daybreak. Must have been dark, especially with these canyon walls blocking the sunrise."

"Must have been."

"Maybe he rode out with someone."

"Maybe." Norton killed the engine and pocketed the keys. They climbed out of the truck and Norton led the way ten yards beyond the turnout. "Baker boys followed this path."

Zack regarded the trampled ground, the bright green centers of snapped twigs and clumps of grass with flattened blades. "Why here?"

"What's that?"

"Why'd the boys choose this spot to go down to the creek? Something draw their attention?"

Norton scratched his chin. "Can't say. Path is pretty well used, that's for sure. We even brought the body up this way." He edged past. "Jacobs interviewed them. Let's ask him."

Shadows deepened as they descended the short distance to the creek bed, the sun slipping behind the canyon's western barrier. Finches chirped and darted between scrubby trees, swallows zigzagged overhead. Zack breathed in the earthiness of moisture sucked from manzanita and bitterbrush.

"Found him twenty yards ahead." Norton turned upstream, skirting jumbled, waterlogged fallen branches with more agility than Zack would expect from a heavy man who must be nearing retirement.

He followed as they trudged across fist-sized rocks, eventually reaching finer gravel in an area cordoned with yellow tape strung between orange traffic cones.

"Jacobs?" Norton hollered.

"Here," came the reply from a rock outcropping sheltered by a spindly oak. A uniformed man of average height emerged from behind the boulders with a tug at his zipper. "Nothing yet, Chief," he said as he approached, raising his sunglasses and securing them on top of thinning blond hair, blue eyes intent on Zack.

"This is Detective Zack Dalton, San Francisco PD."

Zack stepped forward to shake hands as he returned the officer's wary glare.

"I'll explain later," Norton continued. "For now, just know that Detective Dalton is familiar with the dead man and will be assisting in our investigation."

Another reminder to Zack of who was in charge.

"Walk him through."

"Yes, sir." Jacobs crunched across gravel to a hole dug in the middle of the cordoned area. "Body was buried here."

"Not deep," Zack remarked as he moved to stand beside the officer.

"Probably why the dog found him."

"Not a good place to bury a body you want to stay hidden. Any chance Riordan was shot somewhere else?"

"Coroner doesn't think so." Jacobs rubbed his whiskerless chin. "Blood pooled in the abdomen. If the body was moved, it happened soon after death, so we're supposing the deed was done in the vicinity. Lucky for the killer. The creek bank is one of the few places around where you can dig without hitting bedrock right away."

"Lucky or planned."

"Could be the killer intended to move the body later. Never got the chance."

"Could be. Where were his effects?" Zack asked.

"Wallet in his pocket. Pack of cigarettes. Nothing else but the clothes on his back."

"Car keys?"

"In his cabin at the Bluebell."

Norton addressed Jacobs again. "Detective Dalton wonders why this particular spot along the creek. You interviewed the boys, Baron. They say how they chose the path?"

"Just seemed easy."

The chief nodded to Zack. "Want more than that, you'll have to ask them yourself."

"I might." Zack pointed at reddish-brown blotches on the stones. "Blood concentrated in the hole?"

"Yep."

"I haven't examined all your photographs yet. Did you find drag marks? Distinguishable footprints?"

Jacobs hesitated and glanced at Norton, who folded his arms across his chest and nodded consent to continue. "Hard to tell. The ground was disturbed."

"So I've been told."

The officer's cheeks flushed as he started to rise to his chief's defense.

Norton intervened. "Never heard of a pristine crime scene. This one's no different. What's done is done. We work with what we've got."

Jacobs clenched his fists and watched the two men as if waiting for a signal to hustle the interloper out of the area.

Zack chided himself again for impatience. If he didn't need the old man, he'd kick him and his baby-faced officer out on their asses; but he had no jurisdiction, no rights in the investigation. Instead, his own ass was in danger of being kicked. He vowed to keep his thoughts to himself and emotions in check. "Continue."

Jacobs took his time responding. "We searched the scene, but found nothing of significance. Marked the location of blood. Not much of a pattern; probably disturbed when the body was buried."

Zack directed his gaze to Norton. "All Riordan's blood?"

The chief shrugged. "Tested quite a few samples, all type A negative, same as the victim. Can't say it's all his, but the type's rare enough to suppose so. Damn television shows got everyone focused on DNA evidence, which is too damned expensive. Give me the budget and I'll submit for more tests than you can shake a stick at."

"Understood," Zack replied. "Jurors expect you to solve cases with a scalpel and a microscope, not realizing the cost or how long tests take."

Besides, forensic investigation wasn't always the answer. As jurors and criminals and attorneys demanded physical evidence, police departments and academies increased training on ballistics and blood splatter and proper handling of a crime scene, which made for more efficient, by-the-book investigations. But, sometimes, as Lonnie often complained, investigators relied too heavily on textbook solutions, neglecting imagination, letting incorrect assumptions and interpretations lead them astray.

Snap on latex gloves, Lonnie would say, but don't snap off your mind.

Zack walked the area as Jacobs retrieved a metal detector. "How big a swath have you searched?"

"The shot was fired close range, but I've gone at least twenty feet."

Norton motioned to Jacobs. "Time you called it a day. Eleanor will have a conniption about overtime we can't afford." He removed his hat, ran a hand across the stubble of his buzz cut. "City treasurer believes her job is to ride my ass for every taxpayer penny." He snugged on the Stetson and turned to retrace his steps along the creek. "Don't have the manpower to guard the scene night and day. Doubt very much this tape is keeping folks out, so any evidence we find now will be tainted. Might as well remove it, Baron."

"What if," Zack began and the chief stopped, sporting an annoyed frown. "What if the shooting took place farther up the bank and the shooter carried the body down here where he could dig?" He pointed to a copse of scrawny birch jutting from a rock outcropping. "The casing might be up there."

Norton chewed his mustache a moment before shrugging and nodding to Jacobs. "No harm trying. Tomorrow."

***

Chief Norton marked two ticks on a tally sheet held by a magnet to the refrigerator door, profaning Eleanor's name and speculating on just where the bean counters might end their pesky days. He withdrew two colas and handed one to Zack.

An evidence box containing plastic bags was centered on Deputy Jacobs' tidy metal desk. "Been dusted and cataloged," Norton said. "Paw through all you like." He excused himself to answer the office phone, mumbling about how the hell his meager staff managed to be gone all at once and stick him with the phones.

The identification tag on one bag indicated the contents were found on the body: a crumpled pack with two broken Camels, a book of matches with *Woodsman Tavern, Hope, Oregon*, printed on the flap.

"West of town," Norton offered as he returned to stand by Zack. "Last place anybody's reported Riordan alive, leastways who's saying they saw him at all. He left around eleven o'clock. Not particularly drunk, although the bartender puts him there for a couple hours. Seems the man could hold his liquor. Witnesses say he headed east, direction of the Bluebell. No one saw or heard anything more."

The evidence bag also held a brown leather wallet, edges rubbed white and stitching loose, but stamped with a designer logo Zack knew to be expensive. A Nevada driver's license in the name of Edward Freeman was tucked inside, but the photo was of Riordan, pockmarked cheeks and bloodshot eyes recognizable, though he'd abandoned his customary goatee and thin mustache. Zack ran a finger along the laminate, checked for raised edges, glue lines or uneven surfaces, examined the printing for fuzziness. "High quality fake."

"Appears that way."

He set down the license and flipped through the empty wallet. "No credit cards?"

"Nope. Ought to be insurance cards, business cards, damn punch cards for Dunkin' Donuts. Nothing. Guy lived a simple life."

"Or a crooked one. Only ten dollars on him."

"Plus another twenty we found in his shave kit."

"Looks like Riordan had fallen on lean times."

"Which you figure he came here to rectify."

"I'm certain of it." Zack replaced the evidence and lifted another bag containing items found in Riordan's car. An Oregon map was creased open to the southeast quadrant, an uneven circle drawn in blue ink around the small dot representing Hope. He waved the map at Norton with indignation. "Definitely not an accident Riordan showed up here, which you've known all along."

Norton shrugged. "You're bound and determined to mold this case into the result you desire, namely that one or both of the other kidnappers met Riordan at the creek and shot him. I got no problem so long as that's the truth. Let's just say I'm allowing you to discover certain facts on your own, see what you make of them. Match my thoughts, probably got it right. Don't match, we keep looking."

Exactly how Lonnie would run the show and, therefore, how he'd run it himself since he'd learned most of the practical side of investigations from his former partner. But, he didn't like the tables turned and being the one in the dark.

Zack examined a basic black cell phone and a Nevada vehicle registration listing the owner as Edward Freeman with a Reno address.

Norton shook his head. "Checked with the Reno police. No such street. Phone appears to be fairly new. No contact numbers stored. Tried the recent incoming and outgoing numbers, but nothing of significance. I can talk with the district attorney about getting a full report, but that'll take some time."

The dead-ends were exasperating, as they had been for three years. Even before the kidnapping, Riordan had been a chameleon; changing names and addresses at the first sign of trouble, slipping past bill collectors, police and angry jilted lovers with a pocketful of identities and no emotional attachment to possessions, apprehended only when he let down his guard.

Which he'd apparently done for the last time by the creek.

The final bag contained effects from Riordan's cabin: car keys on a metal ring with shamrock-emblazoned green plastic fob advertising "Lucky's," receipt from the Bluebell Café and Inn for three nights lodging, cash paid in advance, checking out on the morning he was killed; crumpled back issue of *Time* magazine; two pair of pants, four shirts, underwear, socks and a brown suede jacket, expensive brands but well-worn. A ragged black leather toiletry kit held a razor and can of shaving cream, toothbrush and paste, a cheap comb missing several teeth, nail clippers and a small pocketknife.

Norton scratched his chin and pointed to the items stacked before them. "Belongings were neatly stored in the duffle, which was at the foot of the bed."

"Like he was packed to leave." Zack ran his hand along the inside of the duffle, tipped it upside down, dropped it to lift the toiletry kit. Something rattled. Noting a hole in the cloth lining, he used a pen to poke at an object lodged next to the seam, upended and shook the kit until a metal disk the size of a half-dollar clinked onto the desk.

"Well, now," Norton said as he bent to examine the etched silver, a swirl of leaves and flowers ringed with alternating points and scallops, a screw on the back side. "Concho."

"What's a concho?"

"What you're looking at. Decoration for leather goods, everything from hat bands to belts to saddles. Typical on cowboy gear."

"Strange thing for Riordan to carry."

"Doesn't match his belongings, that's for sure."

"Expensive?"

"Run from cheap knockoffs to custom design, like this one seems to be."

Look for the square pegs, Lonnie always said, the incongruities, the facts you can't jab into neatly aligned round holes. Something to be learned from square pegs.

Zack rotated the disk with the ballpoint, contemplating how Riordan had obtained the concho and why he'd squirreled it away. No reasonable, significant answer came to mind. "Want me to dust?"

"On my way," Norton said over his shoulder as he trudged to a closet at the back of the office. "But don't hold your breath. We dusted every inch of Riordan's belongings, his car, and the cabin. We got a smudged, unidentified partial from the wallet. Not clear enough to use. A couple solid prints from his room. Probably from the cleaning girl. The car was a mess. Lots of prints. None very clear and none identified, except Riordan's. County forensics team found fibers and hairs, none of which will do us any good without a suspect to match them to."

Zack stared a moment at the concho, then pushed the chair away from the desk, stood and replaced Riordan's effects in the evidence bags. "Guess I'll leave you to it."

Norton shuffled over carrying a cardboard box with fingerprinting equipment. "Suit yourself. Called Doc Foster. He's available first thing in the morning if you want to view the body."

Zack knew he'd not learn much by examining the body. Even a small-town, part-time coroner was bound to know more about gathering evidence from a corpse than a detective who'd spent most of his time working two-bit white-collar crime. Still, clues often turn up in the strangest places and he was itching for something concrete. "Sounds good," he replied.

"Meet me here half-past seven. I'll take you over."

"Okay. Where's the best place to stay in town?"

"Only got three. Starlight Motel's three miles east. Old Skinflint Lambert's not put a dime into the place since his missus died nine years ago. Wouldn't recommend it. The Budget Motel is better. And, there's the Bluebell."

"You said Riordan stayed in a cabin there?"

"Yep. The one in the middle."

Zack nodded and walked to the door.

"Remember," Norton called after him, "I'm cooperating with you because I don't like someone getting away with shooting a law enforcement officer. But, this is my investigation."

Zack raised his hand in salute and hurried out.

***

Zack rolled down the car window and drank in the soft, warm early-evening air as he drove through Hope and turned into an empty parking lot by the Ace Hardware store. He killed the engine and clamored out of the Ford before speed-dialing Lonnie.

"Yeah."

"It's me," Zack replied.

"Who the hell else would call me at home?" A bachelor, Lonnie claimed no family and few friends, notwithstanding poker buddies from the precinct, who were most useful, Lonnie was quick to explain, when he took their money every other Thursday night. He was contrary and opinionated, brusque and stubborn, and sharp as a tack. If only he'd given a rat's ass what others thought and not been so quick to express contempt for incompetence, the higher-ups might have stood by him after the shooting. "Tell me you got something."

"I'll view the body tomorrow and confirm for sure, but it's him."

"Locals let you in, huh?"

Zack watched a GMC ease by, the driver staring at him with curiosity. "Chief's no dummy. He'd already called McKesson, so I played for sympathy. Seems to have worked, although he'll keep the leash short."

Lonnie grunted. "You got a good internet connection?"

"Sporadic. Chief'll let me use an office computer, but it's not private, so I'm relying on you."

"Figured as much. Fire away."

Zack summarized what he'd learned, mildly surprised when Lonnie brushed off the contaminated crime scene, saying probably not much to learn there, anyway. "Riordan had a key chain from a place called Lucky's, most likely a casino. Might help pinpoint where he's been these past years."

"I'm on it."

"Not much else to go on."

"My gut's talking to me, Zack."

"Your gut's always talking, Lonnie."

"And it's usually dead on, right?"

Zack laughed and replied, "Sure." His own gut was screaming just as loud and clear as Lonnie's, which was why he'd worked on McKesson until she agreed to his vacation, why he'd stonewalled his wife's objections and wheedled his way into Norton's investigation. The bastards were close, he was sure. "Okay. I'll check in tomorrow."

Lonnie grunted again and disconnected.

Zack climbed back into the car, started the engine and drove slowly through town. He turned into the graveled lot of the Bluebell Café and Inn, parked and exited the Ford, noting the *Closed* sign in the café window. He walked around the side of the building, searching for an office.

The crunch of hurried footfalls on gravel made him turn.

A lanky, grizzle-faced man jabbed a shovel at Zack's chest.

He leapt to the side and shouted, "Hey!"

The man growled and retracted the shovel to take a swing.

CHAPTER 3

"Leroy!" Annie hurried down the porch steps as her scruffy friend reared to swing the shovel. "Stop!"

He turned at her voice, a split-second distraction. His target lunged, wrapped strong hands around the weapon and pulled. Leroy's feet skittered in the gravel as he fought to regain the shovel and his balance.

"Let go!" Annie demanded, heart pounding at the wildness in Leroy's wide eyes, the tensed muscles of the stranger's forearms, his jaw set in cold determination. She ducked her head as the metal blade wobbled in the tug-of-war, yanked on Leroy's arm until he released his grip.

She pulled Leroy Montrose back a few steps until he shrugged her off and bent to rest hands on thighs as he sucked awkward, wheezing breaths. Annie stared at the tall man now holding the shovel across his chest, narrowed eyes upon her, lips drawn in a thin angry line. She caught her breath and hoped she'd just thwarted the right person.

"What the hell was that?" he shouted.

Leroy rose and pointed a shaky finger. "You get off Miss Annie's property."

She leapt between the men, pressing her hand to Leroy's chest as he stepped forward. "What are you doing?"

"Caught this guy sneakin' 'round."

"I just want to rent a cabin, for Pete's sake."

"He's up to no good, I tell you."

"You're crazy, old man." The stranger set the blade on the gravel, cupped the handle with both hands and leaned on the tool.

Annie noted auburn hair swept in a cut that Jim Mitchell, the town barber, surely could not reproduce, and the crisp lines of a professionally laundered blue shirt. "Leroy's just a bit overprotective."

"Does he swing a shovel at everybody?"

"Only those I catch sneakin' 'round!"

Grabbing Leroy's arm and holding him still, Annie softened her voice and scanned his face until he made eye contact. "I don't think he was sneaking around, but thank you for being on guard." She nodded at the largest of the three log cabins flanking the parking lot. "Go on home. Everything's fine. Sarah's probably got your supper ready."

He mumbled and glared before shuffling unsteadily toward the cabin.

She turned to the man still leaning on the shovel. "Please accept my apologies. He meant no harm."

"That's not how I saw it."

"Well, there's not much I can do but apologize, which I've already done. If that's not enough, then perhaps you'd best leave."

His eyebrows rose at her reply.

Annie fought to stand her ground, to deny the sudden urge to race to her house, fling open the screen door and escape inside.

"I really did come to rent a room and I'm still interested, unless the maniac is going to attack me every chance he gets."

She motioned at the shovel. The man hesitated before relinquishing it. "I'll talk to him. He won't bother you." She strode to the café, leaned the tool against the bright blue wall and turned again to the man who gazed after her. "I've got two cabins available. One with a queen bed, the other two twins."

He pointed at the middle cabin. "Which is that?"

"Queen."

"Good. I'll take it."

"For how long?"

"A week, maybe longer."

"Fine," she replied and wondered why her limbs would not obey silent, anxious commands to stomp past him to the safety of her home.

So strange. Until a few days ago, she'd never felt anything but safe in Hope.

A coyote howled somewhere in the nearby hills, the sound carried on a breath of air to tickle her nerves. She focused again on the stranger, drawing herself upright, shoulders back and level the way her mother had insisted. "Paperwork's in the café," she said in her most business-like voice as she led him inside.

***

Annie flicked the switch by the café's back door, the ballasts crackling overhead, flooding the kitchen with stark light. She blinked in the glare until her eyes adjusted. Stepping past shelves stacked with crockery and large metal mixing bowls and plastic bins of flour and sugar, she pulled out a folding chair and sat at a small wooden desk.

"Smells good in here."

His voice startled her, as though she'd already forgotten his presence and why she'd come to the café, awareness succumbing to routine, like she was in the kitchen for the reason she always was there. "Pardon?"

"Some spice. I can't place it."

She slid open a desk drawer and withdrew a multi-copy receipt book, the pages stamped *Bluebell Café and Inn*. "Cardamom," she replied as she selected a pen from those bunched in a coffee mug, wrote the date on the top receipt. "Four hundred," she said as she entered the amount.

"Huh?"

"The cabin. Four hundred a week."

"Oh, yeah. Fine."

She initialed the bottom of the form, twirled the book to face him. "Please fill in your name and address."

A mistake, she realized as he towered over her before bending to write. She pushed back the rickety folding chair and scrambled to her feet, edging away until she bumped into the long stainless steel table dominating the middle of the kitchen. She watched him straighten, drop the pen and offer the receipt book.

Zack Dalton, he'd written in block letters. San Francisco address.

She tore out the customer copy and slid it as far as she could along the metal prep table, watching from the corners of her eyes as he reached in a back pocket and withdrew a wallet. "Half in advance," she said.

He shook his head and collected the receipt, leaving four bills in its place. "I prefer to pay now."

Annie eyed the money. No secret she could use the income. Running the Bluebell was harder than ever as the town population dwindled—the elderly dying off, young people pulled away by jobs or pushed away by boredom. She couldn't remember more than a handful of folks who'd moved to town over the last five years, but scores who'd left. Those who remained frequented the Bluebell, but how many pies and cinnamon rolls could they eat? Plus, except for a few ranchers, Hope was not a wealthy town. She kept prices low, at first worried about scaring off her customers, then admitting to herself they'd most likely come anyway, but she'd be overwhelmed with guilt, as if swiping money right out of their pockets.

Mark always said she had no head for business.

Which was a cruel irony, given how she'd been stuck with this one.

Her new guest cleared his throat and extended his right hand.

"Oh, um, yes. Annie O'Connor," she muttered as she slipped her hand into his.

"Pleased to meet you. I'm Zack Dalton."

"I know."

"You do?"

She nodded at the receipt book.

"Oh, yeah. Sure."

He had not released her hand, long fingers cupped around hers, and she blushed at the thought of her skin, rough and wrinkled from countless hours of baking and scrubbing. She withdrew and hid her hands behind her back.

He wriggled his fingers as a mischievous smile dimpled his cheeks. "Key?"

Annie sighed. "My mind must be someplace else." She moved past him to the desk, grabbed a key on a chunky wooden fob.

"Where?"

She frowned. Why was she having so much trouble holding a normal conversation with this man? "Where what?"

He laughed, a hearty baritone that reverberated through the kitchen. "We seem to talk in circles, don't we? My fault, I'm sure. My mind has been elsewhere, too. I was wondering where yours had gone."

She brought hand to cheek. "I have no idea. Sometimes it just doesn't seem to be here." His grin relaxed her. A little. She leaned against the steel table and tucked blonde strands behind her ear. "What brings you to Hope?"

"I'm a free-lance journalist doing a story on small-town police chiefs. You know, last of a dying breed, that sort of thing. I got a lead to Chief Norton and came to follow him around."

"He's a decent man, for sure, but I doubt anything in Hope is exciting enough to be written about."

"Maybe not, although it seems I came at a good time, with some guy murdered in the canyon. Could be interesting."

Annie pushed away from the table and wandered to the shelves, straightening a flour tin, angling another. She kept her back to him as she asked, "You came because of the killing?"

"No, just a fortunate turn of events. Oh, sorry. Not fortunate for the dead man. I hope I haven't insulted a friend of yours."

She squared a tin before facing him. "I'd better get on with my chores."

He appeared startled, as he had out in the parking lot. "Oh, sure. Sorry. Standing here like an idiot. Probably keeping you from dinner with your family."

"No," she said quietly, "it's just me," and immediately regretted the words resounding pitifully in her ears.

"Well, sorry, anyway. I'll go settle in. Can you recommend a place to eat? I mean, your café appears to be closed."

"The Burger Hut and King Yan's Chinese are downtown but you'd be better off at the Roadside Tavern. East end of town."

"The Roadside it is," he said and walked to the door, pausing as he grasped the handle and flashed a quick smile. "Enjoy your evening."

She watched him step out into the night, sank onto the creaky chair and ran a finger across his signature before sliding the receipt book into the desk drawer.

**

A path led from the café to Annie's two-bedroom ranch-style house, the concrete pavers uneven, edges ragged because Mark had insisted on digging the earth and leveling sand by himself—one of the many building projects he'd tackled in his haphazard fashion, with more enthusiasm than skill. Inevitably, Annie had to fix his messes— scraping away globs of white silicone after he recaulked the shower, covering old brown paint visible beneath his streaky brushstrokes. Sometimes, they hired someone to finish a project Mark abandoned in frustration, but there were many times when she melted at his downcast expression, weighed the importance of a repair versus the damage to his self-esteem and simply lived with his slapdash workmanship.

Like the irregular path she now walked.

She glanced up to see Leroy approaching her front porch.

"You okay, Miss Annie?"

"I'm fine," she replied as he shuffled past to plop down on a porch step.

"Made a mess of things again."

She eased onto the step beside him, patted his shoulder gently. "I appreciate your concern, but you need to show some restraint."

"Guess I get carried away."

She smelled the sweet-sour of alcohol on his breath. "We talked about this, Leroy. No more booze."

He clasped hands together and frowned. "I can handle it."

No, she thought, you cannot, but wearily dodged a conversation they'd had too many times to count. Leroy would swear he'd give up drink forever, remain true to his promise for a day or two. One time, he stayed dry almost three weeks before blaming his fall off the wagon on a well-meaning but misguided friend at the tavern who'd insisted on buying a round.

And what, Annie had asked, were you doing there?

Usually, Leroy was a convivial drunk, telling stories and laughing with his drinking buddies at the Woodsman, more likely to pass out than start a fight. Attacking Dalton with the shovel was out of character; a consequence of stress, Annie supposed. "You know you've got to lay low for awhile."

He shrugged and nodded like a child reluctantly acknowledging a mother's reprimand.

They both paused at the sound of a car engine starting up, watched Dalton ease his Fiesta out the driveway and turn east on the main road.

"Still say he was sneakin' 'round."

"He's just renting a room, that's all." She wondered if she believed her own words. Two strangers in two weeks renting the cabin. Coincidence? Could be.

Leroy grunted and stood on wobbly legs. "I'll be lookin' out for you."

Annie rose and climbed the last steps to the porch. "How's Sarah doing?"

"Not sayin' much."

"Tell her I'll come over a little later and knit with her."

He grunted again and ambled toward his cabin.

Annie opened the screen door to her house, switched on a bronze lamp atop a glass end table and surveyed the small living room: the stone fireplace with the rugged juniper mantle she'd adored at first sight, the plaid couch she'd hated from the day Mark drove up with it roped into the truck bed, so proud of his find she hadn't the heart to declare the green and rust colors old-fashioned, the bold squares overbearing. The couch had been one of those times she'd simply gritted her teeth. It's just a couch, she'd told herself, not near as important as the twinkle in his eyes as he replayed how he'd gotten the best of the bargaining.

She should replace the darn thing. Nothing was stopping her. Yet, there it sat.

Buffy, the stray tabby who'd wandered in years ago and instantly been adopted, mewed and rubbed silky fur against Annie's legs.

"Wish you were only glad to see me, but what you really want is dinner, isn't that right, silly cat?" She bent to scratch behind the cat's ears before Buffy padded toward the kitchen, turning once to make sure Annie followed.

As she scraped cat food into a bowl and refilled the water dish, Annie glanced around the small kitchen. Whitewashed cupboards lined two walls, the counters topped with the same speckled blue and white laminate as in the café, part of the deal Mark had wheedled at a warehouse selling seconds and outdated colors.

Money had been tight; was tight now, too, but not as bad as when they'd first signed the mortgage to purchase the land and buildings that became the Bluebell Café and Inn. She'd been nervous as she carefully penned her name next to Mark's scrawl, but he was full of hope and confidence and she'd wondered why she was always such a spoil-sport, why she worried and fretted. She had no answer except to square her shoulders and return his beaming smile, giggling as he lifted her from her feet to twirl in celebration.

Buffy gobbled her food as Annie examined the contents of the refrigerator, rejecting the leftover baked ham and potatoes she'd planned to eat, pawing through plastic bags in the vegetable bin, finally extracting a strawberry Yoplait. She retrieved a spoon from a drawer and returned to the living room, pausing by a silver-framed photograph on the sofa table. She rested the spoon in the yogurt cup, set it on the table, lifted the frame and used her shirt to wipe away dust.

Such a lovely couple, people had said, what with his dark eyes and curly hair, her Scandinavian coloring. They did look handsome in the photo, she admitted: young and trim and vibrant, his strong arm draped over her shoulder, a perpetual five o'clock shadow outlining his jaw, the top of her head coming to his chin, a dimple above her high cheekbones.

They looked happy.

She replaced the frame, picked up her yogurt and settled into the brown leather recliner that had been Mark's favorite place to sit. She tried unsuccessfully to clear her mind, focus on something light-hearted and unimportant. She'd been unsettled all day: startled when the phone rang, jumping at a car's backfire, tense as customers chatted. Leroy's antics had drained her last drop of energy and she'd returned home thinking only of escape, of time to relax and recover.

Instead, she was restless, edgy.

She'd thought she was used to the quiet, that she had embraced solitude as compensation for the years when time to herself was inconceivable. The perfect chance to unwind. To read if she felt like reading, hum if she felt like humming. Eat yogurt for dinner if that's all she felt like eating.

But tonight, solitude only seemed…alone.

She set the yogurt cup on the end table, raised the recliner's foot pad and leaned back to stare at the ceiling.

CHAPTER 4

He could've been almost anywhere. Kentucky. Idaho. Texas. No way to tell from the dimly lit interior of the Roadside Tavern: dark wood-paneled walls, the scrape of metal table legs on linoleum and the smack of a cue ball on the eight. Men jawed and clutched thick plastic mugs of lager. Young women huddled by the juke box. A skinny waitress scurried to tables, balancing a heavy tray, tossing fleeting smiles between grimaces.

Accents would differ by location, of course; words twanged or drawled or clipped. But, Zack would take bets on the conversations: the damn price of fuel these days, the damn referee who didn't know his ass from his elbow, the whole country going to hell in a damn handbasket.

A few heads turned as he closed the heavily-varnished wood door, but most of the patrons ignored him. He surveyed the room and inhaled kitchen grease and fried onions, aftershave, sweat and beer.

If you sit at a bar, Lonnie said, folks will talk to you, which is exactly what you want in an investigation. They might not have shit to say regarding your case, but then again, they might. You'll never know unless you get them talking.

Zack bypassed empty tables and headed for the long bar, nodding to two men seated to his right.

"Hello, handsome, where you been all my life?" A rotund woman behind the bar leaned flabby forearms on the lacquered wood.

"He weren't even born most your life, Kitty," quipped the guy next to Zack, a wizened old-timer who grinned and ducked the wadded napkin she threw his way.

"I want your two cents, I'll ask," she said as she balled another napkin.

"Better watch out, Gaylord, she'll cut you off," said his gap-toothed companion.

"No, she won't. Ain't never seen Kitty turn away a thirsty man with a dollar."

The woman waved him off. "Crazy old fool. Now, where were we, hon?"

Zack smiled and slid onto a stool. "Miller sounds good."

She bent to retrieve a chilled mug from a refrigerator below the bar, pulled a tap and filled the mug, placed it before him.

"Lookie that," said the man called Gaylord. "She gave him a special mug. How come you don't give me one of them, huh?"

"You ain't special."

"Was a time you thought otherwise."

She turned down the corners of her heart-shaped mouth. "Was a time I thought a lot of things I'm not thinking now. Hush up and let me attend to this young man." She regarded Zack with piercing blue eyes above full cheeks. Her pouty lips were outlined in bright pink lipstick that clashed with the unnatural ginger of her wiry hair. "You got a name, hon?"

Zack set down the mug and extended his right hand. "Zack Dalton."

"You're making me wish I was thirty years younger and a whole lot thinner." She grinned at him and clasped a meaty paw around his. "Kitty Anderson. I own this dump. Pleased to meet you."

"Pleasure's mine."

"Sure wish it could be, hon."

He laughed and withdrew from her grip. "Got a menu, Kitty?"

"It's Wednesday," piped in Gaylord.

Zack turned a questioning look to him.

"Meatloaf on Wednesdays. Can't beat it."

"Meatloaf it is."

"Anything you want, hon," Kitty replied as she moved to a swinging door and disappeared into the kitchen.

Gaylord's moustache twitched as he laughed and raised his mug in a toast. "Gotta love a woman as feisty as Miss Kitty."

"A bit of a character, huh?"

"Son, you don't know the half of it."

Gaylord's companion directed a lopsided smile at Zack. "Get it?"

Zack knit his brows in confusion.

"Miss Kitty."

"He's too damned young for the original, Wendell," Gaylord said as he shot a furtive glance at the kitchen door and leaned a bony shoulder Zack's direction. "Ain't you never seen a Gunsmoke rerun?"

"Sure, I get it. My father was a big fan."

The two men grinned as Gaylord confided, "Ain't her real name, you know. Parents christened her Gertrude. When she and ol' Joe bought this here place, she said if she was gonna work behind a bar, she'd call herself any name she wanted. Been Kitty ever since. You want to get on her bad side, call her Gertrude." He winked and quickly hid a grin behind his beer mug as the door from the kitchen swung open.

"You up to no good, Gaylord?"

"Just passing the time of day."

She harrumphed, dragged a stool from the end of the bar and lowered her bulk to sit across from Zack. "So, what brings you to town?"

"Maybe he's somebody's beau from one of them computer dating things," chipped in Wendell with a wise nod that wobbled loose skin bagging beneath his chin.

"What do you know about computers, Wendell?" Miss Kitty scoffed before raising her eyebrows at Zack.

He shook his head.

"Sales?" she asked.

"Nope."

"You're not a damned IRS auditor come to harass me, are you?"

"No, ma'am."

The waitress emerged from the kitchen carrying a white plate heaped with steaming food. "You got a special ordered, Kitty?"

"Right here, Helen." She hoisted off the stool and reached below the bar for tableware and napkins, set them next to the plate Helen slid in front of Zack.

"Looks good," he said and pointed to his empty mug. "Gentlemen, would you join me in a pitcher?"

It had been years since he'd eaten meatloaf. He'd happily left meatloaf days behind when he moved for college. Not an adventurous cook, his mother had inexpertly followed Betty Crocker's recipe several times each month. Although Zack inwardly groaned when a fresh meatloaf appeared, he followed his father's example, stifling complaints as he poured ketchup on the bland concoction.

Perhaps he should be grateful for his mother's culinary ineptitude. Deprivation might have triggered his keen appreciation for good food.

"Well?"

Kitty jolted him back to the present. He swallowed and said, "Delicious."

"Thank you. But, I meant what are you doing in Hope?"

"Free-lance reporter," Zack replied as he loaded the fork with mashed potatoes and gravy.

"You probably wouldn't of guessed that in a million years, Kitty."

She pursed her lips before replying, "You got that right, Wendell. And, just what are you reporting on in Hope?"

"Gotta be the murder," Gaylord guessed, his heavy-lidded eyes intent on Zack.

"Not exactly. I'm writing an article about small-town law enforcement and came to interview Chief Norton. Just a coincidence to be here shortly after the murder, but it gives me a chance to observe him in action."

Kitty caught a signal from Helen and rose to fill two pitchers of Miller Lite. "John's a good man, although I'm not sure he's got much of a story in him."

"That's what Ms. O'Connor said."

"You staying at the Bluebell?"

He nodded and sipped his beer. "Checked in this evening, under the watchful eye of a crazy old goat swinging a shovel."

"That'd be Leroy," Gaylord said. "He come after you?"

"Nothing I couldn't handle."

"Must've been hitting the bottle," Kitty said. "I keep telling Annie he's more trouble than he's worth, but she says he and Sarah got no place else to go. Sarah's his granddaughter, you know." She waddled toward the kitchen carrying a red glass tumbler. "Need me a refill."

Wendell snickered and a strand of saliva slid from the corner of his weathered lips. "Keeps her own gin in the back. Good stuff she won't serve around here."

"I guess ownership has its privileges."

"Guess so."

Gaylord interrupted, "Now, about Leroy. He's mostly harmless. Some say his mind got messed up from a Viet Cong bullet, but most folks believe it was too much marijuana. If he came after you, he must've been drinking. Hey, Wendell, maybe he was telling the truth."

"You think so?"

"What do you mean?" Zack asked and lifted the pitcher to refill the two mugs eagerly thrust before him.

"You see, only way Leroy can be drinking is if he's got money, which he don't usually got. Not Kitty nor Roland out at the Woodsman gonna sell him booze on credit. The other night, lemme see, must have been Monday, Leroy was in here slugging down Kitty's best bourbon. We figured he was blowing his disability check and would be broke again in no time, but he insisted he'd come into a pile of cash and would be getting himself spiffed up and on the road soon."

Zack pushed away his empty plate and asked nonchalantly, "Where'd he get the money?"

"Wouldn't say," Wendell replied.

"Like he won a lottery or something," Gaylord added.

It wasn't much to go on: a Vietnam vet with a drinking problem suddenly coming into money not long after Riordan arrived in town. Better than nothing. He'd call Lonnie in the morning, have him run a check on Leroy Montrose.

***

The evening's meal rumbled in his stomach as Zack unlocked the car door and eased into the Ford, a good reminder of why he typically ate lighter cuisine. Tomorrow, he'd need an extra tough workout. He was not looking forward to nightly dining at the Roadside.

He tried to straighten his left leg beneath the Ford's low steering wheel, succeeded only in a bent-knee stretch as he dialed Stella.

"Thought you'd forgotten to call."

"No. Just a long day."

"It'll come to nothing, you know. Like every time before."

Zack frowned but did not reply.

"You're like a dog with a bone."

"Nothing wrong with determination."

"I call it hard-headed. And, for what? Won't change a thing."

He sighed and closed his eyes against the harsh neon Miller Lite sign hung crookedly in a tavern window. "Did Claudine come over today?" An obvious attempt to change the subject, which he knew was a long shot. Talk about a dog with a bone—just try to budge Stella Lundgren off a topic before she was good and ready. Not going to happen. Not until she'd torpedoed your arguments with the single-mindedness that had served her well as a litigator. Witnesses, opposing counsel, even judges trembled before the diminutive brunette in a navy blue suit bearing down with a glint in her eyes and them in her scope.

Court appearances had ended for Stella. Now, she honed her argumentation skills against Zack.

"What are you doing chasing ghosts when I need you here? I mean, really, Zack. Where are your priorities?"

"Just a week or two, Stella. You'll be fine."

"Easy for you to say."

"Claudine?" he asked as he shifted in the uncomfortable seat.

She sighed theatrically. "Of course, she came by. Not that she did much good."

"I thought you liked her massages."

"From those scrawny hands?"

"Last week you said how great she made you feel."

"Yes, well, maybe she's lost her touch."

Or, maybe I've lost my mind, he thought before shifting the cell phone to his left hand. He waved to Gaylord and Wendell as they exited the Roadside and lumbered past him to a squat truck overburdened by a rusting white camper.

"I need you, Zack."

"Have Yvonne come over. Chardonnay's in the fridge. You can watch a chick-flick."

"Fine."

"She's your best friend, Stella. Go out and do something together."

Her voice became distant and childish. "You know I can't."

"I'll call tomorrow night."

"Call me in the morning, too."

"Okay. Sleep well."

She'd already disconnected.

***

Three things a good cop needs, Zack had been told: training, experience and intuition. Lonnie was drawn to intuition. He didn't totally ignore training—he simply adapted standard procedures to his liking, but stayed close enough to fly under the radar. Usually.

His maverick mentality did not win friends higher up. After the kidnapping, the brass had been careful not to anger the troops by firing a cop injured in the line of duty, but they snatched the opportunity to relegate him to a desk job. Lonnie had little choice but to accept. He was not a rich man and had eight years until retirement. What the hell else am I going to do? he'd asked Zack. Behind the wheel or behind a desk, being a cop is all I know.

Give the guy credit, Zack often thought. He made the best of a bad situation. The chief probably figured throwing free computer classes at an old technophobe like Lonnie was a surefire way to force him out, but he attacked every class, conquering the systems with up-yours satisfaction. Now, if you needed information for one of your cases and didn't know a database from a spreadsheet, Lonnie was the go-to guy.

The new desk job did not mean he had changed his ways. He still thumbed his sizable nose at rules.

Not Zack. He tended to operate by the book. Made for a strange partnership at first, but they'd worked it out. Most of the time.

Lonnie would snicker at Zack and say, you're more like me than you know, kid.

No way, Zack would reply.

But, he could trust his former partner. No one would do a better job of research while Zack investigated in Hope.

He pulled the car in front of his cabin, scanning for Leroy Montrose on another rampage. No sign of him. Probably sleeping off his latest binge. Zack climbed out of the car and up the three steps to the cabin, unlocked the door, flipped on the lights and tossed keys on the dresser.

The two-room cabin was small but cozy, walls slatted with pine, the wood floor dotted with oval, multi-colored braided rugs like those his mother had kept in their bedrooms. The queen-sized bed was topped with an old-fashioned block quilt in blues and greens and was flanked by twin nightstands and reading lamps.

He had searched the bedroom and adjoining bathroom briefly upon arrival, hoping to find a clue missed by the local police and whoever cleaned the place. He'd run his hands around the inside of dresser drawers, scanned the empty medicine cabinet. He would search more thoroughly now: examine beneath the mattress, check behind the pine headboard, shine a flashlight along the shelf in the small closet. It was a long shot, but he hadn't much else to do and would feel like an idiot if he missed a clue because he lazily skipped this step.

He patted shirt pockets for his cell phone, recalled placing it on the Ford's passenger seat. Better get the darned thing in case Stella called. He trudged out to the car and grabbed the phone, relieved that no new messages awaited him. As he relocked the vehicle, his attention was drawn by movement at Annie O'Connor's house. He paused and squinted, his eyes adjusting to the moonless night until he discerned the to-and-fro of the porch swing he'd spotted earlier. The creak of heavy chain confirmed that someone was gently rocking.

Probably her, relaxed against the thick slats, perhaps eyeing the mélange of stars overhead, one foot tucked beneath her, the other poised to press and maintain a peaceful sway.

He walked around the car, took two steps her direction before hesitating, absentmindedly fingering the smooth casing of the cell phone he clutched. A wisp of air carried the sound of the creaking chains. For a moment, he thought he heard her breathing; a soft in and out, a barely perceptible sigh.

He slipped the phone into his pocket and mounted the steps to the cabin.

CHAPTER 5

A narrow strip of pearl white radiated like an aura above the canyon wall, widening moment by moment into the inky sky overhead, tips of hidden sunrays slipping along basalt to light the road at Zack's feet. Ankle-breaking rocks and crevices became more visible and he picked up his pace from a careful, slow jog.

Probably hadn't been the smartest idea, starting his run before daybreak on the winding, shoulderless canyon road; a speedy driver rounding a curve would send him scrambling in loose rocks or careening down the bank. But, he'd woken early, mind and body refreshed, eager for exercise, breath as tranquil and warm as the morning air. He'd laced on Nikes and hurried out of the cabin, noting lights on in Annie O'Connor's house and the café.

He lengthened his stride, puffed quick, explosive breaths to match the strike of soles on asphalt, arms pumping, eyes trained on the road, pushing himself for no better reason than the sheer joy of running. He ran until quads and lungs burned, gradually slowing as sweat dribbled down his face and back.

How long had it been since he'd run all out? Had washed away cares and concerns in a flash flood of endorphins? Although he never broke his fitness routine, jogging and free weights four times a week, stretching daily, he hadn't pushed himself like in his college days when he and his roommate, Terry, ended their runs with competitive sprints. He ought to do this more often. He ought to call Terry.

Truth was, he didn't have the energy. Last night was the first solid eight hours he'd slept in more than a year. He managed to get by, stumbling along half-asleep, embracing routine to guide him, watching his actions as if out of body. Not good for a cop.

Stella slept fitfully, if at all, and he supposed he'd fostered her dependency on him. He'd been so attentive through her surgeries and months of rehabilitation, beside her at the slightest whimper or sigh. Now, she demanded companionship, even if disrupting his sleep. One time, he eyed the guest bedroom with longing, but the mere suggestion of nighttime separation generated tears and accusations that drained his resistance and he climbed into bed beside her for another restless night.

The ribbon of light along the ridge bulged, illuminating the greens of cottonwoods and manzanita. Crows soared overhead as he reversed direction to jog back to the Bluebell. The euphoria he'd experienced in his sprint subsided in a flush of melancholy he shoved angrily away as he jogged past the path he walked with Chief Norton the day before.

He distracted himself from troubles at home with thoughts of Riordan and the other kidnappers.

About this same time in the morning six days earlier, someone shot and killed Edward Riordan. Why had Riordan come out here in predawn darkness? Only one logical reason Zack could imagine—to meet someone. Had to be one or both of the kidnappers. Maybe they lured him with promises of a payoff. Money was behind the whole thing, Zack felt certain.

How did Riordan get here? Might have walked, but the man had not been known for physical activity. He may have ridden out with his murderer, perhaps cautious but confident in his superiority. If he drove out himself, the killer must have returned the Buick to the Bluebell at the risk of being spied by an early riser.

Norton was right—there wasn't much to go on. And, every seasoned investigator knew that the evidence trail weakened substantially with each passing hour. More than 48 hours? Your odds of learning the truth diminished like bank accounts of the unemployed.

But, someone must have heard or seen something. Zack just had to keep digging.

Stella's words circled in his mind and guilt oozed like sweat. Was he letting ego overcome his duty to her? Leaving her alone while he pursued another dead end?

"Not this time," he repeated like a mantra as he walked the final thirty yards to the Bluebell.

***

Zack tugged off his sweat-soaked shirt and socks and tossed them on the floor as he glanced around the room for a coffeemaker and fixings. He hadn't looked for one the night before, only now thinking about coffee with his customary morning urge for caffeine. Nothing on the desk or nightstand or the bathroom vanity. Damn. He really wanted a cup. Recalling the light in the café, he donned a clean shirt, slipped into sandals and locked the cabin door behind him.

No sign of Leroy Montrose or his granddaughter, Sarah, as Zack made his way to the café. Good. Although fully intending to seek them both out and learn whatever he could, he'd as soon do so after savoring the morning and the afterglow of his run with a fresh-brewed cup of java.

Strains of country music filtered through the café door as Zack hesitated, then lightly knocked. He waited, ears tuned for the sound of footsteps or a shout of welcome. Rapped again. No response. He twisted the knob and pushed the door open wide enough to stick his head in and view the kitchen. "Hello? Ms. O'Connor?"

She stood at the stove with her back to him, stirring the contents of a large pot. Her blonde hair was swept clumsily atop her head, held with a net, tendrils curling down her long, pale neck. She swayed as she stirred, oversized shirt with sleeves rolled above her elbows and baggy green sweatpants swallowing the curves he'd admired the evening before.

The aromas were intoxicating: the sweetness of melted chocolate, butter and brown sugar from cookies cooling on a metal rack; the comforting, yeasty perfume of bread baking; a hint of basil and oregano, garlic and onion, which must be seasoning the concoction in the pot. And, like the subdued accompaniment to an aromatic symphony, he smelled coffee.

"Hello," he called, louder this time.

She yelped and spun, spoon in hand, flinging droplets of whatever she was cooking across the floor and stove.

"Sorry," he said, "I didn't want to startle you."

"What?" She shook her head and frowned, rested the spoon on the counter and wiped her hands on a cloth as she hurried to twist a radio knob and silence the Dixie Chicks. "Oh my stars, I think I just aged ten years."

He stepped all the way into the kitchen. "I'm sorry. I really was trying to get your attention without frightening you."

"No, no, my fault. I guess I was lost in my work. I mean, Sarah will be here soon, but I wasn't expecting her yet, or anyone else for that matter, and I suppose I had the music on a bit too loud, but I do love that song so I was focused, well, maybe not focused but immersed…" She momentarily closed her blue eyes, opened them and drew herself tall. "Is there something you need?"

"Sorry to bother you, especially making you jump that way, but I was wondering if it's possible to get a cup of coffee."

She frowned again and cocked her head. "The coffeemaker in your room?"

"Can't find one."

"Why, it's on top of the…" her voice trailed as she brought a flour-dusted hand to her lips. "I forgot. The pot broke. I meant to replace it. My turn to apologize. I assure you we'll get one this afternoon."

"That would be fine."

"Yes, good."

He waited.

"No problem. I'll see to it."

He sniffed the coffee fragrance and arched his brows.

She crossed her arms over her chest and smiled at him a moment before exclaiming, "Oh, of course. I have some right here. Would you like a cup?"

"If it's not too much bother."

She grabbed a large mug, filled it from a silver carafe. "Cream?"

"Black is fine, thanks."

She handed him the mug and brushed a flaxen strand from her face. "It's not so good, anyway."

Zack sipped and replied, "I think this is quite delicious."

"Oh, no, I mean the packaged coffee for the in-room service. It's never seemed to matter to our guests, so I only supply a standard brand and grade."

"Ah. Well, then, lucky me that the pot broke." He did feel lucky to stand in the warm, aroma-drenched kitchen, steaming cup of smooth, dark coffee in hand, beautiful woman before him.

Was she beautiful? Perhaps not classically. High cheekbones underscored half-moon eyes, patrician nose a bit long, mouth wide. She was not heavy, but not model-thin. Sturdy, his mother might have said. Broad shoulders, large hands, shapely legs. She wore no make-up he could detect, yet her cheeks were rosy and lips full.

A complete contrast to Stella's dark litheness and haunting brown eyes, perfectly enhanced with the finest cosmetics. Even now, on her most distraught days, she carefully layered on foundation and powders, blush and shadow.

"Ethiopian."

"Pardon?" he asked, the mug poised at his lips.

"It's an Ethiopian coffee I finagled out of a supplier. He told me about it one day and I begged him to bring some on his next visit."

"Your customers must love it."

"Oh, I don't serve this coffee in the café. I keep this for myself."

"Which now you've shared with me."

"Yes, well," she said and reached up to pat her hair, seemed to suddenly remember the net and ripped it off in a cascade of blonde silk, several pins clinking to the linoleum floor. She squished the net in her hand as he bent to retrieve the pins. "Thanks. Not my best day, I guess."

"From the wonderful smells in here, I can't image any day better."

She regarded him a moment. "Refill?"

Zack smiled and extended the mug. As Annie poured coffee, he wandered to the stove and inhaled deeply. "Minestrone?"

She nodded as she handed him the mug, slipped on the net and picked up the spoon. "Mrs. Moretti's recipe. Well, not a written recipe; just her special combination of ingredients. She lived next door when I was a girl. I used to walk her dog, so she taught me to cook."

"Pancetta?"

She raised her eyebrows in surprise. "How'd you guess?"

"Mrs. De Luca was my Mrs. Moretti, except she didn't have a dog. I mowed her lawn instead."

Annie smiled as she stirred and adopted an exaggerated Italian accent. "Minestrone is not a soup, my darling girl. It is art, and you are the artist."

He laughed and nodded. "Yep, that's Mrs. De Luca."

"Pancetta fried in olive oil until crisp and golden. Onions translucent."

"Not leeks?"

She shrugged. "When I can get them. Not easy to buy the right ingredients in Hope."

"Kale?"

"Spinach."

"A pinch of thyme."

"And fresh basil." She dropped the large spoon into a cradle on the counter, selected two smaller stainless steel spoons from a tray and offered him one. They dipped and tasted.

"Excellent."

"More salt, do you think?"

He closed his eyes to savor the chicken and tomato base laced with garlic, smoky bacon and herbs. "Why ruin a masterpiece?" Annie looked pleased and he found himself happy to have pleased her.

A timer buzzed on the stove. She hushed it, grabbed mitts and hurried to extract four loaves of bread from the oven.

"You do all this by yourself every day?"

"Sarah helps." She adjusted the loaves on a cooling rack. "I got an early start and figured I'd let her sleep. I have a routine after doing this for seven years, so it's not too hard. I find cooking by myself to be rather peaceful."

"And I intruded on your peace and quiet."

She turned and stared at him a long moment before nodding at the radio. "Not so quiet."

He laughed and carried his mug to the industrial stainless steel sink. "I will leave you to your peace."

"I didn't mean…"

He held up his hands to stop her. "I appreciate the coffee and the conversation, but we've both got work to do."

"Your article about Chief Norton?"

He sidled toward the door. "I'm riding along with him today, so I'm bound to learn something." He pulled open the door, half-turning to wave as he exited. She stood by the sink, wiping her hands on a cloth and staring at him with an expression he could not fathom.

***

"It's like a refrigerator in here," Zack said as he shivered and paced Norton's office.

"Finally got the darned air conditioner on and now can't turn it off. Just wait until Eleanor sees the electric bill, let alone the repair bills." Norton grimaced as he rummaged through a desk drawer. "She's always ranting how she could run this place better than me. About ready to take her up on it."

"Pull the electrical plug."

Norton grunted and tapped a file on the desk. "Dang-blasted contraption probably'd never come to life again and I'd be sweating like a proverbial pig this afternoon."

The front door creaked open, followed by a female voice. "Oh my God, it's a friggin' icebox."

Norton grimaced and stepped past Zack into the main office. "I've got a call into Lincoln Matthews to come take a look," he said to a middle-aged, hawk-faced woman clutching a thin sweater over scrawny shoulders and shivering theatrically.

"Thought he fixed it yesterday," she replied as she eyed Zack standing behind her boss.

Norton waved his hand behind him as he walked to the hat rack and retrieved his Stetson. "Penny Chester. Keeps this place in order. This here's Zack Dalton. Going to be tagging along with me a few days."

"Pleased to meet you." Zack stepped toward her.

"Likewise," she replied and brushed his palm in a distracted semblance of a handshake, hazel eyes regarding him like a fox watching a chick. "Here for a few days, huh?"

"Yes, ma'am."

"Penny's the person to go to if you need anything," Norton added as he secured the Stetson and headed for the front door. "Matthews should be here soon. In the meantime, you might use the portable heater from the storage room."

"Eleanor will have a fit about running a heater and the air conditioner at the same time," Penny snickered and rolled her eyes.

"What Eleanor don't know won't hurt her. We're heading out. Call if you need me."

Zack followed Norton out the office door. "Going to be as hot as yesterday?"

"So they say. Whoever the hell they are."

Hay-scented air swept through rolled-down windows and rustled papers on the dashboard as Norton steered the truck through town. Zack inhaled deeply as if trying to store in his nostrils the pungent sweetness of grain.

Still not powerful enough to overcome the sharp smell of disinfectant that hit him as he and Norton entered the storage room at the mortuary; a lifeless, cold room of white-painted walls, grey flooring and stainless steel. A six-corpse refrigeration unit stood against the far wall.

"Got him ready for you, John," offered Dr. Foster, the part-time coroner, after shaking Zack's hand.

"Up to Detective Dalton."

The doctor opened the thick steel door and slid out a roller rack supporting a sheet-covered corpse. He looked expectantly at Zack, who adopted a stern expression and approached the body. "I'd appreciate you telling me what you've found, Doctor."

Foster pulled back the sheet to reveal the body's head and upper torso and Zack fought not to flinch. The initial shock of viewing a corpse always stole his breath, as much from the rawness of mortality as the pallid, chilled skin and inert muscles sagging on bone. Not that he'd done this often. He'd only been involved with death a few times on the job and mostly as a peripheral player, gladly leaving unpleasant tasks to medical examiners and senior detectives accustomed to clinical evaluation and emotionless detachment.

He had watched his mother die of cancer, his father of a massive stroke three months later. Although heart-wrenching to lose them, he'd garnered some relief from the intimacy of holding hands, wiping brows, talking even when they no longer responded. Entirely different than viewing a body in a morgue.

"That him?" Norton asked.

Foster glanced up, startled. "Thought you'd positively identified him from the fingerprints, John. You telling me he's not who you thought he was?"

"No, it's Riordan all right. Just asking Detective Dalton if this is the man he's been looking for."

Riordan's arms rested on the rack along his sides, hands covered by the white sheet. Zack glanced at Norton before lifting the sheet to expose a left wrist and forearm decorated with a string of tattooed black spiders. "It's him."

Foster pointed to the corpse. "One gunshot to the chest. Missed the big organs but severed an artery. He bled to death. Residue on the clothing and shape of the entry wound lead me to believe the shot was fired at close range. Maybe a foot or two; not more than six. Found fragments of a small caliber hollow-point bullet, but nothing large enough for identification. Of course, I'm no expert at firearms."

Norton nodded and scratched his neck, his ruddy cheeks slightly pale. "Anything else you can tell us?"

"Everything's in the report. No bruises or other signs of a struggle. Submitted for toxicology reports, but nothing back yet."

Zack stepped away from the rack. "Guess that's it, then. Thanks for your trouble." He walked out ahead of the other men, heard Norton remind the physician to keep Zack's true identity a secret, at least for the time being.

The morning air was warm and thick in Zack's nostrils as he leaned against the truck waiting for Norton. He ran a hand along his neck and evaluated his emotions. How did he feel seeing Riordan's inert body? How should he feel? Satisfied the bastard got what was coming to him? Triumphant that the good guys won in the end?

He searched within for jubilation, for righteousness, for compassion or pity even. Found only numbness.

Norton trudged out of the mortuary, adjusting his Stetson and jingling keys. He climbed into the Ford and waited for Zack to join him. "Never do like coming here. Just as soon do budget-to-budget combat with Eleanor. Need a cup of coffee to clear my mind."

"You've got that right," Zack said as Norton started the engine and backed the truck into the street.

***

Zack slid into a red vinyl-covered booth opposite Norton in the Downtown Diner, carefully avoiding what appeared to be sticky syrup on the laminate-topped table.

"Here, let me get that for you, hon." The gravely, smoker's voice came from over Zack's right shoulder as a skinny arm thrust past him with a frayed towel. He leaned back as the waitress wiped in counterclockwise circles, gathering some crumbs in the honeycombed cloth, scattering others around the booth. Gone was the syrupy-sweet of someone else's meal, replaced by the industrial scent of Pine-Sol.

Her name was Gladys, or so said blue letters on the white plastic badge pinned on a stained apron pulled tight with a crooked bow. Her wrinkled lips were painted bright red, hair fastened with fancy chopsticks into a knot on top of her head.

"Morning, Gladys. You got some coffee in that pot over there?" Norton asked as he placed his Stetson on the seat beside him.

"Don't I always?" She turned to Zack. "Cream or sugar?"

"Black's fine," Zack replied and watched Gladys scurry to the counter, retrieve the pot and return to set two mugs before them, pour steaming coffee from high above the table without spilling a drop, as she probably had a million times, adding a bit of flare to her humdrum job. Zack sipped the coffee, thought of changing his mind on the cream, ruefully comparing the bitter brew to Annie O'Connor's delicious Ethiopian.

"How's Donny?" Norton asked Gladys as he relaxed in the booth with a satisfied sigh.

"Gout gets him, mostly 'cause the stubborn old goat won't heed the doctor's advice. Says he's gonna die eventually, so what difference does it make when or how, might as well enjoy the ride. Except, he ain't enjoying no ride 'cause he's miserable."

"Hard to get some people's attention."

She muttered and moved to another booth, brandishing the coffee pot.

They sat in silence a few moments before Norton said, "Never forget the first corpse I viewed. Like to sweat my body dry, I was so nervous."

Zack frowned and shook his head. "Not something I relish doing. I suppose you've got to have a certain mental capacity to be a coroner. View things clinically, like a scientist."

"I suppose."

Gladys returned to top off their coffee. "Anything to eat, gentlemen?"

Which reminded Zack his breakfast had consisted of a protein bar he'd retrieved from his duffle before hurrying out the cabin door. "We got time?"

Norton shrugged. "Fine with me."

"Special's two eggs, three bacon, hash browns, toast and coffee."

Apparently, specials were the way to go in Hope. "Sounds good. Eggs over easy and whole wheat toast," he replied and Gladys left to place his order.

"Those tattoos what you were looking for?" Norton asked.

Zack traced the coffee mug handle with his thumb. "Yeah."

Norton stared at Zack and waited.

"The only clue we had to identify the kidnappers. Took too long to get even that one clue."

The hunt started out according to standard procedures. A fellow officer had been shot, which made the search top priority. An APB was issued for the van. There'd been no license plates, so patrols kept a sharp watch for any and all white vans. But, there were too many winding, narrow roads in the California hills, too many places to hide a vehicle, too many ways to access crowded freeways. The van was finally located two days later on a private graveled road, burned to a crisp. The kidnappers must have stashed a second vehicle there or had an accomplice waiting.

The fire in the van destroyed any surface evidence. They might have learned something from a more comprehensive forensic search but, before they could order one, the case was closed.

With Lonnie in the hospital calling the shots by phone, and Zack temporarily suspended, other detectives tried to interview the victim. They got nowhere. She claimed she never saw the kidnappers' faces. The few times she was not masked, they wore masks themselves. She yielded no details as to stature, coloring or accents, nor could she recall anything to help pinpoint where she'd been held. A drama queen given to hysterics, she hid behind her highly-paid physician's sleeping pills and orders that she not be disturbed. The only clue the detectives gained came from drug-infused mumbling about horrible black spiders.

"They stopped the investigation two days later," Zack told Norton. "Waited until sure Lonnie was going to be okay, then reassigned everyone. I went storming into the captain's office and got my butt chewed. Case closed, no questions to be asked."

"Peculiar."

"Like I said, the victim's husband had strings to pull."

"Yes, but why'd he pull them?"

Gladys appeared to slide Zack's breakfast in front of him, slap the check on the table and perform her daredevil coffee-pouring feat.

Zack watched Gladys make her rounds with the coffeepot. "That's what we wondered. You'd think the guy would've wanted the kidnappers caught. Instead, he said the publicity of an investigation would upset his delicate wife, that she was safe and the money in the briefcase was meaningless. We figured he had something to hide, just never found out what."

Norton swigged coffee and placed the mug at the end of the table. "The black spiders?"

"Couldn't make heads or tails until one day I was swapping stories with a parole officer friend of mine. He's laughing about the stupid things criminals do and get caught. Mentions a guy who got nabbed because of his unique tattoos."

"Which gets you to thinking."

"Yeah," Zack said between bites. "This was several weeks after the kidnapping. Everyone else had moved on, except Lonnie and me. By then, the woman was up and showed no signs of stress from her ordeal. So, I faked a chance encounter at a department store." Zack chewed and waved his fork. "At first, she didn't recognize me. Then, she got nervous, glancing around as if afraid someone might see us together. Just one question, I said, and I'll leave you alone. She waited, so I asked if the black spiders were tattoos. She backed away, not saying a word before she fled, but the look on her face told me I was right."

"How'd you tie the tattoos to Riordan?"

"My friend, the parole officer. He canvassed his colleagues and one of them mentioned a former parolee. Said the guy used to refer to himself as the Black Widow."

"Clever."

"Right."

"You try to reopen the case?"

Zack pushed his plate away and leaned back in the booth. "No dice. Captain said the evidence was too slim. Lonnie and I worked on the side to build a case. Riordan had finished his parole and split, whereabouts unknown. Without an APB, he was impossible to find. Showed his picture around and found a bar he had frequented in the city. We cased it for awhile but nothing happened."

"Victim identify him?"

"Not in so many words. I approached her again. Unofficially. Showed her the photo. She went ballistic; shoved the photo away and created quite a sensation with a fainting spell. Her husband threatened to sue for harassment."

Norton sniffed and reached into a back pocket for his wallet, but Zack stopped him with a wave. "On me." He laid several bills next to the paper check on which Gladys had scribbled unintelligible hieroglyphics.

The chief nodded and grabbed his Stetson. "Seems you've got a penchant for unofficial investigations."

"Just this case."

"Because it's personal," Norton added as he hefted from the booth and waved farewell to Gladys. "Clouds one's judgment, you know. Best to let someone else handle the matter."

Zack rose and fixed green eyes on the chief. "Nobody to call on. Except you."

The older man bent his head to regard Zack over the top of wire-framed sunglasses before pushing past him toward the exit. "You always such a troublemaker?"

***

The sun beat on Zack's shoulders and back as he leaned against the F-150 and waited for Norton, who'd been waylaid by a passerby outside the diner. Wouldn't be long before the citizenry of Hope shuttered themselves in cooled buildings, or slipped beneath the umbrella of a protective oak, sipping iced drinks and biding their time until sunset moderated temperatures. But, for now, the streets and sidewalks were full of ranchers and housewives, toddlers and silver-haired retirees.

Zack rolled his shoulders, feeling the sun's heat like a sauna melting stress-tightened muscles. He watched people going about their business—a middle-aged man in white shirt and blue tie entered the bank; a young woman in heels and sundress sifted the stack of mail she carried; a bearded, skeletal man hesitated a moment outside the diner, scanning the patrons through the picture window before shuffling past.

Zack shifted beside the truck and thought of Norton's question. Was he a troublemaker? Probably appeared that way. But, he'd been truthful about this case being an exception. Otherwise, he was mostly a by-the-books cop. That's how he approached life—steady and straightforward, with a staunch sense of duty and responsibility and loyalty. Who could tell if he held these characteristics intrinsically or as a byproduct of his upbringing?

Maybe both.

Walter and Elizabeth Dalton had been late-comers to parenting—Zack's conception a surprise, living with a child an enigma. They'd mostly interacted with him as an equal, aghast when he threw a tantrum or failed to understand their discourse.

He didn't care if they were different than other parents. He loved them and felt no desire for the more tumultuous home life of his friends. His parents gave him respect and freedom; he returned obedience and trustworthiness.

Not that he didn't get into his share of scrapes. There'd been a couple fights at school and teenage experimentation with alcohol. But, he supposed he'd been an easy child to raise.

Even after their deaths, he fulfilled his duty to his parents: brushing away brown, crackling leaves from their graves, arranging sprays of forget-me-nots by the mute granite markers.

So, no, he'd have answered Norton, if the man truly wanted an answer. No, I'm not a troublemaker.

The chief shook hands with the man in Levi's and a plaid shirt who'd been jabbering at him for ten minutes, walked to the truck and motioned for Zack to get in. "I guess every job has its downfalls. Listening to Howard Lemming is enough to drive me out of mine. Nothing much to say, but not shy about saying it."

Zack grinned and stared out the windshield at the man standing on the sidewalk with his mouth moving, as if still bending Norton's ear. "Don't listen."

Norton steered the Ford into traffic, tipped fingers to his hat and nodded Lemming's direction. "He's the mayor."

Zack laughed. "Hell, I should write an article about you and your job. Might be interesting."

"Like watching paint dry. But, you know what?"

Zack didn't think the man wanted a response, so he waited.

"It's got moments."

They'd reached the east end of town and Norton swung the truck onto a northbound side road.

"Where to now?" Zack asked.

"See a guy about that concho."

***

Gene Harris ran a tack shop in an outbuilding on his one-acre property five miles from town. He repaired stirrups and harnesses, restitched panels and replaced straps with a practiced hand and meticulousness bordering on compulsion. Only one way Harris did anything—his way, and at his own speed, too, which was excruciatingly slow for some impatient ranch hands whose livelihood depended on retrieving their repaired tack. Still, he was the best in the county, so they dropped off worn straps and battered halters with an anxious admonition that they surely needed the item by the end of the week, their words skittering like grass seed in a whirlwind past the slender craftsman with unkempt hair and a rip in the pocket of his grease-splotched shirt.

Zack breathed in the leather smell of the shop and eyed rows of straps hung from nails along the walls, shelves heaped with stirrups and bridles, saddles lined up on a long workbench in a makeshift assembly line. The chaos probably struck fear in a customer's heart that their beloved gear might be buried beneath halters and pads and ropes, never to be seen again, but Zack guessed the stooped man squinting at them through thick glasses knew exactly where every braided rein and saddle nail was stored.

"John," said Harris as greeting, not moving from the stool on which he sat at the workbench, tool poised above a swath of leather.

"How're things, Gene?"

"Can't complain."

Norton rubbed a saddle and whistled at the softness. "Mighty fine piece."

"Yep."

"You keeping busy?"

"Yep."

Norton pawed through leather-working tools jumbled in a metal box and said over his shoulder, "This here's Zack Dalton. He's tagging along with me for a few days."

"Nice to meet you," Zack said, offering his hand. Harris regarded him a moment, then frowned as if contemplating whether he had to put down his tool in order to be polite. Zack retreated. "Don't want to interrupt your work."

"That's right," Norton added. "Won't keep you long, Gene. Just got something to show you, find out if you've ever seen it before." He pulled a plastic bag from his pocket and tipped the silver concho onto the workbench.

Harris lifted the concho and held it close to his face, squinted and rotated the piece in his hand. "Ain't new. Scratches along the edge. Off a saddle?"

"Not sure."

"A bit large to come from a hatband or belt."

Norton nodded. "You ever work with one like it?"

"Like it, yeah, but not exact. One thing's for sure, ain't off no working man's saddle. This here's meant for a show saddle with lots of silver and tooling. Costs more than most folks around here care to spend."

"Know of anyone in the county who owns such a saddle?"

Harris shook his head and handed the concho to Norton. "Not likely they'd bring it for me to work on." A sneer and a twitch by his left eye signaled his disgust for rich land barons so stupid as to reject his services.

"If a person wanted to buy such a saddle, just where might they head?"

"Couple mail order places. Or, one of them custom makers in Texas. Not around here."

Norton grunted and dropped the concho into the plastic bag, which he stuffed in a shirt pocket. "Much obliged, Gene." He tipped his hat and walked to the door. Zack followed, glancing behind to see Gene Harris hunched over his leatherwork, his visitors perhaps already an unimportant, forgotten interruption.

As Norton pulled out of Harris's driveway and turned back toward town, Zack leaned his arm on the truck door and furrowed his brows. "Someone around here must have a show saddle."

Norton glanced at him. "You're assuming Riordan didn't bring the concho with him. He could've picked that piece up in a Nevada poker game, for all we know."

"Or, he could have found it here."

"Maybe. Never noticed a fancy saddle in our Fourth of July parade or heard of anyone riding for show."

"Something to ask about."

Norton rubbed his temple. "Yeah."

They rode past an out-of-business auto repair shop and gas station, a chain link fence enclosing the pit left behind when pumps were dug up to comply with environmental regulations. An unnecessary deathblow to a long-time business, according to Norton. "Never a problem with the station or pumps, so why in hell go mucking around? Now, look what's left." He motioned in disgust at graffitied plywood covering broken windows and waist-high weeds rising from cracks in the asphalt. "Poor Maloney. Run out of business by those what don't even live here. Damn shame, that's what it is."

The chief eased the truck into the parking lot by the police station and killed the engine. Zack reached for the door handle, glanced sideways to see Norton with lips drawn thin and arms folded, staring out the front windshield. With the air conditioner off, the cab heated quickly, but Zack breathed the dense air and waited.

After a few moments, Norton sighed, nodded his head and cocked an eyebrow, as if reaching a conclusion he'd rather not reach. "About this investigation," he finally said. "If I was in your situation, I'd probably be hot under the collar and out to set things straight, just like you. Instead, I've got the district attorney wanting answers. The only help in the department is from part-time officers, the best being Larry Kincaid and Harold Dorsey, the rest good for directing traffic, although some days I have my doubts. Officer Jacobs is scheduled for two weeks of vacation, starting tomorrow, and I'll be danged if I'll delay a man's pleasurable appointment with a rainbow trout. Could call on the county sheriff, but Bud Whitaker's never been one to take on difficult jobs. That leaves me. Not enough hours in the day." He shrugged and sighed again. "Got other things on my mind, too. So, bottom line, there's little I can do. The state police have plenty on their plate, but they'll step in if I call."

"No, don't," Zack pleaded. "They'll shut me out. You said you'd give me time."

The older man removed his sunglasses and rubbed his eyes. "Not proper procedure. What if you come up empty-handed? Case'll be deadly cold before anyone official steps in. How am I to explain?"

"I know, but I'm close on this, I can feel it. Give me what support you can. Don't worry, I won't run off with your case. I'll do the legwork and consult you with my findings. You understand this town, these people. Help me analyze what I learn and I'll share everything, I promise."

Norton regarded him through narrowed eyes. "You're putting me in a tight spot, son."

"I won't let you down."

The chief grunted and opened the truck door. "You damn well better not."

CHAPTER 6

A bell chimed overhead as Zack pushed open the glass door to Mitchell's Barber Shop and smiled at the nostalgia of the place, a throwback to the shops his father had taken him to as a boy. Mirrors stretched above a counter with glass containers of black combs and scissors, electric razors sat in their chargers. John Wayne movie posters in thin metal frames collected dust on the opposite wall.

Roy Rogers posters had decorated the walls of Patterson's Barber Shop when Zack was a kid. He used to stare at Rogers in the mirror, wishing he was watching the movie instead, reading the reflected, backwards words until they were all too familiar.

Two of the three vinyl swivel chairs were occupied; three pairs of eyes acknowledged Zack in the mirror as his shoes squeaked on shiny linoleum squares. The wiry, middle-aged barber waved his scissors and motioned Zack to the unoccupied chair. "Here for a trim?" he asked in a high-pitched voice.

"If you've got time."

"Oh, sure, sure. I already cut Troy, so you just have a seat. I'll finish up on Mr. Isley here and you'll be next."

A blue cutting cape swathed Isley's bulky frame. He regarded Zack beneath heavy lids and bestowed a disinterested nod of greeting. The slender man of about Zack's age slouched in the adjacent chair and averted his eyes. Father and son, Zack guessed, noting resemblance in their small mouths, aquiline noses and wide-set grey eyes.

"Now, as I was saying, Mr. Isley," Mitchell deftly switched from scissors to comb in his right hand, "my cousin, Bernie, he's right good at raising these pups and charges a reasonable price. Why, considering all the food and medicine he's put into them dogs, he's almost giving them away. He won't pay me no mind when I try to explain about overhead and making a profit, but all's the better for you 'cause, I'm saying, you'll get a good deal. Might you could use one out on the ranch?"

"We don't need another dog."

"Maxie's not getting any younger, Pa," Troy said.

Isley shot his son a piercing glare. "You so hot for a damned dog, buy it yourself."

Mitchell turned hopefully to Troy, who sniffed and swiveled the chair with the heel of his cowboy boot. Mitchell shrugged, set his tools on the counter and grabbed a whisk to sweep hair particles from Isley's neck.

Zack stared at the movie posters, remembering how Mr. Patterson would hand him a cherry sucker, which he'd crunch as he spun in the chair, lost in his make-believe world as Roy Rogers' trusty sidekick while his dad was lathered and shaved. He smiled now as he considered whether instead he'd become Lonnie's sidekick and just how different Lonnie was from Roy.

He missed the question thrown at him, only peripherally aware he'd been addressed. "Pardon?"

Isley checked his haircut, ripping off the cutting cape as he stood. "I said that you must be a movie fan, the way you're fixated on those posters."

"Just taking me back. My dad was a big fan. We watched every classic cowboy movie he could find."

"I've seen 'em all, too, I'd say," said Mr. Mitchell. "*Billy the Kid Returns*, now that was a goodie. Or, *Sons of Katie Elder*. 'Course, it come along later." He retreated to the back of the shop to grab a broom.

"A bunch of crap," Troy grumbled as he rose from the chair and retrieved a hat from the rack near the front door. "Fake gunslingers acting tough. Nothing like a real cowboy's life." He nodded at Zack. "Don't suppose you know much about that."

Zack shook his head. "Nope. Not my calling."

Isley senior slapped bills on the counter. "No? What is your calling?"

"I'm a writer."

Troy scoffed. "Cushy. Figures."

The guy seemed itching for a fight. Zack had no idea why he'd been singled out, except by virtue of being a stranger in the path of an eruption. He'd have called the guy on his rude behavior, but worried he'd jeopardize his cover.

Isley glared at his son. "Walk a mile in a man's shoes." Troy's mouth turned down and his face reddened as his father approached Zack with hand extended. "Ray Isley." His grip was firm and commanding.

"Zack Dalton."

"Forgive my boy. He's got a hard on today, for some reason I can't figure. You new to town?"

"Pulled in yesterday."

Mitchell had returned and was sweeping grey and brown strands into a pile. "Heard tell he's writing a story about Chief Norton."

A good reminder to Zack that news travels fast in a small town like Hope and secrets are difficult to conceal—exactly what he was counting on to solve the murder, but also what he must avoid to maintain his cover.

"That so," Isley replied, a statement, not a question.

"Should make an interesting story," Zack said.

"I suppose." He retrieved his hat and joined Troy, who sulked by the door. "Norton's a good man, which I say as someone who considers himself an expert judge of character. I can peg a person right away." He nodded at Troy, who pulled open the door and set the bell tinkling. "Which is why you're a bit of a puzzle, Mr. Dalton. You don't seem much like a writer to me."

Zack shrugged and spread his arms as if to bare all to the unbelieving.

Isley grunted. "Well, pleasure to have you in town. Good day, gentlemen." He exited, Troy like a herd dog nipping at his heels.

Zack chewed the inside of his cheek, replaying the conversation and gathering impressions of father and son Isley.

Mitchell swept cuttings into a dustpan and dumped them in a wastebasket. He returned and picked up the money Isley had tossed on the counter. "Ain't that the way." He snorted and waved the bills at Zack. "It's the rich what don't leave a decent tip."

Zack shook his head in sympathy as he moved to the chair Isley senior had vacated.

He didn't need a haircut; he needed information.

He'd recalled Norton referring to Mitchell as a talker and the bright-eyed barber was only too willing to gossip. "There's a few thumb their noses at the good, honest folks in town. High and mighty with their customized trucks and big houses."

Probably shouldn't let him get worked up, Zack thought as he watched the barber whack away.

"All them tax dodges. Screwing the government out of millions. Now, I'm no fan of taxes. They're too high, for sure. But, every shady deal by the rich means the government just collects more from us hard-working folks."

The worst offender was Ray Isley, who apparently symbolized to Mitchell every wrong imposed on those at the bottom of the heap. "Too full of himself," Mitchell declared while snipping.

"You still cut his hair," Zack said.

Mitchell shrugged and mumbled about taking a dollar when a dollar is due.

Zack managed to change the subject to Ed Riordan.

"That's something, ain't it? A murder right here. Now, I never met the man, but I seen him around and heard aplenty, that's for sure. Not a trustworthy type. Kinda slippery, if you know what I mean." No, he hadn't noticed Riordan talking to anybody in particular. "Just a waitress or two, that sort of thing. Strictly business. Although, some said how Riordan had himself a little female companionship in town. Never heard a name."

Twenty-five minutes later, Zack ran a hand over his shorn head. Pierre, his San Francisco stylist, would have a fit, which might be entertaining. Pierre's real name was Timothy, but he swore his fake French accent and snooty manner attracted well-heeled customers and upped his tips. Zack smiled at the thought of walking into the salon, Pierre shrieking and cursing the *imbécile* who ruined his fine taper.

Oh well, his hair would grow back. The shortness would be welcomed in the heat and help him blend into Hope.

Zack left the barber shop with sunrays penetrating stubble to his scalp, but with nothing new to help solve the case.

***

More dead ends annoyed him when he returned to Norton's office. Officer Jacobs had wielded the metal detector all morning, expanding the search even wider than Zack had suggested.

Nothing.

Just ancient fishing lures and car parts and the usual assortment of coins. He did locate a pretty gold ring; now in the lost and found and a call made to Faye at the local paper to run an announcement. Norton thanked Jacobs and shooed him on his way to a well-deserved vacation, Zack agreeing there was no need to do more at the crime scene.

Next, Zack scoured Riordan's car, parked a block from the police station in a pole building where they stored equipment and an old cruiser. He hoped to find something Norton and his crew missed, as he had with the concho.

Nothing.

Probably a silver lining there—finding a clue would have shown up the locals again; surely not the way to be on the chief's good side.

They discussed possible suspects, Norton coming up empty, Zack grasping at straws. "What do you think about Leroy Montrose?" he asked.

"Leroy?" The chief glanced up from the stack of reports he idly fingered. "You mean for the murder?" Deep pores fell into crevices as he wrinkled his nose. "Guess anything's possible, but I don't see it. Leroy's harmless, unless he's been drinking. Even then he's more danger to himself than others. Spent a few nights here sleeping one off." He thumbed toward the block wall separating the main station from the holding cells. "You get to know a man when he frequents your cells. He's got some demons left over from the war, but I don't think of him as criminal or violent."

"Came at me with a shovel."

"That right? Well, as I said, anything's possible, but I don't like him for the murder."

"I heard he might have come into some money."

"And, you're thinking he took it off a dead man?"

"As you said, anything's possible. Montrose a local?"

Norton drummed his fingers on the desk a moment before leaning back in the chair. "No. Moved to town about two years ago. Brought his drinking problem and his granddaughter with him. Don't know much about him before then. Annie O'Connor's most likely to know him best. She more or less adopted Leroy and Sarah, let them move into one of her cabins. You might want to learn what you can from her, unless you're going to go at Leroy directly."

"Might do both."

Norton nodded, then scrunched his face a moment. "Don't figure Leroy for premeditated murder. Guess he could have done it while on a binge, but that sort of leaves you high and dry, doesn't it?"

Zack squirmed on the straight-backed chair, gave up trying to find a comfortable position and stood, stretching his arms overhead and rotating his torso to loosen kinked muscles. "How so?"

"Shoots the hell out of your kidnapper theory."

"Montrose could be one of the kidnappers."

Norton shook his head. "Don't see it."

His view of Montrose matched that of Gaylord and Wendell at the Roadside Tavern the night before. If Leroy Montrose was a seasoned criminal, he was doing a bang-up job of hiding behind a harmless drunk façade. Still, Zack had left a brief message for Lonnie to investigate the man.

"What's your next step?" Norton asked.

Zack ran a hand along his cheek and mentally checked his options—a short list, given the lack of evidence. "I'd like to interview the boys who found the body. Their father, too. They might have remembered something useful."

Norton shrugged. "Nothing came up when Officer Jacobs talked to them, but perhaps you can wriggle out a forgotten detail or two. Start with Kent Baker. Get his permission to chat with the boys." Norton glanced at the wall clock hanging askew above his desk. "Most likely getting off work and heading home. He's a private man who might not take to a supposed writer interrupting his evening. If I were you, I'd catch him tomorrow."

"Any idea where I can find him?"

"Works out on the Rockin' I Ranch owned by Mr. Ray Isley."

Zack nodded. "We've met," and added to Norton's quizzical look, "at Mitchell's."

"Ah," Norton replied as he wrote down directions to Isley's spread.

**

There was a certain irony to posing as a journalist—writing did not come easy to Zack. He'd bumbled through required English classes in high school and college, earning average grades because he completed assignments on time, if not eloquently. The technical aspects of writing didn't bother him; he was fair at spelling and grammar. For sure, his police reports appeared as fine literature compared to the misspelled, rambling constructions of other officers.

No, the difficulty was concocting a story. Teachers assigned essays about the greatest hero in your eyes or demanded a short story about a lost dog. He'd beat his brain for days trying to envision what the damn dog looked like and why the hell it was lost in the first place, let alone what happened along its journey home. How should he know? Go ask the dog.

And, forget description. 'The dog barked' said all Zack intended to say. He remembered his fifth grade teacher placing a red brick on the desk before her, instructing the students to list everything they might do with the brick. Zack bent over his paper, printing options—build a house or a walkway, put it in the toilet to change the water level, like his father did. When the teacher called time, he was proud of his single column of practical uses for the brick, until he noticed the double-sided scribbled pages of the girl beside him. A doll? How the heck did you make a doll out of a brick?

It wasn't until the police academy that Zack bettered his skills of observation and description. What color eyes did the perp have? He carry two bags or three? Move to her right or left? How far?

From Lonnie, he'd learned to suppose.

Suppose the perp ran down an alleyway; where would he head next? Suppose you wanted to hide cocaine in your ramshackle apartment; where would you hide it?

Supposing was what he was doing now, parked on Canyon Road, leaning against Lonnie's car, trying to envision the morning Riordan was shot. He breathed in pollen-coated air, pushed away from the vehicle and moved to the path he and Norton had walked the day before, willow cotton drifting around his head like wayward snowflakes, a lizard crinkling dry leaves beneath newly-greened branches.

Norton was right—many scenarios were possible. Could have been an accident. Perhaps a careless hunter, now too scared to confess. Except it wasn't hunting season and the autopsy report pointed to a small caliber bullet.

Could have been target shooting or firing off rounds to test the gun's action. Or, simply shooting for the hell of it and Riordan got in the way.

None of which jived with why Riordan would have been in the canyon at the crack of dawn. No matter how Zack supposed different scenarios, he concluded that Riordan had met someone who had not wanted to be seen, most likely one of the other kidnappers.

He stepped along the shoulder, examined the ground at his feet for dark brown spots of dried blood and kicked aside large rocks, sending platoons of red ants scurrying for cover. He found nothing to indicate the killing had taken place by the road; at least, not within thirty yards of the turnout. Dr. Foster was probably right—the murder happened down by the creek.

Why leave the road? Simpler to stay up here, still a private location, the odds against anyone driving by at that hour. Why scramble down the bank and across uneven terrain before the light of dawn?

Only one reason Zack could suppose: Riordan had no choice.

Zack inched down the path to the creek, searching for clues, imagining Riordan stumbling over rocks and roots, a gun pointed at his head or jammed into his back. It was the only sensible supposition and led to one conclusion: the murder had been planned. Recalling Officer Jacobs' remark about bedrock in the area and the relative ease of digging along the bank, Zack concluded that the killer had chosen this spot carefully; planned to shoot Riordan and bury him here.

Risky. But, murder is always risky.

Perhaps the murderer intended to bury the body deeper in the silt, but he was slow and the swelling morning light spooked him, jump-started worry that someone would rise early and drive the canyon road, notice his car parked at the turnout. So, he convinced himself he'd dug enough, dragged Riordan's body into the shallow hole and hurried away.

Which brought up another point: Riordan's car. The chief found the Buick parked at the Bluebell, but Zack thought it unlikely Riordan walked to a rendezvous in the dark. If there was to be a payoff, he'd have planned to collect the cash and drive south to the state highway, turning east or west as whim dictated, disappearing as he had three years prior. Probably couldn't shake Hope dust off his worn Rockports any too fast. Get the money and get out.

For the same reason, he wouldn't have ridden out here with someone else. Criminals aren't the most trustworthy individuals, which no one would understand better than a slimeball like Riordan. He'd have wanted to be in control, not jump in a car with someone entirely too much like himself.

Who returned Riordan's car to the Bluebell? Could have been the murderer but, if acting alone, he'd have needed to return the Buick, then hoof back up the canyon to retrieve his own vehicle. Too risky, too time-consuming. He could've walked to the meeting point in the first place, but that would afford no quick escape should something go wrong. Equally risky.

What if two people met Riordan? They could have driven out together, committed the murder, each driven a car back to town.

Zack realized he always visualized the killer as a man. No evidence pointed either way, whether the killing was connected to the kidnappers or not. He and Lonnie had identified two kidnappers as male, but they hadn't glimpsed the driver. Could've been a woman. Maybe the same woman drove for this meet, too.

Zack walked along the creek, hesitated a moment and turned a slow circle to survey the area, convinced he'd arrived at the crime scene. Jacobs had removed the bright orange cones and yellow tape and filled in the hole where the body had been buried. The investigation was finished here, except for Zack's fruitless meandering.

They'd failed to find much evidence and weren't likely to, even if they searched for weeks on end.

He circled the area, but nothing new attracted his attention and he shook his head in frustration. He gathered a handful of small, flat stones, eased onto a log wedged between boulders, rolled his neck, the pops and cracks loud in his ears, sighed and skipped a stone into a glassy pool.

The place reminded him of hot summer days visiting his pal, Joey, in the Sierra foothills. Two weeks of swinging from a rope tied securely to a thick oak limb, catching butterflies in a net, caramelizing skinny arms and knobby knees with hours in the sun. Broke his twelve-year-old heart when Joey's parents sold their property and moved to Kansas. He missed Joey, for sure, but he sorely missed summer adventures in the hills—a million stars in the jet-black sky, or the moon like a powerful flashlight as they sneaked out to the lopsided fort they'd built in the afternoon.

A whoosh overhead drew Zack's attention. He raised a hand to block blinding sunlight and saw a hawk circling in the currents, wings flapping powerfully between long glides. Master of your territory, aren't you, Zack thought, wondering if the bird flew by to assess danger or for simple curiosity. He followed the hawk's traverse along the canyon, flight casual and sure, perusing with the patience of familiarity, knowing where to find food, where to nest and perch, the direction from which enemies might come. At home in this rugged place.

A flush of envy surged through him as he lowered his hand and stood. Crazy to be jealous of a bird.

He hadn't planned on moving to the city after college. Hadn't planned on becoming a cop. Truly, he hadn't planned much in his life, seizing opportunities as they sprang before him rather than doggedly pursuing goals. He lived as if faced by a series of climbing walls, grasping tentative handholds before hauling himself to a ledge, only to find another wall before him. He did not gaze up and predetermine a path; he simply reached for the next convenient hold.

A scholarship dictated his choice of college, where he'd been happy enough as he squeaked by with a geography major. The job market had been tight as he graduated, so when a classmate extolled the benefits of law enforcement, Zack interviewed and tested for the police academy, surprised to be accepted. He moved to San Francisco when he received his one and only job offer.

You let everyone else run your life, Stella once said.

Including you, he'd thought.

He couldn't deny her accusation, yet it was only recently that the truth rubbed against his emotions like scratchy clothing, irritating and distracting.

In the beginning, he was excited to live in the city, but the excitement vanished when he realized that the pleasures to counterbalance city-life hassles were beyond his finances. Still, he clung to his job, climbed the career wall hold by hold, unable or unwilling to choose a new course.

He didn't remember what impressions of law enforcement he'd first harbored, if any. Probably a fanciful vision groomed by television. In reality, much police work was far more mundane than the blood-pumping, adrenaline-surging investigations in the movies. Even so, some officers got off on the potential for danger or on being a figure of authority. Not Zack; at least, not any more. As a rookie, perhaps he'd been captured by the headiness of locking away bad guys and cleaning up the streets. But, years of dealing with the poor and the addicted, the wretched and the wicked, and he wearied of a never-ending, fruitless task.

Unable to afford the delights of the city, Zack had spent most of his free time visiting his parents. When they passed away, he was unattached, unencumbered and unexcited by the life he was leading and seriously considered moving on. He contemplated a career change, perhaps a law enforcement job in a smaller town or getting out altogether. Maybe he should travel, explore the world, ski in Colorado, cast a line in Montana.

Stella changed everything. They met when he testified at a trial, bearing the full force of her interrogation. Perhaps because he didn't squirm under her intensity, stuck to his account and fended off her stealthiest jabs, she'd ended with a slight smile and a piercing stare. She called him the next day and insisted they meet for dinner.

Once again, he embraced the opportunity presented, dropping his musings about leaving his job and the city, burying any thoughts of what he really wanted in life. He slipped into Stella's world without much consideration of the consequences.

Those consequences now gnawed at his insides as he slogged back to Lonnie's car. He was surprised to find three bars on his cell phone there in the canyon. He sighed and punched in her number.

"Thought you'd never call," she said.

"You can call me, too."

"Not that you ever answer." A soft slurp helped him envision Stella slouched on the sofa with a full glass of expensive Chardonnay. "Oh, let's not argue. Just tell me you're coming home tomorrow. No, better yet, come home tonight. You know how much I miss you."

They managed a ten-minute conversation. Household details. A movie she'd watched. Whether she should get a dog; a small one, soft and cuddly. A puppy would keep her company, be more loyal than people. A puppy would be good therapy. But, she'd need his help to train it. She'd need him home.

At least she was less confrontational than the day before.

Zack reached for the ignition key and frowned as his phone rang, hoping she hadn't called back. He blew out a breath in relief. It was Lonnie's number on the display.

"Quit goofing off and get to work," Lonnie said.

"Aw shucks," Zack replied, "you interrupted my poker game and just when I was dealt a full house. What kind of a friend does that?"

"The kind who knows you're too much of a wuss to bet a buck on cards."

"Merely smarter than the average bear. I take it your game didn't go so well last night?"

Lonnie harrumphed. "Bunch of damned cheaters, you want my opinion."

"Don't play with them."

Harrumph.

Zack laughed and changed the subject. "Got anything?"

"Tracked Riordan to Minden, Nevada. Lived with a cocktail waitress, name of Arlene McIntyre. Got the car from her before he wore out his welcome. Not one kind word does she say about ol' Edward Riordan. Claims he spent money fast and furious. First his, then hers. Blew a fortune at craps until she kicked his skinny ass out of her house."

"So, he'd have been looking for a new source of funds."

"You got it."

"Any known associates?"

"Negative. Arlene says Riordan was too much of an asshole to have friends."

"Bitter woman."

"Sounded like she's led a bitter life. I'm thinkin' she needs a shoulder to cry on."

Zack chuckled and slouched into the tuna can's worn upholstery. Lonnie was a bachelor, not a celibate. "Maybe she'll buy you a new car. You sure could use one."

"Nothing wrong with a classic Ford."

"This heap is not a classic, Lonnie."

"Is to me. Nothing of consequence yet on Montrose."

Typical of conversations with Lonnie, swinging topic to topic, his zigzags making perfect sense to him. It had taken Zack several months as Lonnie's partner to learn how to dissect his ramblings, which proved helpful as Zack became their main spokesperson with the brass, the press, anybody of authority. On the other hand, Lonnie conducted most interviews, his wandering style often befuddling suspects into contradictions and admissions.

"You there, cowboy?"

"Yeah, sure," Zack responded as he peered out the windshield. The hawk had returned, dipping and rising in widening circles overhead. "Montrose."

"He's got a record; piddling charges of disorderly conduct, public drunkenness, trespassing. Nothing to make him for something big like kidnapping."

The hawk had flown out of view. "That's what Norton said. Still, there's the question of coming into money recently. I'm hoping to corner him this evening, see if I can learn anything."

"You do that. I'll keep tracking Riordan. Must have associated with someone besides Arlene."

"Maybe you better go interview her in person."

Lonnie emitted his third harrumph of the conversation.

***

Zack seemed to lose himself recently, tripping over redundant thoughts, skipping past any he didn't care to recognize. Lonnie called him a friggin' space cadet. Stella complained he daydreamed instead of listening to her.

Lost in thought again, he parked in front of his cabin at the Bluebell without much recollection of driving there. Not good for a cop. Not good, in general.

He climbed from Lonnie's car and dug into a pocket for the cabin key. Movement by a poplar caught his attention and he saw a female form retreat behind the tree. Not Annie. Shorter, plumper, darker. He stared at the poplar as a round face peeked from behind.

He scanned the area again but caught no sign of Annie or Leroy, so he walked slowly across the parking lot. "Hi. I'm Zack. I'm staying in a cabin here." He hooked his thumbs in the front pockets of his jeans and smiled. "You must be Sarah."

Brown eyes stared as first a leg, then an arm, emerged until she stood before him, one hand pressed against the tree. "Yes, I'm Sarah."

He nodded and offered his hand. "Pleased to meet you."

She hesitated before inching forward to pump his hand twice and retreat with her hands shoved under her armpits.

Zack twisted to point at the largest of the three cabins. "You live over there, don't you?"

"With Grandpa."

"Sure is beautiful in Hope. You like living here?"

A slow shrug. "It's okay. Annie's nice."

"Yes, she is. You help her in the bakery."

"I'm good at baking. Annie says so."

"Well, must be true. What's your favorite thing to bake?"

"Blueberry pie, I guess. You eat any?"

"Not yet, but seems like I'd better."

Joey's sister, Teresa, was three years younger and a constant pest when Zack and Joey planned their summer escapades. She'd sit on their carefully sketched maps, grab a crayon and obliterate the location of the buried treasure. She'd squirm between them as they glued model airplanes.

When Zack complained to his mother, she hushed him. Teresa's different, she said, it's not her fault. She a retard? he'd asked. No, and don't use that word. She's just slower. You must treat her kindly.

Sarah stared at him now with Teresa's eyes.

He'd not thought of Teresa in a long time, had not imagined how a teenaged Teresa might appear. Perhaps something like Sarah, an uneasy amalgamation of a woman's body and a child's innocent face.

"You come out by these trees often?" he asked.

"Sometimes." She inspected her foot tracing lines in the fine dirt splattered with pine needles and dried cones.

"Really tall, aren't they?"

"Yeah."

He leaned back and craned his neck to stare at the treetops. "Sure would be fun to get up there."

She mimicked his stance, peeked sideways at him before looking overhead. "Like the squirrels."

"You think they climb that high?"

Dark brows knit in a frown as she lowered her head. "They have to get cones to store for winter."

He whistled. "You're right. Guess if I have questions about wildlife around here, I know who to ask."

Her eyes clouded as she sucked in her lips, turned and sprinted toward the hills backing the property.

"Hey, Sarah?" he called. What had spooked her? He followed her flight between trees until she rounded a hillside and was lost to view.

He turned and saw Leroy Montrose trudge down the steps of his cabin and gather a watering can. Zack approached him cautiously, surveying the area for shovels or other handy weapons. "Hey, Leroy. How's it going?"

"Huh?" the old man squinted against fading sunlight. The can rocked away from the faucet as he rose from a crouch and water gushed over his loafers.

"Here, let me get that." Zack grabbed the green plastic handle and guided the can under the spigot. "Guess I startled you. Sorry about your shoes."

Leroy retreated, peering at Zack. "I know you?"

"Sure. We're neighbors. I'm staying in the cabin next door."

"Don't mean I know you."

Zack turned off the faucet. He checked the man's eyes and sniffed for alcohol, concluded he had probably tipped a glass or two but was not drunk. "Guess not." He shifted the watering can to his left hand and held out his right. "Zack Dalton, sir. Pleased to meet you."

Leroy sniffed and hunched his shoulders before clasping Zack's hand. "Pleasure."

"The water for these?" Zack motioned to planter boxes fronting Leroy's cabin, bright red geraniums seeming to extend parched flowery tongues.

"Miss Annie says to keep it off the flowers."

Zack carefully poured between the stems. "I'm sure she knows what she's talking about."

"Always does."

Zack smiled and returned to the faucet for a refill. "Sounds like you're a fan."

"Ain't no better people than Miss Annie. She's good to me and my granddaughter."

"I can tell. Of course, you give her a hand around the place."

Leroy puffed his chest. "I don't accept no charity. I work for my stay."

Zack set the can on the porch, slipped his hands in his back pockets and rocked on his heels. "Must be hard work, with three cabins and the café and all. Been doing it long?"

"About two years. I brung my granddaughter where she can smell the roses. She and me, we don't belong in a big city with all the crazy people."

"What about her parents?"

He grimaced and walked up the steps to lower himself onto the porch. "They're the crazy people I'm talkin' about. Care more for their drugs than their daughter. Never raised my son to be that way. Leastways, not when I was around. Guess he come by it when I took to the road to get work. Figured his mother would do him right. Figured wrong."

Zack leaned against the stair rail and rested a foot on the first step. "Only so much a man can do."

"You got children?"

He shook his head.

"Don't bother. More trouble than it's worth." Leroy stretched his legs and seemed to rise several inches from his slouch. "All gonna change now. Got me a stake and I'll be makin' something of my life. Provide for Sarah, too. You wait and see."

Zack chose his words carefully. "It's a fortunate man who's got the wherewithal to get ahead."

"I figure you can do quite a lot if you've got money and an ounce of sense what to do with it."

"Takes me forever to save enough just to get my car engine tuned. Forget about replacing the heap." Zack nodded at the Fiesta.

Leroy closed one bloodshot eye against sunlight bouncing off the side window of Lonnie's battered Ford. "Not much worse than my rig. Got my eye on one of them Chevy Silverados."

Zack whistled. "I'd love to drive one of those. Hey, maybe you can share your secrets of success. You been saving a long time? You probably invested in gold or something, huh?"

Leroy wrinkled his nose on one side like he'd sniffed an unidentified yet familiar odor. He pointed a crooked finger. "I remember now. You're that fellow who was sneakin' 'round here yesterday."

Zack raised both hands in surrender. "No, sir. I was just needing a place to stay."

Leroy pondered a moment, flicked his wrist as if swatting a fly. "No harm come of it."

"No, sir. I understand you were just doing your job. I swear I'm a trustworthy guy. But, not every man is. Even up here in a small town like Hope, I'll bet you get your share of no-goods."

"Humanity is humanity," Leroy said, nodding with satisfaction at his wisdom.

"Take that guy who was murdered last week. Out by the creek? I'll bet he was a rascal if ever there was one. Why else would he get himself killed?"

Leroy turned away and grunted.

"I was told he stayed in the same cabin where I'm staying. Did you run into the guy?"

Leroy shrugged. "Time or two."

"He seem like a scoundrel to you?"

He shook his head vehemently.

Zack shifted his position at the railing. "A bit of excitement in town about the murder, I guess. Were you around when he got shot? Seems like the sound would echo through the canyon a long way. Did you hear it?"

"I believe I was takin' a shower 'bout then. Couldn't hear nothin' but water runnin'."

"Boy, you're an early riser. They say he was killed before daybreak."

"Come to think of it, maybe I was still asleep." He stood and clomped across the porch to yank open the screen door, mumbling over his shoulder, "Yep, I was asleep. Didn't hear a thing."

"I sleep like a baby when I've been working hard all day." Zack stepped from the porch and faced Leroy with a grin.

Leroy stared a moment before the door rattled closed behind him.

Zack sighed and turned toward his cabin. He'd get no more from Leroy today. Seemed Gaylord and Wendell were right—Leroy had come into money, though he hadn't offered how.

Lonnie had reported that Riordan's luck had run out and he was flat broke. There'd been little cash in his effects, so he died in Hope as poor as when he arrived. If he received a payoff, the money was gone. Leroy? He could have handed over a payoff, shot his former accomplice and taken the money back. But, where would he have gotten the money in the first place? Hard to believe he'd have hoarded his share of the ransom for three years and let his thirst for liquor run dry.

Head down, Zack walked toward his cabin, thoughts circling like a cat chasing its tail. His gut grumbled about something wrong in his logic.

He couldn't buy Leroy as one of the kidnappers. The man's drinking problem had not started yesterday; not likely he'd have been straight enough to plan or participate in the kidnapping. That did not eliminate him as a murder suspect. They could be looking at a robbery gone wrong, plain and simple, with no connection to the kidnapping.

Norton was right—that was not the answer Zack wanted.

He glanced up and saw Annie head to a weathered Weber grill listing on an uneven brick patio by her house. She tugged off the lid and stared into the grill a moment. Zack took a step that direction, hesitated, then strode toward her. "Can I help?"

She turned, a startled, worried frown slipping into a rush of pink in her cheeks.

Zack cringed. "Seems I'm forever making you jump."

"Oh, no. I mean, yes, you do tend to pop up unexpected."

"I could wear a bell."

The roses in her cheeks brightened as she laughed. "I don't want to treat you like a cow."

"Good. I'm not ready to be put to pasture." He lifted the lid off the barbecue, scrutinized the charred, rusted insides. "Nothing a good wire brush and a hot fire won't cure."

Annie wearily swept hair off her forehead. "Perhaps another day." She sighed and raised her face to the sky, followed the flight of swallows dipping and rising, then returned her gaze to him.

Her blue-grey eyes captured his and he stood inanimate a moment, the gritty wooden handle of the grill lid squeezed in his hand, aware only of the crinkle of fine lines at the corners of her eyes, the dimple by her mouth as she smiled. He finally inhaled and lowered his arm, the lid clanging against the grill like a gong.

Annie flinched.

"Whoa. Startled you again. Sorry."

"No, it's me. I'm just a bit jumpy these days."

Zack rubbed the back of his neck, apparently calling her attention to Mitchell's handiwork.

"You cut your hair."

He grinned and wrinkled his nose. "Short, huh?"

She hesitated, as if considering compliments for Zack's shorn-sheep style, gave up and laughed. "Well, you fit in with the locals now."

Zack joined her laugh and motioned to the Weber. "How about I clean this up?"

"Oh, I couldn't ask you to."

"You didn't. I offered. Tell you what. I'd really prefer not to eat at the Roadside every night. Not that the food was bad. But, it's such a warm evening, perfect for grilling. Show me to a wire brush. I'll clean this baby and head to the grocery store. Would you join me in a little summer barbecue?"

"No!" the word an explosion of breath. Her eyes darted from his as she moderated her tone. "I mean, thanks for asking, but I…I've got dinner already on the stove." She inched toward the porch steps. "Very kind of you to offer."

"I'll bet what you're cooking is way too good to pass up." He straightened the lid on the grill and brushed dust from his hands, barely able to hide his disappointment. He turned toward his cabin, stopped and faced her, momentarily refrozen by the last of the day's sunrays reflecting gold in her topsy-turvy hair. "Maybe tomorrow."

He took three long strides.

"I've got chicken breasts in the fridge and greens for a salad."

He spun back around with a grin. "Got any cumin?"

CHAPTER 7

Beware, lest the devil control your tongue!" Annie's father would bellow, his voice exploding with the fervor of conviction.

"Amen!" her mother would shout, and Annie would clamp lips tight against the impulse to speak. If she held her tongue to the roof of her mouth, could the devil yet waggle it in deceitful words? If she clenched her teeth like a fortress, could she trap bad words within?

She rarely spoke, even to herself. Teachers shuffled her to the back of the classroom, convinced her silence stemmed from some unknown and unchangeable learning disability, discouraged they had no solution. She made few friends; spent recesses and lunch hours slumped beneath a tree watching schoolmates chase and skip rope and laugh.

Books were banned in their house; readings from the Bible the only entertainment her father allowed. Annie grew tired of these stories and wondered about the sinful content in the books her parents derided, until curiosity finally won out over fear of reprimand. One afternoon, she slipped into the school library. Mrs. Yarnell, the librarian, became Annie's closest friend, guiding her selections and encouraging first whispers, then full volume as Annie ceased to listen so intently to her father and learned to trust her own voice.

But now, when words escaped that she'd never intended to say, she swore he'd been right and a mischievous devil controlled her tongue.

Why in the world had she invited Zack to dinner?

She'd meant to send him away—an emphatic but polite refusal, donning independence like armor. Where had the words formed? Surely, not in her brain.

You're stuck now, she thought as she wiped a tattered rag across the redwood-stained picnic table, scattering brittle leaves and scrubbing away bird droppings, embarrassed at the chipped, neglected condition of her patio furniture. She peeked at Zack crouched over the Weber, tunelessly whistling as he scraped with a wire brush and unfastened the pan to dump grease-splotched charcoal remains.

"Haven't used this in a while," he said as he reassembled the grill and built a base of briquettes.

"Doesn't seem worth the effort."

"But you were thinking about it tonight."

She shrugged and draped the cleaning rag over her shoulder. "Seemed to fit the evening."

"Well, allow me to do the honors." He grabbed a clean rag from those she'd heaped on the table, swiped at grease and soot on his hands, frowning at his efforts. "Going to take soap and hot water before these are presentable. Mind if I wash up?" He nodded toward her house. "Then, I can get the chicken breasts and start cooking."

"No!" the word rushed and harsh. "I mean, don't bother. I'll bring out the chicken and the spices you need." She held her breath, hoping he wouldn't question her rude behavior.

He only regarded her a moment before saying, "No problem. I'll wash up in my cabin." He walked off with a glance over his shoulder, perhaps expecting her to change course as she had before, now retracting the dinner invitation.

She hadn't felt those words coming either, but this time she was convinced of her intention. It was one thing to dine on a warm summer night with an attractive man like Zack; it was another entirely to invite him through her front door. She'd kept her home off limits to all males for almost three years.

She gathered the rags and strode into the house, stepping around Buffy, who tried to slow her for a treat. "I fed you, greedy little cat. You can't persuade me with those big green eyes. I'm a rock, you hear?" Buffy mewed and circled until Annie laughed. "Okay, okay. You win," at which Buffy positioned herself before a kitchen drawer. "You're a sly one, aren't you?" Annie added as she delivered a treat and stroked Buffy's ears.

She washed her hands at the sink, staring out the kitchen window at the flower beds Mark had built from redwood planks he'd haggled for at the lumberyard. A bargain, he'd told her. The guy didn't know what he had. Later, as she listened to him curse about knots and uneven thickness and bent boards, she did not mention that, perhaps, the lumberyard man knew exactly what he had. Instead, she praised his handiwork and shoveled soil into the beds, mixed in manure and compost, pressed in geranium and marigold starts, kissed him and reveled in his satisfied smile.

Toby had loved the bright reds and yellows. He would toddle across the patchy, weedy lawn to point a chubby finger at a bloom, turn to make certain she was suitably impressed, her 'ooh' or 'ahh' the signal for him to work his way down the row. "Don't touch," she'd warn, which worked until one day when she'd been preoccupied with the bills stacked on the kitchen table. Her absent-minded approvals apparently did not satisfy Toby, who managed to dislodge or decapitate several plants before she realized what he was doing. Her startled cry precipitated his red-faced wailing.

She'd not been angry, had not scolded her son, only rocked him in her arms and whispered that flowers are living things, too, and we need to take care of them. His tears subsided as she let him help reset plants and pat soil around their insulted roots.

She ought to rebuild the planter boxes. Mark's bargain redwood planks, strong and sturdy as the tree itself, had survived snow and rain and blistering sun, but nails had given way and boards uncoupled from the sides, the original rectangle now a haphazard jumble. It only made sense to pound the boards back together in autumn after removing shriveled plants, or before planting fresh-leafed starts in spring.

Somehow, she never got around to it.

Maybe this fall.

Maybe the planter boxes were fine just the way Mark and Toby had left them.

The scrunch of footsteps on gravel sent her scurrying to the refrigerator. She took out a package of chicken breasts, salad greens and assorted vegetables, quickly assessing freshness, tossing a slimy cucumber into the garbage can. She arranged their dinner ingredients on a metal tray, added salt, pepper, and the cumin he'd asked about, grabbed the tray and hurried out.

He'd changed his shirt.

She sniffed a light fragrance of aftershave.

Great.

She'd avoided the hall mirror, knew the wicked thing would reflect a harried woman with mussed hair, wearing an oversized, shapeless blouse, probably with a dirt smudge on her nose. Now, she wished she'd not only peeked, but repaired the damage.

A squirt of lighter fluid from a rusted can and several matches later, Zack had the charcoal glowing and closed the lid to heat the grill. "Thanks again for letting me invade your space. Nothing's better than grilling on a summer night like this. A guy thing, I guess."

"Must be," she replied with a laugh. "Mark always grinned like a cat with cream when he cooked on that old grill." She registered the question on his face. "My husband."

"Oh," was all he said but she saw his eyes flicker to her left hand.

"My rings don't fit the way they used to. I took them off one day and haven't gotten them back on." She rubbed an indentation on her left ring finger. "He died almost three years ago."

She hadn't meant to tell him that, either. Not that she tried to hide her loss, but there was no call to lay everything out to a stranger.

He lowered himself to the bench opposite and she found herself grateful for his choice, leaving the wide table between them. "I'm so sorry."

She shifted and stared at oaks and Ponderosa pines at the rear of her property, the dirt below littered with brown needles and sharp cones, husky grey squirrels chasing each other with the skitter of claws on bark. Long, heavy ropes dangled from a thick oak branch where Mark had shinnied up to affix a swing, the wood seat now rotting on the ground.

"Not so high," she'd implored as he chuckled and pushed against her.

"You a scaredy cat?" he'd teased. "I'll push you high enough to catch a moonbeam."

When she wrenched her attention back to the present, it seemed she'd been lost for hours. Zack sat quietly, following her gaze into the trees. She straightened and brushed hair behind her ear. "Hey," she said and mustered a bright smile. "How about that chicken?"

Another trip into the house to gather more spices, which he combined in a small bowl.

"Cinnamon? You're sure?" she asked.

"You're doubting my surefire rub?" He thumped his chest as if thrusting a dagger into his heart. "That hurts." He grinned and placed the spiced breasts on the grill.

As the chicken cooked, they shared recipe ideas and cooking techniques, laughed at their similar experiences with Mrs. Moretti and Mrs. De Luca, Zack saying perhaps they should get their old Italian neighbors together, Annie declaring that would be way too many cooks in the kitchen. They sheepishly described their worse culinary disasters, one-upped until agreeing that Zack pouring cleaning fluid instead of red wine into his stew took the prize.

"It was my roommate's fault," Zack defended himself. "He drank my Merlot and filled the empty bottle with cleaner."

Dinner was delicious. It had been a long time since Annie paid much attention to what she ate. Funny thing to admit, as she baked and cooked for a living, but cooking for herself held no appeal. Meals were for nourishment only. Favorite recipe cards, splotched with dried sauce or coated with flour, languished in a kitchen drawer beside half-filled boxes of birthday candles.

She had many dinner invitations after Mark died: well-intentioned phone calls from church ladies concerned with the welfare of a woman alone; occasional approaches by men, young and old, single and married. She turned them down politely, at first begging time to adjust to her new situation, later using her odd working hours as an excuse. The invitations ceased after awhile, except for a few men in town who still hoped she'd give them a chance.

Sometimes, she dined with Leroy and Sarah, which hardly led to tantalizing conversation. Leroy was either too drunk, hung over or preoccupied to offer much of interest, and Sarah's discourse was limited.

Kitty occasionally lumbered in, poured two glasses of Chardonnay and settled to gab as Annie cooked. They talked about anything and everything that came to Kitty's mind. Quite often, that included Annie's marital status.

"You need a man," Kitty would declare.

"I need nothing of the kind," Annie would fire back.

"Hell," Kitty would say, "I'm older and fatter and uglier than you, but I'd take a man if there was a decent one around."

"Well, you can have them all."

By the time Kitty waved a flabby goodbye, they'd have polished off a meal and the Chardonnay, conversation finally run as dry as the bottle.

Evenings with Kitty were good times.

Annie cleared the table, waved away Zack's offer to help and balanced the heaping tray as he held the screen door open for her. She placed the tray on the kitchen counter, retrieved three chocolate brownies left over from the day's goods, opened a bottle of Chilean red wine and returned outside. The sun had slipped below the pines but the afterglow tipped the needles with gold. The evening was still; blades of grass like soldiers at attention, manzanita leaves frozen in space, as if the only rush of air came from beneath swallows' wings as they circled and swooped for supper.

"It's not much," she said as she poured wine into two glasses.

"I'm not hard to please," and at her doubting frown, "well, not too hard."

She sat lengthwise on the redwood bench, hugging her knees to her chest. "I'd guess you're a wine snob."

It was difficult to tell if he was genuinely stunned or only bantering again. "Me? What in the world would make you think that?"

She shrugged and reached for her glass. "The way you sniffed and swirled the wine. I saw you check out the legs."

He laughed and brandished his glass. "You've found me out. I'm a legs man." He seemed to rethink his remark. "With wine, I mean. Well, maybe in other ways, too."

"I see." She let a pause carry whatever meaning he wished to assign, found herself grinning at his schoolboy fluster. It had been so long since she'd joked with anyone except Kitty. "And, how are the legs tonight?" she said, instantly regretting her boldness.

He fixed intense green eyes on her. "Superb."

She sat motionless a moment, then swung her long limbs under the table. "Well, I'll bet you've sampled a lot of them. Wines, I mean."

He sipped and shrugged. "Some."

"I'll bet you've even got a wine cellar."

"Not me." He stared over her shoulder a long moment and she began to think she'd carried the teasing too far, when he sighed and returned his attention to her. "The cellar and all its contents belong to my wife, Stella."

She didn't need to glance at his left hand; she'd already noticed the absence of a ring or telltale fading. Lots of married men don't wear rings, for safety at work, or because they can't adjust to the feel of a metal band. Then, there are men who deliberately misrepresent their marital status. She didn't picture Zack as the type to play that game.

"You make a wine cellar sound like a bad thing," she said.

He slumped a bit and tapped his glass lightly on the table. "Not at all. She's got some delicious wines."

His mood had turned gloomy and distracted, so Annie searched for a new topic. "How's your article coming?"

His thoughts must have been very far away because the moment stretched before he refocused on her. "What?"

"Chief Norton?"

"Oh, right." He straightened and grinned. "He's a character."

She breathed silent relief that the awkward moment had passed. "Hope has a lot of characters, some good, some not so much. Chief Norton, he's one of the good ones."

"I'm just gathering information right now. You never know what'll end up being important until you figure your angle. For instance, I'm thinking it might be the murder. How he investigates and how he's affected personally."

Night had begun to swallow the twilight, their faces obscured, nuances masked. Even so, Annie averted her eyes. "It's late," she said, withdrawing her legs from under the table and swiveling on the bench. "I should be getting to sleep. Tomorrow's Saturday."

If he showed any surprise at her abrupt dismissal, she could not detect it in the dim light. "Saturday is special?" was all he asked.

"Cinnamon roll day. I start early."

He rose. "I've overstayed. My apologies."

"No," she replied in a rush. "It's fine."

He walked along the table, took a hesitant step toward her. "I'm afraid I got carried away. It was just so nice."

She wrapped her arms around her chest. "Yes. It's only now getting chilly."

"Not exactly what I meant," he said as he turned away. "Goodnight, Annie."

She watched him walk away, then called out, "Thanks for cooking."

He kept walking, waved an arm above his head.

A bird landed on the roof of her house, perhaps the same mockingbird whose medley had floated through an open window the night before. She peered through the dark as the bird hopped away. When she twisted Zack's direction, he was entering his cabin. The mockingbird warbled and chirped and mimicked as Annie gathered the wine bottle and glasses.

***

Night had not yet yielded to morning; the cool air opaque, like gauze pulled over the world's eyes. The slightest sound was clear and reached far into the darkness; nocturnal creatures were already retired, daylight's inhabitants yet to rise. Annie breathed in the prologue to a new day as she walked the path to the café, knowing where to step even with only faint outlines of what lay ahead.

She'd walked this path so many times, greeting the world before most folks yawned and opened their eyes. In winter, she hurried against the numbing cold, but on clear summer morns like this, she hugged a sweater to her chest and tarried, thoughts awakening in slow syncopation with each step.

She should be tired this morning, her normal seven hours of sleep reduced to barely more than five; yet, somehow she felt fresh and alert. She'd been keyed up after Zack left, had cleaned the kitchen and dusted the living room to try and wear herself out so she could sleep. But, her thoughts banged off each other like bumper cars.

She ought not to trust him. She ought to keep her distance. This was not the time to let down her guard. After all, what did she know of this man? Of his past or his motives?

Yet, it was such hard work to distrust him.

The more she told herself to calm down and quit worrying, the more harried her thoughts had become until she'd finally tumbled exhausted into bed, Buffy curled into the empty space at her side.

When they'd first opened the Bluebell and learned how early she needed to begin preparations, Mark had worried aloud about her safety walking to the café in the dead of night. Who knew what wild animals were around, let alone lowlife humans. He insisted on staggering out of bed, sleepy-eyed and tousled, to escort her the seventy-five yards to work.

That lasted a week.

His solution then was to install a timer-driven light above the kitchen door, illuminating the landing in pale yellow so she could spy any dangers. She'd shaken her head but expressed only gratitude for his concern.

Not once had she been threatened on her morning walk. Not once had she seen a human or animal skulking by the door.

Until today.

She blinked at the apparition of a man sitting on the top step, hunched into a jacket, legs stretched before him.

Zack raised his head at her approach. He stood when she reached him, grinned and said, "I've always wanted to make cinnamon rolls."

CHAPTER 8

Sharp, spicy manzanita should have assaulted his nostrils as he ran down Canyon Road, Nikes striking asphalt, arms pumping. He should have caught a whiff of balsamroot flowers or pungent juniper or even his own sweat. Instead, he still smelled the cinnamon and yeast of Annie's kitchen.

"More flour?" he'd asked.

She'd sprinkled a teaspoonful over the mound before him. "Not too much or it'll be tough. The dough needs to be sticky but still come off your fingers."

He'd bent low and focused on kneading. "How long?"

"About five minutes. Until it feels right."

"Feels right?"

"Spongy. Stretchy. Not too wet or dry."

He raised an eyebrow and grinned.

"You just get so you know."

As the dough was rising, she brewed a pot of the delicious Ethiopian coffee and instructed him in combining sugar, cinnamon and spices. Her special recipe, she told him—a touch of nutmeg and cardamom. When it was ready, she divided the dough and worked the first half to demonstrate, then stood by as he tried to emulate how she flattened the dough with her palms and stretched it into a rectangle with quick, light stokes of the rolling pin. His rectangle bent kidney-shaped. He grimaced and yielded the rolling pin to her. "I'll do better next time."

The words had come naturally, but the promise in them dangled like a spider web in a breeze.

If she noticed, she hid it well. She rolled dough from the corner, snugged the lip over filling, moistened the final edge with egg wash and pinched to seal the seam. At least he did better at this step, his log tight and even. They sliced off wheels with a pastry knife, lined them on baking sheets and covered them with a damp cloth to rise again.

Like the previous evening, conversation was easy: favorite kitchen gadgets and spices; dogs versus cats as the best pets, he a dog lover for sure, she extolling Buffy's virtues. He learned nothing of consequence about her, yet now reflected on what he did learn: how she blew a soft breath over her top lip to remove a tickling blonde strand, how she hummed to herself when she forgot his presence.

He asked if she had any gut feelings about Riordan. Smart? Trustworthy? Sleazy? She brushed aside his question with a noncommittal shrug. She sloshed soapy water in the sink and said she wasn't in the habit of forming opinions about her guests.

The kitchen door had creaked open. Sarah was several steps into the room before registering his presence, her startled brown eyes locked on his, childlike directness amplified by the droop around her parted lips. He called a good morning, slugged the remainder of his coffee and thanked Annie for the baking lesson.

She wiped her hands on a blue cloth. "Now you can make them at home."

He rinsed the mug in the sink. "Seems like a lot of work if you're only feeding one or two."

She wrapped wax paper around one of the blueberry muffins she'd baked while waiting for the cinnamon rolls to rise. She handed the muffin to him. "Which is it?"

He quickly peeled back the paper and licked gooey melted berry. "Huh?"

"One or two?" she asked as she darted a look at Sarah.

The muffin warmed his hand as he watched her swipe the dishcloth across the countertop. When she stopped to peek his direction, he caught and held her gaze. "Officially two. Mostly one."

Which summed up the loneliness of his marriage.

The words replayed now as his muscles fatigued and gait slowed. He grunted in disgust at his own weakness, unaccustomed to feeling sorry for himself, bewildered these days when he could not stem that tide.

An electronic chirp resounded from the cell phone he'd shoved into a pocket. He slowed to a walk and glanced at the display. "Yeah."

"Well, top of the morning to you, too."

"Not everyone's Susie Sunshine like you, Lonnie."

"You should try. Throws people off when they expect grumpy and you come out with dimples and twinkles and stuff."

"Okay. My, such a beautiful morning!"

"Now, you're pathetic."

Exactly what he'd been thinking.

Zack closed his eyes against the sunlight slinking between jagged rocks on the ridge. This was conversation with Lonnie—nothing so important as to preclude introductory bullshit. Usually, Zack enjoyed their banter. Today, he was annoyed. "Got anything?"

"Who twisted your shorts? Okay, okay. I get the picture. Just demand I stick to business."

"Stick to business, Lonnie."

"Leroy Montrose. You get anywhere with him?"

Zack ran his free hand through the wasteland of Mitchell's haircut. "He claims to have come into money, which matches other reports. Seems too much of a coincidence with Riordan showing up in town. But, I'm not liking him for the murder."

"Well, he ain't one of the kidnappers. At the time you and me were exchanging bullets with sleezeballs, Mr. Montrose was residing in an Arizona detox clinic, part of a plea bargain on a drunk and disorderly charge. One of those places locked tight as a drum."

"Doesn't seem like the program worked."

"Usually don't. Big game they're playing, you ask me. Prosecutors and defense attorneys in cahoots with touchy-feely docs so they can bill the state for pretending to change what can't be changed."

"Some people do quit drinking, Lonnie."

"Most don't. Anyway, makes no difference whether your man Leroy dried out or not. Point is, he was not one of the kidnappers. So, if he is the murderer, then we might be up a creek pissing in the wind."

Lonnie was great at mixing metaphors.

Zack walked in circles, trying to head off muscle cramps after the run. "I'll keep working on the money angle. If Leroy got money from Riordan, then Riordan first got it from someone else in Hope, unless your Ms. McIntyre was wrong about him being broke when he left Nevada. Leroy's money might not be related to Riordan at all. Maybe he worked for it."

"Or, dug up dirt on our boy and demanded payment, later covering our boy with said dirt."

"In either case, he may have information we need."

"He's all yours. I'm still tracking Riordan, but nothing interesting is coming to light. What's your plan?"

Zack sighed and shook his head. "Keep talking to people. Follow up on that concho I told you about. Not much to go on. Damned dead ends are starting to piss me off."

Lonnie chuckled. "Cheer up, Susie Sunshine."

Zack cut the call and gripped the phone in his sweaty hand as he walked toward Main Street, head down, eyes focused on the asphalt. This trip to Hope was beginning to feel like another failed attempt to identify the kidnappers.

The sound of sluggish footsteps coming toward him drew his attention.

The kid approached cautiously; oversized, untied hightops scuffing along the uneven asphalt, blemished chin lowered and shoulders hunched, a nervous twitch under his left eye. He waggled the fishing pole he held, as if testing its flimsy length like an epee.

"Nice morning, huh?" Zack said.

He sniffed and shrugged, apparently having some conversation with himself, probably deciding how best to handle running into a stranger. He was a bit unkempt—fine brown hair sticking up on one side of his head, like he'd lost his comb months ago, T-shirt partially tucked into grass-stained shorts, arms and legs disproportionately long for his narrow early-teen frame.

Something about him reminded Zack of his childhood friend, Joey. Maybe the freckles across his nose.

Zack pointed at the fishing pole. "Going to fish the creek?"

The boy shrugged. "Yeah."

"Do any good here?"

Another shrug. "Sometimes. Fishing's better upstream or over to McPherson River, but this is close enough I can walk."

"Better than nothing, huh?"

"Yeah."

Something in his eyes, the tilt of his head. More than the freckles was Joey-like. "Hey, I'm Zack Dalton," he said and extended his hand.

A skinny arm reached and a youthful hand grasped. "Rory Archer."

"You come here often?"

"When school's out."

Zack spread his feet, arms crossed over his chest in a casual, just-two-guys-talking stance. "Sure was something, that guy getting killed last week. You hear about it?"

"Who hasn't."

"I guess word gets around, huh?"

"My dad says you can't fart without making the headlines."

Zack laughed and raised his hands in innocence. "Better he say that than an outsider like me. But, hey, you might have been fishing the morning of the murder. Could have landed right in the middle of things. Now, that's a scary thought. I mean, were you? Out here?"

"Maybe."

Zack wanted to attack, to scare information from the kid, if any existed to scare up. Instead, he drew a slow breath. "They say the guy got killed before sunrise. Probably you were still in bed. I mean, fishing's better late in the morning, right?" he asked, knowing the opposite, baiting the kid.

"No way."

"No?"

"Early bird gets the worm."

Zack nodded. "You've got a point. Wow, imagine if you'd run into the murdered man, huh? Wait a minute. You didn't run into him, did you?"

"No."

"Well, I bet your father's relieved about that."

Rory stared out to the creek.

"The shot must have been pretty loud, echoing off these canyon walls. Did you hear it?"

"Nope."

"Guess you weren't here when the deed was done. Maybe you got here later."

"Maybe."

"Like I said, good thing you didn't get mixed up in it. Hey, what do you use for bait?"

Rory turned down the corners of his mouth as he shook his head. "This is a fly fishing rod. My dad says there's no skill to fishing with bait. He says only wimps use worms and stuff."

"He's a good fly fisherman, huh?"

A fourth shrug. "Yeah, but I'm better."

Zack laughed and nodded at Rory, "Feels good to beat the old man, doesn't it?" The only contest his own nonathletic father had favored was chess and Zack still recalled with a flash of triumph the first time he yelled checkmate, too excited to maintain the decorum Walter Dalton insisted was part of the game.

He'd probably gotten all the noncommittal answers he'd get from Rory at the moment, but the kid tweaked Zack's investigative senses. He may have nothing to add, but Zack wanted to try again another time. "Hey," he said, "I've got an idea. I must confess, I've always been a wimp fishing with worms, but I'd love to learn to fly fish. Would you teach me?"

Rory regarded Zack, sucked in his lips a moment before squaring his shoulders. "Okay." He shifted the tackle box in his hand, a flush rising along his cheeks.

Zack's grin was sincere. "Deal. I'll pick up a license. Guess I'd better get some gear, too."

The final shrug of the conversation. "Nah, I got enough for both."

"Same time tomorrow?" Zack asked and, at Rory's nod, gave a thumb's up and continued his run down the road.

***

Two hours later, he had a whole lot of nothing to show for his information fishing expedition. He'd dangled bait in front of the hardware store clerk, pretended interest in buying a little chunk of Hope paradise in order to question a realtor, even threw a line to the county librarian, who nibbled but was not nearly the catch he'd hoped.

He bought breakfast again at the Downtown Diner, leaning back in the booth as Gladys poured coffee from on high. With each person, he circled the conversation to Riordan. Each time, he walked away empty-handed.

Not entirely true. Although he failed to gather concrete evidence or leads, he succeeded in building a picture of Riordan's time in Hope. One thing was certain: the man had not earned friends. Seems he was loose with comments about backward country yokels.

"Like he was so all-fired sophisticated," said Gladys with a sniff. "I seen how the fabric of his pants was all pilled and the cuffs frayed. He had no call for superiority."

Zack learned more about Police Chief John Norton than of Riordan. He began each conversation with queries about the chief, shoring up his cover as a journalist. Norton was a popular figure in Hope.

"Couldn't put the town in better hands," said Lance Jordahl at the hardware store. "He has good sense, which is more than you can say for some."

"Did he tell you about Owen?" Gladys rested the coffee pot on the table and ignored a wave from the corner booth. "Owen Harding's a good man but not too quick on the draw. Got himself mixed up with some swindler who came visiting with a big bruiser in tow. Chief Norton was not one bit afraid. He faced down the crook and sent him and his bodyguard packing. Owen was mighty grateful. The chief just told him to be more careful."

Each time Zack spoke with someone about Norton, he received a shake of the head, a sigh, and a reference to his long marriage to Amelia, the gentlest woman you'd ever meet. His informants eyed Zack expectantly, sure that he was privy to the trouble with Norton's wife, so he feigned understanding and silently vowed to learn more.

Stopping by the Roadside Tavern to pump Kitty for information on Norton and Riordan was on Zack's agenda for late afternoon. He figured Wendell and Gaylord would be warming their favorite stools. They'd certainly been willing to talk two nights ago.

For now, he slowed Lonnie's Ford as he rounded a bend in the road. A graveled side road was crowned by thick timbers and a wrought iron sign with the Rockin' I Ranch brand. He turned in and drove toward buildings far ahead. Circular irrigation systems sprayed the crop on his right, young shoots bright and refreshingly green against the steely-blue sky. Cattle grazed in the field to his left, the inevitable greener-grass seeker munching tall weeds through the barbed wire fence.

A wide drive circled before a log house with an impressive stone chimney and picture windows like enormous bug eyes. The wooden porch was outlined by rails of knotty, twisted tree limbs. The massive double doors were carved with the Rockin' I Ranch brand.

A man in dirty coveralls glanced up from the bucket of stain he'd been stirring, rested his stick on the lid and nodded a greeting. "You here for Mr. Isley? He's out for the day."

"Actually," Zack said as he eyed the outbuildings flanking Isley's house, settling on the barn a hundred yards behind, "I was hoping to speak with Mr. Kent Baker and was told I could find him here."

The man pointed his stir stick toward the barn. "Most likely seeing to the horses. Drive on back."

"Thanks," he replied and eased the car past a four-car garage and a large pole building, stopping by the red two-story barn with giant doors yawning open.

Horses whinnied as Zack stepped carefully across the dirt floor, scanning for fresh manure. He needn't have worried—the place was immaculate. Five stalls along one side, four chestnut heads bobbing. Tack hung neatly on the opposite wall. For sure, the barn smelled of manure and hay and animals, but you'd be hard pressed to find a stall unmucked or a horse unbrushed.

A man groomed the fifth chestnut at the far end of the barn, rubbing a brush along the silky hide, muttering to the horse as they both watched Zack approach. "Can I help you?" he asked in a soft voice.

"I'm looking for Kent Baker."

"That'd be me."

Quiet strength was the impression Zack got of the man: intelligent blue eyes shielding his thoughts, facial muscles relaxed around thin lips, a determined set to his jaw. He stood no more than five-eight, with a lean torso and muscular forearms. His Wranglers and plaid cotton shirt were soiled from dust mingled with sweat, but his auburn hair was trimmed neatly above his ears, moustache carefully shaped, cheeks stubble-free.

Zack offered his hand and noted Baker's firm grip. "Zack Dalton. Pleased to meet you. Got your name and where to find you from Police Chief Norton. Hope I'm not interrupting."

Baker stroked the horse as he spoke. "What can I do for you?"

So far, Hope residents seemed to buy his cover story, but Baker's steady gaze worried him, as if the man's bullshit meter operated at high frequency. Zack chose his words carefully. "I've been working with Chief Norton on the investigation into the murder victim your boys found. He's got a lot on his mind these days, so he asked me to follow up, in case you've thought of anything to pass along."

Baker would make a terrific poker player. Not a facial muscle twitched. His unblinking eyes bored into Zack's. "Told him all I know."

Zack rubbed the horse's nose and stared into a huge, wary brown eye. "Guess he's just being thorough, checking with everybody twice. People sometimes remember details after a time."

Baker nodded and circled to brush the other flank, the horse throwing back its head and pawing a forefoot. "Easy, Tara," he said. "Not much to tell. My boys were pretty upset. Carried over to me, I suppose, so I didn't notice much except that arm sticking up from the gravel."

"That'd be a shocker."

"I assumed my boys had it wrong. But they didn't."

"No signs of someone else having been there?"

Baker stopped grooming the horse. "Like what?"

Zack shrugged. "Tools used to bury the body? Papers that fell out of a pocket? Anything out of place."

"Not that I recall."

"Signs of a struggle? Long marks left by something dragged through the gravel?"

"No, sir. Like I said, I was focused on my boys. Not thought much of the crime since, except to worry about them."

Zack decided Kent Baker truly had nothing to add to their meager body of evidence. "Must have been traumatic for them."

"They're doing all right, I guess. Couple bad nights to start."

"I can imagine."

"You got kids?"

"No." It was one of his regrets in marrying Stella, who said she was far too old for motherhood. "May I speak with your boys? Ask them a few questions?"

"Don't see what you'd accomplish. They told the police everything. Kids forget quickly."

"Something could trigger a memory."

Baker squinted at him. "Chief Norton asked you to do this, huh?"

The man was no fool. A stranger doing the chief's job? Zack had been right to tread carefully and now drew on the one excuse he could conjure, hoping he didn't have to get into details. "As I said, he's got a lot on his mind these days. His wife, you know." He waited for Baker to reply no, he didn't know, and could Zack kindly fill him in. Instead, Baker nodded and shushed Tara as the horse whinnied. Relieved, Zack added, "Officer Jacobs is on vacation and there's too much work for John to handle. I told him I'd help out."

Baker gave Tara a pat and walked to the workbench to set down the brush. Finally, he turned to Zack. "Not sure what good it'll do, but go ahead. I don't want them upset, understand?"

"Absolutely," Zack replied.

"They told their tale many times in the beginning. Got to be neighborhood celebrities, all the other kids hanging on every word. That calmed down after a few days and they've moved on."

"I'll be careful."

"You do that." Baker led Tara to her stall, clicking with his tongue and speaking softly as he closed the door. "When do you want to talk with them?"

"This morning would work."

"I'll call my wife."

"I'm sure John will appreciate your cooperation." He regarded the remaining stalls. "Beautiful horses."

Baker came to stand beside him. "That they are. Real pleasure to work with, except Tara's a might stubborn at times."

"Seems pretty docile."

"You caught her on a good day. She's got a way of figuring what makes my job difficult. Moves when I need her to stand, plants herself in one position when I need her to move."

Zack laughed. "Does Ray Isley ride them all?"

"You acquainted with the Isleys?"

"I've met Ray and Troy."

"Well, Troy rides Chaco, over in the third stall. Mr. Isley prefers Dandy. These first two are getting on in age, so I give them any workout needed."

"And, Tara?"

"Belongs to Mrs. Isley. She rides more than the men of the family. Let's Tara have her head a bit too much for my liking, but they get along, especially when it's time to gussy up for a parade."

Zack had been inching toward the barn doors. He stopped and peered at the tack hung on the wall and the saddles resting on a rail. "She rides for show?"

"Sometimes."

He spied a saddle glinting in sunrays that slipped through the open doors, berated himself for not having noticed the decorated saddle. He'd been too focused on gaining Baker's confidence and had failed to carefully note his surroundings. "That hers? Mind if I take a look?"

Baker watched as Zack ran a hand over the soft leather, examined the rose and leaf tooling, the silver conchos along the fender. A perfect match to the concho in Riordan's shave kit. "Beauty," he said as he moved around the end of the rail.

Sometimes, he did get lucky.

"There's one missing here."

"What?" Baker hurried over to peer at the vacant spot. "Darn things are always coming off. Guess I better look for it."

He could have told him not to bother—the concho was safely stored in a police evidence box. "Maybe it came off when she rode in a parade."

"Not likely. Mostly she rides in the late summer, so she's not been out for months. I checked the saddle good after the last ride." The man was tense now, probably envisioning the thankless task of scouring the barn for the lost concho.

"Maybe it didn't fall off."

Baker frowned at him. "You mean, somebody took it? Easy enough, but I don't think any of the boys around here would risk their job for such a thing. The Isleys have lots of visitors, but most don't come near the barn. No, more likely it fell off."

Zack walked toward the barn doors, stopping as he reached them. "One last question." Baker was toeing the ground beneath the saddle. "Did you ever run into the murdered man, Edward Riordan, prior to finding him buried by the creek?"

Distracted, Baker looked up from his search and shook his head.

Zack saluted in thanks and walked out into the shimmering heat as the horses blew and snorted.

Riordan had in his possession a concho from Mrs. Isley's saddle. How had he come by it?

Zack turned the Ford back down the drive to the log house. The man who'd first greeted him raised a paintbrush in farewell. On a hunch, Zack killed the engine and approached.

"You find Kent?" the man asked as he dipped the brush in a gallon of stain.

"Yes, I did, thanks. Mighty fine animals he's tending."

"You betcha. 'Course, I'm not much of a rider myself. Not like these cowboys working around here. Me, I'm just the handyman."

"I guess Mr. Isley's too busy to do for himself."

He glanced over his shoulder before turning twinkling blue eyes to Zack. "Wouldn't know an Allen wrench from a vise grip. Don't bother me none. Good job security." He chuckled and winked as he dipped the paintbrush.

"Nothing wrong with that. I'm Zack Dalton, by the way." He stepped forward to shake hands but the man waved him off with the wet brush.

"Clyde Driscoll. Pleased to meet you."

"Seems Isley's not much of a horseman and not much for fixing up the place. Must be a good businessman."

Driscoll sucked in his cheeks a moment. "I got no idea about that, except my paychecks keep coming."

Zack kept pace as Driscoll moved slowly down the porch wielding his paintbrush. "Got to admire a man who can run an operation like this."

"I suppose."

"I'll bet he's got plenty of advisors. Financial gurus and lawyers. Probably people coming and going all the time."

"Like a swinging saloon door."

"I wonder," he began and made of show of thinking hard before shaking his head.

"What?" questioned Driscoll, his eyes narrowed and brush held motionless above the rail.

"Nah. A long shot. No need to bother you."

Driscoll straightened and pointed the brush at Zack. "Well, now, how do you know without asking?"

Zack rubbed his chin. "I was just thinking. I've been working with Chief Norton while he investigates the murder down by the creek. Unfortunately, he's getting nowhere fast. Seems most people never even spoke to the victim and don't know why he was in Hope. So, I was thinking, perhaps he had business with Mr. Isley. You never saw him at the ranch, did you?"

Driscoll's chin rose. "What if I did?"

Zack's pulse quickened. He'd gone fishing again, throwing a line into black water with no idea of what swam beneath. If there was something to catch, he couldn't let it slip away. "I'm sure Chief Norton would be mighty grateful for any help." Driscoll's expectant smirk did not change. "Plus, he mentioned a reward for information leading to an arrest."

The weathered handyman's eyes widened. "How much?"

"Not sure, but I can check. John's a bit tied up these days. His wife, you know." He played the sympathy card again and exhaled at Driscoll's slow nod. "He's authorized me to be his eyes and ears. Tell you what, if you've got information, you can pass it along to me and I'll check on that reward." He sensed Driscoll's indecision and chose to work on the man's self-importance. "But, really, I wouldn't get my hopes up. Not likely you know something of value in the case." He nodded and waved as he turned toward his car.

"Now, hold on there. You're judging what I got to say before I say it."

Zack twisted back, head cocked to one side and eyes narrowed.

"You on your honor about that reward?"

"Wouldn't say so if I wasn't."

Driscoll sniffed and nodded toward the barn. "He was here, that guy what got himself killed."

"When was this?"

"Couple days before they found him."

Zack shook his head. "I asked Kent Baker if he'd seen the man. He said no."

"Well, he don't work every day, now does he?" Driscoll smirked. "That's how come I was in the barn. One of them damn horses went and kicked his stall door and bent a hinge. Normally, Baker fixes stuff there, but him being off, young Isley ordered me to do it. I was getting supplies from the storage room when I heard the voices."

"How do you know it was Riordan?"

"Stuck my head around the corner to look. You see, they weren't having no pleasant conversation. Nothing I wanted to get in the middle of. So, I peeked but kept my presence to myself. Couple days later, I opened up the local newspaper and his face was front and center."

"How come you never told this to Chief Norton?"

Driscoll grinned and wiped spittle from his mouth. "He never asked."

And, no one offered a reward, Zack added, pretty sure the man would have kept quiet about the encounter without monetary enticement. "Could you hear what they said?"

"Well, my hearing ain't exactly what it used to be. Got my hearing aids in now, but not that day. Damn things drive me crazy. Besides, seemed the wiser choice to stay the hell out of whatever they were into. Like I said, it wasn't a friendly conversation. But I could make out when Isley yelled, 'You'll get no money from me.' That's what he hollered before he stomped out."

"Did Riordan follow him?"

"I suppose. I ducked back around the corner a minute or two before looking again. Guy was gone."

Zack regarded Driscoll, judging his reliability. The man might be fabricating the encounter to secure the reward, but Zack didn't think so. Riordan being in the barn could explain the concho in his shave kit. "I'll pass your information along to the chief."

"Don't forget that reward."

"Yes, sir," Zack replied as he walked to his car. "I'll check right away. Chief Norton knows how to get hold of you?"

Grey-stubbled flesh wobbled beneath Driscoll's chin as he nodded and bent to the paint can, a satisfied grin forming around yellowed teeth, probably already planning how to spend the reward money.

Deceiving people wasn't Zack's favorite thing to do but, if necessary for the investigation, he'd do it. Should he let Norton in on his subterfuge? It'd be one more wrongdoing not likely to endear him to the man.

Letting Driscoll down later would be easy. Heck, he'd hand over a couple hundred of his own money if the argument between Isley and Riordan helped lead him to the kidnappers.

As Zack stopped the Ford under the Rockin' I Ranch entryway, he speed-dialed Lonnie.

CHAPTER 9

Chief John Norton glanced up from papers strewn across his cluttered desk. "Dang-blasted bureaucrats will be the death of me."

Zack sank into the worn chair across from him. "At least you got the air conditioner fixed."

"Now, don't be jinxing me. Matthews said he fixed it for good. But I've never seen a mechanical device fixed for good. Dang things got minds of their own and bust themselves at the most inopportune time. Don't be giving this monster any ideas."

"We could speak in code," Zack said with a grin.

Norton harrumphed and pointed a stubby finger. "Plain ol' English will do."

A uniformed, scrawny man with pock-marked cheeks and a knobby nose appeared in the doorway to Norton's office. "Chief?"

Norton held up a hand to beg a moment from Zack. "What've you got, Harold?"

The officer noticed Zack and hesitated.

"You can speak in front of Mr. Dalton here," Norton said and waved his arm in a hurried introduction. "Officer Dorsey. Zack Dalton."

"Sorry to interrupt," Dorsey said as he shook hands with Zack. "Just wanted to let you know that Oliver at the repair shop says the patrol car's needing new brake pads."

Norton sighed and spread his arms wide. "Isn't anything in this operation working?"

Dorsey seemed to miss the sarcasm. He squinted his eyes in thought a moment before answering, "I do believe the copier's fine this week."

The chief groaned. "A miracle." He rubbed his hand across his chin and nodded to Dorsey. "Tell Penny to prepare the paperwork. Can't have a patrol car with lousy brakes."

"Yes, Chief." Dorsey hurried out the doorway.

"Part-time officer," Norton said. "Well-meaning, but limited." He leveled his gaze at Zack. "You have news for me?"

"First, tell me about Ray Isley."

The chief cocked an eyebrow and stared over the tops of his black-framed reading glasses. "What about him?"

"Background. I understand he's not originally from around here."

"He a person of interest in this case?"

Zack shrugged. "Everyone's of interest."

"That's a cop out, if I ever heard one, excuse my pun. Okay, I'll play your game. As I said before, Ray Isley came to this county about ten years ago, started buying property from people glad to sell. Ranching requires economies of scale these days and many of our small-time ranchers couldn't make a go."

"Isley arrived here with a lot of money?"

"Yes, but don't ask how he came by it. Never had a reason to inquire."

"How's he fit into the community?"

"Like a peacock in a hen house. Which ruffles a few feathers."

"Is his operation profitable?"

"Far as I can tell. Some years probably better than others. That's the nature of the business. Subject to all kinds of influences. Weather, commodity prices, politics."

"How about lately?"

"Good years, which were sorely needed after the last bad spell." Norton closed one eye as he thought. "Four bad years in a row, I'd say, ending about three years ago. A good time to buy up land, if you could afford to. That's when Isley increased his acreage to its present size."

"Three years ago, huh?"

"Now, don't tell me you're trying to tie Ray Isley to your kidnapping case."

Zack ignored Norton's glare and shifted forward in the chair. "Matched the concho to a saddle. Belongs to Mrs. Ray Isley."

Norton tented his hands and riffled thick fingers. "Got any idea how it came to be in Riordan's possession?"

"He was out at the ranch two days before he died. Handyman heard him arguing with Isley, something about money. Maybe Riordan found the concho on the ground, decided to keep a souvenir, or maybe he pried it off the saddle. Doesn't really matter. The point is, he was out at the Rockin' I Ranch. Not a place he'd just stumble upon."

"Doesn't make Isley a kidnapper or a murderer."

"As you said, he's merely a person of interest."

Norton pushed aside papers hiding a monthly calendar desk pad covered with scribbles and ran his finger along entries for the next few days. "Think I'll have a chat with him. Get this squared away. I'm willing to bet on a reasonable explanation."

"I'd like to be there."

"Figured as much," Norton said as he flipped through a book and reached for the phone cradled on the desk. A few moments later, he said, "That was Mrs. Isley. Ray is out of town today and tomorrow. I'll set up a meeting for Monday morning."

The delay was exasperating, especially since Zack had so little to investigate in the meantime.

"You got anything else to report?" Norton asked.

"I spoke with Kent Baker. Nothing new from him but he gave me permission to talk with his sons. That's where I'm heading next."

Norton glanced at his watch. "You will keep in mind they're just kids." At Zack's who-me indignation, Norton leveled a stern glare. "If I were you, I'd tiptoe around Isley. You might fool most folks in town, but he's a different story. You don't get to be the richest man in the county if you're gullible. If you push him, he's likely to push back and he's got the money and lawyers to do so." His desk phone rang and he reached for the receiver. "Leave Isley to me."

***

Zack rang the Baker's doorbell, heaving an exasperated sigh when no one answered. He took a chance and walked along the unfenced side of the house and spied Mrs. Baker by a square, rotating clothesline.

She was startled when he called hello and stood motionless as he approached to introduce himself. She swept flyaway strands of auburn hair behind her ear, fluffed her bangs and smoothed the front of her cotton shirt, regarding Zack from the corners of hazel eyes below worried, knit brows. "My husband phoned to say you might come by."

Good, he thought as he quickly assessed her nervousness and figured she wouldn't act without her husband's permission. Most likely, Kent Baker ruled the family with the calm determination Zack had noted at the Rockin' I Ranch. Zack spoke softly, imitating Baker's cowboy cadence. "Sorry to interrupt," he said, motioning to the plastic basket at her feet. "Let me give you a hand." He grabbed the corner of a blue cotton sheet, heavy with rinse water and smelling of laundry detergent.

"Oh, no, really," she said, but made no effort to stop him.

"Takes me back to being a kid." He matched two corners to fold the sheet in half, secured it on the plastic-coated line with a wooden clothespin. "I'd be in the backyard swinging a baseball bat or running my Tonka trucks and Mom would be hanging sheets on the line. She said it was the only way to get that fresh smell."

She smiled, showing small, even teeth. "My mother always said the same thing."

"Well, Mr. Baker's a lucky fellow that you carry on the tradition." Zack rotated the clothes line and reached into the basket.

She patted her hair again and watched as Zack hung the second sheet. "Kent said you want to talk to our sons about finding the body."

"I've been giving Chief Norton a hand. He's having a bit of a hard time right now." Zack was relieved to see the familiar sad frown when he mentioned Norton. He was sorry for whatever ailed Norton's wife, but took advantage again to gain her confidence. "We're just following up, talking to everyone a second time. Sometimes people remember things after they've had time to think."

"I don't know. They've mostly gotten over that horrible day."

Zack pinned the final corners and turned toward her, hands on hips and head bowed. "Took it pretty hard, did they?"

She wrinkled her nose. "Tommy was okay, I guess. He enjoys being in the spotlight. But, not Timmy. He's, well, more sensitive."

He shook his head. "A dead body is not something a child should find. I'm sure you and Mr. Baker have helped your sons work through this and I promise I'll do my best not to upset them. Sure would aid Chief Norton's investigation if I can talk with them."

The back screen door creaked open as two tousle-haired, slender boys clomped onto the stoop, halting in a mirror-image stare at Zack, a black Lab squeezing between them.

"How do you tell them apart?" he whispered.

She gathered the clothes basket and grinned. "Tommy's a half-inch taller."

***

Kent Baker probably maintained the lushest lawn in Hope—trimmed and fertilized and evenly mown, a soothing green testimony to the man's fastidiousness. Zack sat cross-legged on the grass beneath the skimpy shade of a poplar and eyed the twins huddled before him, Rex stretched out and panting. A half-inch of height was not going to help him distinguish between the boys. "Which one of you is Timmy?" he asked.

"I am," came a quick response from the boy on his left.

Peter and Paul McAvoy lived down the street from Zack when he was growing up. Older by a couple of years, the McAvoy twins used Zack as a decoy for their escapades. What adult would suspect that as they talked with that well-mannered Dalton boy the McAvoys were planting a rubber snake on the back porch? Zack's parents discouraged the relationship as soon as they understood his role, but not before he learned a thing or two about the craftiness of twins.

Peter and Paul were experts at confusing the enemy, swapping identities as needed.

Zack was pretty sure the Baker twins had those same tricks down pat. Such a determined, confident response seemed unlikely from the boy Mrs. Baker described as more timid.

"Pleased to meet you," Zack said and reached out to shake hands, keeping his suspicions to himself. "So, you must be Tommy," he added and moved his hand to the twin on the right, the boy's weaker grasp convincing Zack he was onto their ploy. The question was whether they routinely tried to fool strangers or had a special reason to try and fool him. Maybe a little of both. "Did your mother tell you why I'm here?"

The twins nodded in unison. The one who called himself Timmy narrowed his eyes. "How come you're doing the asking instead of the police?"

"They're just a bit busy."

"You got a badge?"

Zack grinned at him. "Sure wish I did. That'd be cool, wouldn't it?"

The twin who'd answered as Tommy smiled brightly, then turned as the back door opened and Mrs. Baker approached with three soda cans on a tray. "Oh, boy!" he said and leaped up. "I get the root beer!"

"No way!" his brother shouted and scrambled to his feet. "You had one last time."

"I brought three, for heaven's sake," Mrs. Baker said as the boys snatched cans off the tray and popped the tops, guzzling as she shook her head and offered a can to Zack. "I hope this is okay. I don't keep much soda pop in the house. My husband doesn't approve. He says we might as well drip sugar into their veins."

The can sweat icy condensation as Zack swigged. "My father felt the same way. But, it didn't bother me. Just made them taste that much better. Root beer's my favorite." He gulped and grinned at the twins as they settled back on the lawn.

They'd switched positions.

They wore identical T-shirts with a green Incredible Hulk flexing oversized muscles on their undersized chests, and similar khaki shorts. But, he'd noticed a loose shoelace on the sneaker of the boy who'd been on his right. The shoelace now flopped on his left.

Mrs. Baker glanced around as if deciding whether to sit on the grass beside them. Zack spied a plastic lawn chair on a small concrete patio and fetched it for her. She settled into the chair with a grateful smile, waved a finger at her sons. "Now, you answer this nice man's questions, you hear?"

"Yes, Mom," they mumbled in unison.

The syrupy sweetness of the soda coated Zack's throat as he took a final swig. He'd never cared for root beer. He set the can at his feet. "I know you told Officer Jacobs what happened the day you found the body, but I'd like you to tell me, too."

"We didn't find it," said the boy who'd called himself Timmy.

"You didn't?"

"Rex did."

The dog's ears perked and head rose at his name. He panted and drooled before flopping back on his side.

"I guess he's the real hero then, huh?" Zack said.

"Dogs can't be heroes," said the assertive twin.

"Yes, they can," retorted his brother. "Don't you remember those Lassie reruns? Dogs are heroes every day. Right, mister?"

Mrs. Baker frowned. "Boys, I don't think this is what Mr. Dalton came to talk about."

Zack reached over to pat Rex's head. "It's okay. Dogs are often heroes, although sometimes they get help from people."

"Like us," so-called Timmy said, "because, you see, Rex wouldn't even have been by the creek if we hadn't brung him."

"Brought," corrected his mother, then covered her mouth with slender fingers. "Sorry. Habit."

Zack laughed and shook his head. "No problem."

A faint bell sounded from within the house and Mary Alice Baker sprang from the lawn chair. "Oh, dear. I'm expecting a call. Will you excuse me?"

You bet, Zack thought, grateful for time alone with the boys, certain that if there was anything to learn, it would be easier without her present.

Interviewing children can be tricky. Some are too anxious to please, fabricating answers they think you want to hear. Some are scared or intimidated and clam up. Normally, parents are present, unless implicated in the investigation. Interviewing a child alone likely taints any evidence gathered and opens the door to charges of misconduct.

At this point, proper procedure and chain of evidence be damned. Zack was running out of time and patience.

"It's Grandma," pretend-Tommy said. "She calls every week. They'll be on the phone forever."

Zack smiled at him. "Moms and grandmas sure can talk, can't they?"

The boy grinned and nodded.

"We might as well continue. One at a time, okay? Who will describe that day for me?"

"I will," declared the false Timmy, as Zack had expected. "We went to the creek looking for stuff."

"What kind of stuff?"

"Just stuff. You can find pretty cool things sometimes. We weren't allowed to go to the creek by ourselves when we were little, but Dad said it was okay once we turned ten."

"So, you rode out on your bikes?"

"Sure. It's not far."

"You always walk down to the water in the same spot?"

"Nope."

"How'd you choose where to go down?"

Both boys shrugged.

"Did you see anybody else around?"

They shook their heads.

Zack plucked a stalk of silky grass. "So, you walked to the creek. Then, what happened?"

"Rex started barking and carrying on. We kept hollering but he wouldn't come, so we went to get him. It was gross."

"I'll bet. I'm sure the chief's got all the information he needs about the body. You don't need to describe it to me. Some things are best forgotten."

A slight nod from the more timid boy.

His brother swung his arms wide. "We ran to our bikes and rode home. End of story."

"I suppose you've told the story to your friends, too."

"About a bazillion times."

"Like a celebrity, huh?"

He shrugged, but smugness in his bright eyes betrayed how much he'd enjoyed the limelight.

"Oh, yeah, one more question. Did you find any stuff?"

The boy squirmed and his brother's head snapped up, eyes wide and lips parted.

They'd found something.

"What do you mean?"

Zack discarded the grass stalk. "Well, you said you went to the creek to look for cool stuff. I wondered if you found any."

One vigorous, defiant shake. One pair of frightened hazel eyes.

He hunched to be eye level with the disturbed stare. "Did you find anything, Timmy?"

The boy winced as his brother declared, "We told you. I'm Timmy."

Zack ignored him and spoke softly to the boy whose stare had not wavered. "You can get in big trouble by not turning over evidence in a murder like this. Did you know that, Timmy?"

Tommy scrambled up and grabbed his brother by the arm.

"Ow!"

"C'mon. We're leaving."

The real Timmy shrugged off his brother's grasp.

"On the other hand," Zack continued, "you can be a hero like Rex if you help capture the bad guys."

"I said, c'mon," the real Tommy shouted.

Zack risked a glance from Timmy to the house, willing Mary Alice Baker to gab on the phone a few more minutes.

Timmy puffed shallow breaths, then slowly reached into the pocket of his shorts as Tommy plopped to the ground with a dramatic groan. Timmy held his hand out to Zack and unfolded slender fingers to dump a bullet casing into Zack's outstretched hand.

"Best thing we ever found," moaned Tommy.

"Shut up," whispered Timmy.

Tommy's eyes widened as he pulled up handfuls of grass. Zack guessed Timmy didn't rule their relationship often, but Tommy listened when he did.

"You've done the right thing," Zack said to both of them.

"Are we in trouble?" Timmy whispered.

"Not with me or the chief, but I can't be so sure about your parents."

Timmy grimaced as Tommy said, "Dad'll be mad we didn't give it up right away. We'll get grounded, for sure."

Zack nodded and pocketed the casing. "My Dad would've been mad, too. Tell you what. Let's keep this to ourselves, okay?"

Hope lit the mirrored faces before him.

It would suit Zack fine to keep this discovery quiet.

"What are you going to do with it?" asked Tommy with a covetous stare at Zack's pocket.

"Take it to a lab for evaluation." The back door squeaked open and he waved to Mrs. Baker as she peered at them.

"It'll help you catch the murderer?" Timmy asked.

"I hope so," Zack replied as he stood. "But, whether we catch the bad guys or not, giving up this evidence makes you both heroes."

CHAPTER 10

He dialed Lonnie as he hurried down the Bakers' walkway.
"I always said you've got cop instincts."

"Never heard you say that, Lonnie."

"You weren't listening. Me, I'm full of compliments."

"You're confusing compliments with bullshit."

"Okay, Boy Genius, what's your next move?"

Working outside the confines of protocol was Lonnie's definition of a good cop. How the hell else do I get things done? he'd ask when Zack questioned his methods. Yet, he knew his bounds—expert at snuggling the line between doing his damn job and screwing up an indictment; a master of knowing exactly how much wool he could pull over a superior's eyes.

Zack had never mastered Lonnie's devious arts. He'd learned to work with him in the only way he could—follow due process and ignore Lonnie's shenanigans.

Now, the rule-breaking decisions were his.

He hadn't told Norton about the bullet casing.

He rationalized that Norton was too busy and distracted to deal with the evidence and he did the chief a favor by handling it himself. But, in truth, he wanted quick answers, which he wouldn't get if he turned in the casing.

And, he might not want to share what they learned.

If the casing matched those they'd squirreled away three years ago, he'd have proof he was on the right track. If not, there'd be little evidence tying Riordan's murder to the kidnapping and he'd most likely abandon the investigation.

Lonnie hadn't spent years on the force in a vacuum. Although never popular with the brass, he'd built a cadre of guys who sniffed at the rules as he did. It was a world of debt and repayment—doing favors one day, demanding one the next. He called a friend at the state forensics lab, which resulted in Zack driving two hours from Hope to hand the casing to another of Lonnie's buddies, who would transport it and the kidnapping casings to the lab for comparison. They'd get results the next day.

Now, Zack was headed back to Hope. The meandering highway stretched before him to a pinpoint in the distance, warm air rushing through the open windows, the Fiesta's radio crackling and finally losing signal. The early morning start to the day caught up with him, his eyelids heavy as he shifted in the uncomfortable seat. He noticed a sign for a wayside and pulled in.

Grabbing the bottle of water and bag of chips he'd purchased at a convenience store, he walked to a bulky pine picnic table beneath the octopus arms of an old oak. A Stellar Jay squawked and flit above his head, no doubt hoping the tall man with a tired, pensive look would be careless with his snacks.

Zack sat atop the table and drew his feet up on the bench. He uncapped the bottle and swigged as he watched the black waters of the Tyee River on a high-speed chase to the sea.

The investigation was tumbling like the river: careening off standard procedures, sweeping past eddies of routine and the law. He was off-duty and off-record, hurriedly navigating his own course while ignoring the dangers, unable to maneuver back to safe waters.

But, it was the only way to get answers.

He was sure the casings would match and confirm the only reasonable scenario: Riordan went to Hope to demand money from another of the kidnappers. With that confirmation, he'd need only find the murder weapon and solve both crimes.

Keep digging, he told himself. You're almost there.

Fatigue settled like heavy dew dripped from leaves above. In a puzzling turn of emotions, his need to solve the crime and save face was fading the closer he came to achieving his goal. Yes, he wanted to follow this breakthrough to its conclusion. But compulsion was slipping behind a malaise that took more and more effort to overcome.

If the casings didn't match, Zack wasn't sure he'd have the energy to try again.

Wouldn't Stella laugh.

He opened the bag of chips, the crackle of plastic drawing squawks from overhead.

He'd called her as he began his return drive to Hope.

"Sounds like you're driving. Are you on your way home?" she asked.

"Not yet. I've got a good lead."

"You've said that before."

"I'll be back as soon as I can. Why don't you get out of the house? Go to dinner with Yvonne."

"Don't be so cruel, Zack."

He sighed and tightened his grip on the phone. "Sorry. I understand."

But, he didn't.

He'd never know if she actively participated in the jury tampering that got her disbarred or if she was only caught in the fallout. It really didn't matter. The case was high profile, with an ambitious district attorney ready to make political points. Someone had to go down.

When the disbarment was announced, Stella retreated behind the walls of her San Francisco condo. "I can't face them," she'd screamed.

"Who?" he'd asked.

"Anybody. Everybody."

She'd been standing before the full-length mirror in their bedroom. She shrieked and hurled a bulky ceramic vase against the glass, shards tinkling to the floor.

Zack was patient, at first. She's a strong woman, he thought. She'll find her stride again.

But things got worse.

He supposed her injured pride left no room for flaws. A beautiful but aging woman, Stella must have seen and hated flaws she saw reflected in the mirror.

One botched surgery later, the skin of her face was over-taut, her smile constrained.

"It's not that bad," he told her and meant it. Her face was not grotesque. Just a bit odd.

"I'm hideous," she screamed.

Of course, she sued the doctor, but what good was money to a wealthy woman?

Unwilling to face the stares and whispers she feared, she entombed herself and relied on Zack to entertain her, commiserate, share a nightly bottle of wine. As her demands of him increased, so did his resistance. The condo's granite countertops and faux marble walls blinded like strobe lights as he crossed the threshold; the city lights beyond the massive picture window beckoned him to be anywhere but there.

With a frustrated sigh, Zack slid off the picnic table and slugged the last of his water as the raucous jay swooped overhead. He crushed the chips in the bag and turned it upside down to scatter crumbs on the ground.

"Knock yourself out," he said to the noisy bird and returned to Lonnie's car.

***

People are creatures of habit, Zack thought as he strode across the Roadside Tavern.

Gaylord and Wendell were perched on the same stools as when he'd met them two nights before.

"Well, if it ain't the writer. You won a Pulitzer yet?"

Zack shook hands with the men, both licking lips in anticipation of another shared pitcher of beer. "Not yet."

"How's a person win that thing, anyway?" Wendell asked.

Zack shrugged as Kitty flung open the swinging door and emerged from the kitchen.

"Thought you'd left me for good, sugar," she said, a smile puffing her glowing cheeks.

"No man in his right mind would leave you."

Wendell whooped and punched Gaylord in the arm. "Ain't he a charmer? You ought to take lessons."

Kitty frowned at Wendell. "Some things you can't learn. I doubt Gaylord's got a charming bone in his body."

"There you go again, not recalling proper, Kitty," Gaylord began.

"Don't you be reminding me of times I'd as soon forget, old man." She shook her head and turned to Zack, the twinkle in her eyes betraying how much she enjoyed bantering with the two barflies. She motioned to the taps. "Pour you one, darlin'?"

He laid a twenty on the counter to the contrived disinterest of the men beside him. "Let's make it a pitcher. Will you gentlemen join me?"

"Mighty neighborly of you," Gaylord said as Wendell bobbed his head. They hurriedly drained their mugs and slid them to Zack for refills.

"How's your story coming on John Norton?" Kitty perched on a stool and rested her forearms on the bar.

Zack set his mug on the cardboard coaster she tossed before him. "I'm learning a lot by watching him work, but he's not one for talking about himself. It's hard to add a personal aspect to the story, which is pretty important."

Gaylord nodded. "I know exactly of what you speak."

"Oh, you don't know anything of the kind," Kitty retorted.

"Heck I don't. I'll have you know I subscribe to eight magazines. Best stories are the ones got the personal aspect Zack here's talking about."

"Well, aren't you full of surprises."

Wendell chuckled, deep crevices forming by his eyes, as Gaylord squared thin shoulders and saluted Kitty with his beer mug. "Yes, I am. Happy to introduce you to more surprises any time you're of mind."

She harrumphed and hefted off the stool to wait on a young man in paint-splattered coveralls. She filled two pitchers of Miller Lite and returned to lean on the bar across from Zack. "John tell you about Amelia?"

"His wife? I sense something's wrong, but he's not saying much."

"That's like him. Not one to wear his heart on his sleeve. Don't suppose he'd be very happy with me for speaking out of turn."

"Could be he'd be grateful for someone else to do the telling," Wendell suggested.

She eyed him a moment before returning her attention to Zack. "Every so often one of these two yokels says something sensible." She waved off their protests. "Amelia's come down with cancer and the outlook's not good. Been how long, you reckon, Gaylord?"

"First heard back in February."

Flesh wobbled under her chin as she nodded. "Poor dear. The doctors took her female parts, but the cancer had spread more than they hoped. Sewed her back up and shook their heads is what they did. Said there's not much they can do except keep her comfortable until the end."

Wendell leaned across Gaylord. "I remember John coming into the tavern the night they got the news."

"That's right," Gaylord added. "Sat hisself down at the table over yonder by the jukebox. I never seen a man so dejected."

"Broke my heart," Kitty said. "They were high school sweethearts from the next county over. They got no kids, so when she goes, John'll be all alone."

Zack sipped his beer and reflected on his time with Norton, sorry he'd complicated a life already complicated enough. On the other hand, the murder happened whether Zack showed up or not, so perhaps he really was doing the chief a favor by leading the investigation.

Several men in dusty jeans and soiled plaid shirts entered the tavern and tromped to the pool table, hollering out a beer order. Kitty slapped mugs on a tray and tucked plastic-covered menus under her armpit. "She's a good woman, Amelia is. It's a crying shame."

The three men sat in silence until Zack motioned to their mugs. He drained the pitcher and set it on the bar, raised his mug in salute. "Here's to your health."

"Damn straight," Gaylord clinked with Zack and then Wendell. He drank and wiped a shirt sleeve across his mouth. "Well now, being's you been on the front line with the chief, tell us, how goes the murder investigation?"

Two reasons Zack had stopped at the Roadside Tavern after his long drive. True, an ice cold beer sounded good, but he wanted to learn what he could about Norton's wife and dredge up additional information on Riordan. "It's a tough case. Seems the man wasn't in town long enough for folks to get to know him; at least, not that they're admitting."

Gaylord jumped at the bait. "Well, we talked with him plenty, didn't we, Wendell?"

"Two or three times, I reckon. He come in and sat right where you're sitting now. But, he wasn't the gentleman you are."

Meaning he hadn't sprung for a pitcher. "What did you talk about?"

Gaylord bowed his head in contemplation. "Well, now, nothing jumps out as important. The weather. The beer he preferred."

"He weren't particularly interested in anything we had to say." Wendell's pockmarked nose wrinkled in disgust. "Plum full of himself. A big braggart, you ask me."

"What'd he brag about?" Zack asked.

"Money," Gaylord said.

"And women."

"Claimed he was coming into a fortune. Said he'd be heading to Nevada because he had it all figured out how to beat the odds." Gaylord snorted and reached for his beer. "Fool and his money. No one beats the odds for long. Won't catch me throwing my money away at a craps table."

Zack had already heard of Riordan's claims about money, which supported the kidnapper payoff theory. On the other hand, he'd heard only the slightest tidbits of a love interest in town. If such a relationship existed, he wanted to find the woman. "He talked about women, too, huh?"

Gaylord leaned in close. "Claimed he had a sweetie right here. Now, I'm not saying it's true. Just repeating what the man said."

"I wouldn't think he'd make up something like that. Word might get around and land him in trouble."

"He was so full of hisself, he most likely never give it much thought. Just spouted off how women couldn't resist his charms." Wendell did not hide his distaste for Riordan.

Zack shrugged and goaded the men. "I'd have called him on it. I'd have told him to quit maligning the local women."

"Exactly what we done," Wendell said. "Told him the women in this town are good Christians and not likely to be taking up with a stranger."

Gaylord pushed aside his empty mug. "He dropped all kinds of hints about lonely widows, but if he was hinting at Mrs. O'Connor, he'd stretched his story too far."

Annie?

"Well," Wendell mumbled.

His friend frowned at him. "Well, what?"

Wendell rubbed sandpaper whiskers. "Well, I did see him and her nose-to-nose."

Gaylord's eyebrows rose in surprise. "You never said nothing about this."

"Figured it was none of my business. Still isn't. Should keep my mouth shut."

Zack aimed a piercing stare at Wendell. "Funny thing about investigations; you never know what might help solve the crime."

Wendell sighed. "Mind you, I didn't see much. Wouldn't have thought nothing of it if we hadn't just listened to the man's bullshit. I was driving by the Bluebell and seen him in a discussion with Mrs. O'Connor. Couldn't hear what they said. But, just as I'm getting past, he laughs and walks away. Her face was so red, I expected steam rising, she was that mad. No idea what it was about." He paused and stared defiantly at Gaylord. "You see why I never brung it up before?"

No way Zack could imagine Annie in a romantic relationship with Ed Riordan. However, she'd first evaded his subtle inquiries about the man, then claimed little contact with him, which did not square with Wendell's observation. Why had they argued? Riordan might have been slow to pay his bill or smoked in his cabin, but why hide so ordinary a confrontation?

He gave an elaborate shrug. "Probably nothing, like you said."

"Yep." Wendell pushed up from his stool. He'd apparently had enough of their conversation. "Much obliged for the beer." He tipped his John Deere cap and hobbled toward the door.

Gaylord nodded appreciation to Zack and hurried to catch up with his friend.

Zack gathered his change, minus a healthy tip for Kitty, as she returned to the register behind the bar.

"You need a menu, hon?"

"No, thanks. I'm heading to the supermarket for steaks to grill."

"Well, where in the world…" She paused and narrowed her blue eyes before pushing the cash drawer closed with her rump, a Cheshire-cat grin spreading across her face. "Tell Annie hello for me."

CHAPTER 11

He asked for a mortar and pestle.

"No problem," she replied.

Oh, my stars! she thought as she hurried into the kitchen, willing the utensils to signal their location, to fly into her outstretched hands like a sorcerer's broom.

She should be more organized.

Yes, but when was the last time she'd used the small stone mortar and chunky pestle Mark bought at a garage sale?

Should be with the spices.

Not there.

Perhaps behind the roasters and platters, relegated to the cavernous darkness of a lower cabinet between an equally unused soufflé pan and dusty pasta maker.

With a startled cry, she flung open the door to the cabinet housing a hodgepodge of thrift-store china. She rose on tiptoes and searched behind the mismatched patterns, snatching the mortar and pestle in triumph.

Zack was stacking briquettes in the barbecue and seemed unconcerned by her prolonged absence. She nonchalantly exhibited the tools, acknowledged his approval and blew air across her upper lip to riffle corn-silk bangs. She returned to the task she'd begun before his request sent her flying to the kitchen: bathing zucchini and red peppers and mushrooms with olive oil, salt and pepper. She slid the slick wedges on metal skewers.

They were silent as they worked—a silence he apparently felt no need to fill as he lit the briquettes and opened the vent in the lid to his desired level. She skewered the last of the vegetables and wiped her glistening hands on a paper towel.

Now, the silence between them tickled her nerve endings until raised like the fur of a fidgety cat. He swung a muscular leg to straddle the bench opposite her and leaned his elbow on the redwood planks between them. She licked her lower lip and reached for a wine glass as she nodded toward the mortar. "So, what are you going to do?"

He'd been staring at her with a twitch at the corners of his mouth, as if a smile was working to the surface. "Ah!" He extracted a small opaque bottle from a paper bag. "Peppercorns," he explained, gold-flecked eyes scanning her face for approval. He opened the jar and dumped hard, green corns into the mortar, scrounged in the bag and pulled out two more bottles. "Rock salt and cloves." He added these ingredients, grabbed the pestle and began to grind the spices to coarse granules.

She reached for the bottle of peppercorns, turned it in her hand to inspect the label. "You didn't buy these at the Hope supermarket."

"Nope. Found a place in Klamath Falls."

She wrinkled her brow. "Today?"

He was focused on grinding. "Yep."

"You drove there today?"

The pestle halted as he glanced up. "I had an appointment."

She drew a breath and blushed. "I'm sorry. I sound like I'm doubting you."

"Not at all," he replied but she thought his voice held a slight edge.

A capricious breeze rustled the paper bag, which she corralled and anchored with the jar of peppercorns. "It's just that I don't get away often."

"You have a lot to handle here." His eyes did not leave her face.

She toyed with a pine needle stuck between two chipped table planks. "I guess."

He returned to his grinding, finally nodded in satisfaction, rose and carried the bowl to where the steaks rested beneath waxed paper. "Seems like a nice town," he said as he spread the spice mixture on a platter, placed the meat on top and pressed gently to coat.

"I suppose."

He glanced at her and flipped the steaks until evenly covered on both sides.

"Is this your own previously-secret recipe?" she asked.

"An imitation. Sometimes, I try to recreate excellent dishes I've ordered in restaurants. Not always with success, I might add. This one took me several tries and it still needs tweaking."

"I'm sure it will be delicious."

"If I get busy. Otherwise, I'll be cooking in the dark and who knows what'll happen."

"You should have time. It's light so late here in summer."

"I noticed that. I rather like it."

She sipped wine as Zack removed the grill cover, lined the skewered vegetables above the heat and checked his watch. She suddenly giggled, drew a hand to her mouth and shook her head as Zack's raised eyebrows questioned the joke. "Sorry. I was thinking about when we first bought this place, Mark and me." She set the wine glass on the table. "I wasn't enthused. Afraid, I guess. I mean, what did I know about running a café? Mark told me he'd work sun up to sun down and, in the beginning, he tried. But, he was thinking of shorter southern days where we grew up, not here with the light lingering so late. After two weeks, he was dragging around with heavy bags under his eyes."

Zack smiled as he repositioned the vegetable skewers and placed the steaks on the grill. "That explains it."

"Hmm?"

"Your accent. You're from the south."

She wrinkled her nose. "Thought I'd gotten rid of my drawl for good."

"Certain words and expressions. Why do you want to change your accent?"

She lowered her feet from the bench and tucked blonde strands behind her ear as she set utensils and plates on the table. "Different place, different time of life I'd as soon do without."

"Not a happy time?"

"Not unhappy, I guess. More like numb. I don't remember feeling much of anything, except with Mark."

He'd been forbidden to her, of course, her bible-thumping father blasting the full power of his preacher's baritone. Ain't no good taking up with a boy like that, he'd bellowed.

Like what, she'd asked.

You know good and well what I mean. The boy is not to be trusted.

Because his hair is long? Because he laughs and dances and sings?

He will lead you to damnation!

"Which is probably why I left with Mark right after high school graduation. He offered everything my father denied me."

Zack declared the meal ready and Annie realized with a flush that she'd been talking for some time. Zack used metal tongs to lift the steaks and vegetables from the grill and set them on the plates. He poured wine and saluted with his glass.

Aromatic juice flowed from the meat as she cut through the crusted spices. "Oh, my stars! Delicious."

He bowed thanks and took a bite, chewing to judge tenderness and seasoning, finally nodding. They ate in silence a few moments before he sipped the Merlot and asked, "Did you come straight to Hope?"

"Oh, no. That was years later."

Good years, she thought, then wondered if she remembered correctly or if those years only seemed good because the last few were so bad.

They'd traveled the country, flitting from one low-paying job to another. No plan. No goals. Mark wouldn't hear of such constraints. Why limit our options? he'd ask. We've got the whole wide world to explore.

She happily joined him, a 1980's version of hippies, making do with meager possessions squeezed into Mark's Volkswagen Jetta. Each time they moved, she stocked groceries in stubby, noisy refrigerators and scrubbed chipped bathroom fixtures in rundown apartments. They rented by the week, even that short commitment sometimes too long for Mark, wanderlust screaming his name even as she carted her Samsonite into new quarters. Several times, they left behind what they'd paid for a week's lodging, money they could ill afford to waste.

They rambled almost four years before she wearied, life's adventures illusive, each new town only a replica of the last. I want to settle down, she told him, work a steady job, buy a house, start a family.

Shackles, he called the stability she coveted. Where's the adventure?

Where's the adventure in living hand-to-mouth? she'd shouted. Where's the adventure in people staring at you like you're a mongrel out to steal their food? Turning up their noses because you so obviously don't have a dime to your name?

She'd slept fitfully the first night they fought, tossing and replaying their argument. Floorboards had squeaked as he paced the stained shag carpet in the living room. The front door had creaked open as she twisted in the sweat-damp sheets. She assumed he'd gone for a walk to clear his head. She was certain he'd return with newfound understanding and envelop her in sticky-skin warmth, his kisses erasing her tears.

He was gone a week.

She took a job in a diner and waited, sitting each night in the drab apartment, the bare walls mocking, her father's voice resounding through the rap music blasting from two doors down. One evening after work, she dragged her tired body to the apartment and pushed open the battered door, caught her breath at Mark's pensive stare and unsure smile, a cheap bottle of wine in one hand, sagging daffodils in the other.

That had been the first time he disappeared, but not the last. Each time, she welcomed him back. But her patience waned.

The last argument was the worse.

"He was gone three weeks," she said and pushed aside her plate. "I thought we'd come to the end. Suddenly, there he was, and I thought, oh no, here we go again. But, he had a plan. One week later, we signed papers to buy the Bluebell. Not a lick of experience between us at running a business, but he figured, how hard can it be? Hadn't I learned from my momma, the best baker in Tennessee? I was so scared, but how could I refuse? He was giving me everything I'd asked for, leaving his wandering days for me."

Zack stacked his plate on hers and leaned back to stretch his long legs under the table. "Sounds like he loved you."

"Yes, I believe he did." She stared beyond him to the fading light sequestered behind western hills, smiled wanly at the swallows zipping overhead. The birds were so like Mark—darting here and there. "He managed to settle down a little, although his head was always filled with ideas and schemes. I think he was happy here."

"How did he die?"

Annie sucked in her lips and closed her eyes, opened them as she stood and gathered the crockery. "Wrapped his truck around a tree." She waved off his help and picked up the tray. "But the whiskey killed him."

***

She took her time scraping plates and wiping the mortar clean. Maybe he'll leave, she thought, then wondered if she wanted him to. She enjoyed his company. Which was the problem. She'd harnessed her emotions for so many years, it scared her to unleash them.

Especially now.

Well, don't then, she thought. You don't have to spill your heart to this man. Stick to the weather, cooking, sports if he's interested. She'd never particularly cared for sports, but she could fake it to keep conversation on safe ground.

Yet, it buoyed her heart to release fear and hurt she'd buried deep. She dried her hands on a cloth and figured she'd stalled long enough.

He had moved to the heavy-planked wooden swing on her porch, the chains creaking as he pushed off with his foot. He acknowledged her with a smile. "Hope you don't mind. It looked comfortable."

"Of course," she said, eyeing the space beside him on the swing, choosing to lower herself to the porch, knees bent and feet resting on the top step. Her mind raced with topics to broach. Lovely evening, isn't it? What do you think of oregano?

He didn't help, apparently content to sway like a mysterious sphinx, until he called out, "Hello, Sarah."

Annie's shoulders tensed and she focused on Sarah peeking from around the corner of the house, astonished eyes locked on Zack sitting in the porch swing where she'd never seen a man before.

You think of her as a child, Annie thought, but she's a woman, too. She's both. The thoughts triggered mother-bear instincts and she wanted to shoo Sarah away from this stranger.

If only she'd been as protective before.

You've gone over the edge, she chided herself and turned a quick smile to Zack before beckoning to Sarah.

She approached slowly, eyes trained on the ground, mouth slack as usual. She'd be pretty, Annie often noted, if not for that slackness and drooping skin below her eyes. Annie's heart ached for the girl. She should be cheering at high school football games, rifling her closet for the perfect outfit and crying in disgust when nothing would do.

She should have a normal teenager's life.

"How are you this evening, Sarah?" Zack asked.

Annie watched Sarah's face for signs of fear, but found none. "It's okay," she said as she rose from the porch and walked down the steps to stand before Sarah, smooth the bangs along her forehead. "You can answer him."

Sarah's eyes flit between Annie and the ground before she replied, "I'm fine."

"Do you know who this man is?"

"He's Zack."

Annie never found the pattern to what Sarah remembered and what she did not. She performed simple chores well, repetition the key. Certainly, the basics of reading and mathematics were lost to her. Annie bristled each time she thought of Sarah's druggie parents: neglectful, ignorant, self-absorbed people who had no right to a special daughter like Sarah.

"We had a great conversation yesterday, didn't we, Sarah?" Zack asked.

A smile lit her face. "He didn't know how squirrels hide food for winter."

Zack laughed and brought his hands up in a gesture of wonderment. "News to me."

Annie returned Sarah's bright smile, reached to straighten the collar of her blue-striped cotton blouse. "You're an expert on squirrels, aren't you?"

A vigorous nod.

Annie peered over the girl's shoulder toward the cabin she shared with her grandfather. "Have you eaten dinner?"

Sarah's smile faded a bit as she slouched and nodded again.

"Did you clean the kitchen?"

"Yeah."

"Why do I even ask, huh?" Annie ducked her head to gather Sarah's stare. "You clean up better than I do, don't you?"

"You skip the sink."

Annie laughed and said over her shoulder to Zack, "She gives away my terrible secrets."

"I'm appalled."

She caught Sarah's hand in hers. "Is he home?"

"He's asleep on the couch."

At this early evening hour, that meant Leroy had tipped a bottle again and lay sprawled on the worn secondhand sofa, snoring off the booze. "Has he eaten yet?" she asked, adding at Sarah's headshake, "Let him sleep. He can eat when he's ready. You have paper and pencils in your room? Yes?" She said to Zack, "Sarah's good at drawing, too."

"I'd love to see your work, Sarah."

He means it, Annie thought, realizing that she'd been listening intently to his voice. One hint of repulsion or indifference toward Sarah and she'd kick his butt out of that swing so fast and hard he'd have to crawl to his cabin. Instead, she sensed genuine concern and patience. She exhaled in a rush as she turned Sarah gently by the shoulders. "Time for you to go home, okay? You know we can't leave your grandpa alone when he's been drinking."

Sarah nodded but dragged her feet with more than one backward glance as she returned to her cabin and disappeared inside.

Annie gathered her hair in one hand and drew it up to cool her neck, released it to float to her shoulders. She returned to the porch and stood with head bowed as she swept pebbles aside with her toe. She finally smiled up at Zack. "Thanks."

"For what?"

"For being kind to her. Not everyone is."

He rose from the swing and came to the top of the steps. "Are Sarah and Leroy relatives of yours?"

"No, Leroy came looking for work. I certainly don't have the time or skills to do everything around here myself, but there was no money to pay him. I started to turn him away when Sarah walked into the café." She moved to a bed planted with dahlias and fingered a soft, newly unfurled leaf. "This one might have the bright red flower. I forget until they bud. You'd think I'd remember, wouldn't you?"

He walked down the steps and joined her by the dahlia bushes. "Funny how some things we remember and others we forget. I've never found a way to control my memory."

She smiled at him. "Probably better off. You'd likely try to remember everything and blow a fuse in your brain." She gave a soft laugh and noticed a dimple on the left side of his mouth as he joined in.

"Wouldn't want a blown fuse," he said. "I guess our minds protect us sometimes, blocking out a past we're better off forgetting."

"But, unfortunately, hiding things we'd love to remember, too. Anyway," she said and released the dahlia leaf, "I couldn't turn them away."

Although the sun had sunk behind the hills, golden light infused the dahlia and the grass beneath her feet and deepened the green of pine needles. A wispy breeze carried the scent of pine and sun-baked foliage. She listened to the rat-a-tat of a woodpecker drilling for dinner and the high-pitched chitter of Sarah's beloved squirrels. Moments like this, she thought, when the day eases into night, heat into coolness. This she never wanted to forget.

She turned to find Zack staring intently at her.

She told herself to be wary and nervous, but it didn't work. Instead, she nodded toward the back of her property. "Go for a walk?"

***

Annie always found solace in walking—a mindless use of feet and legs accompanying her mood and thoughts. Brisk, earth-pounding steps for anger; slow and unsteady for sorrow; lightness and tiptoes and skips for joy. They'd done their best talking, she and Mark, on sidewalks and forest paths.

They hadn't walked together much the year before he died. Too often, he'd been sunk in depression, drunk or on his way to being so, discarding her suggestion of an evening stroll with the wave of a whiskey bottle. She'd walked alone, slipping beneath the barbed wire fence to trudge up the path on the Bureau of Land Management property that adjoined theirs. If not exactly solace, she'd at least found escape.

She'd abandoned the practice lately, not wishing to be alone with her thoughts.

Now, here she was, crouching as Zack separated barbed strands, turning to do the same for him. The path wound along the hillside, steep in sections but mostly on gentle switchbacks that wove between pine and hemlock and juniper.

"Where does this trail lead?"

"Everywhere," she answered. "Nowhere. I've never followed it to the end. Perhaps it doesn't have one."

"Ah, the path to nowhere. Seems I've traveled this way before."

"You?"

"Does that surprise you?"

"You seem so confident. So together."

She halted as they rounded a bend to a narrow meadow. A doe, motionless in thick bunchgrass, eyed them with perked ears before bounding up the hillside.

"Beautiful," he whispered.

She turned with a smile, only to find his gaze upon her and not the deer. A flush swam for her cheeks. She spied a large, flat boulder twenty feet ahead and hurried to hoist herself on top. Zack followed her and they surveyed the meadow, until her nerves, fluttering like butterfly wings, compelled her to speak. "Are you still on a path to nowhere?"

"I suppose the path is leading somewhere. I'm just not sure it's where I want to go."

Annie selected a pebble and rolled it in her palm. "Your work?"

"Somewhat. I guess work's never what it's cracked up to be."

The clay pebble crumbled as she toyed with it. "Your marriage?" He heaved a big sigh and she wrinkled her nose. "Sorry. Forget I asked."

"No, it's only fair. You've told me a lot about you and Mark."

Not everything, she thought, but more than she'd ever told anyone else, including Kitty. For the life of her, she couldn't figure out why.

"Just because I'm a blabbermouth, doesn't mean you have to be one, too."

His laugh was loud and masculine. "Can't say I've ever met a blabbermouth I've more enjoyed."

She tossed him a sidelong look meant to chastise, but spoiled the effect with a grin.

He stared out at the meadow a moment before saying, "Stella is a powerful woman." Shook his head. "Was. She's not well. But she was a dynamo in stilettos when we met. Nothing and nobody intimidated her. Smart. Successful." He leaned a shoulder toward Annie and whispered, "Filthy rich. Could have anything she wanted. Turned out, she wanted me."

Annie searched but found no response, tucked her hands under her thighs and stared at the softening Creamsicle horizon.

"I ate it up. Literally," he said with a quick laugh. "Best tables at the finest restaurants."

She studied her dangling feet in grass-stained tennis shoes, bowed her head, long tresses hiding her expression. She sensed that he was talking as much to himself as to her.

"My father was big on old truisms. Play with fire and you'll get burned, he told me many times." He sniffed and crossed his arms over his chest. "Guess I should've listened."

"You've been burned?"

"Maybe." He jumped down from the boulder. "So, there you have it. Meet the official boy toy. Married to a woman twenty years his senior, living her extravagant lifestyle. She pays for everything. My meager earnings wouldn't cover so much as her chauffeur bill. It's been a wild ride."

Annie lowered herself from the rock and brushed dirt from her jeans. "Do you enjoy the ride?"

"Some of it, yes. It's intoxicating, all the wealth and power. Of course, I knew all along what many of her crowd thought of me. Made me angry, at first, but then I realized I was exactly what they imagined."

"Doesn't matter what others think."

"No, but it matters what I think and I do not like what I've become."

"Is the ride over?"

He grimaced as his green eyes sought hers. "I don't know."

They'd moved so close together, his breath brushing her face as he spoke. She retreated a step. "It's getting dark. We'd better go back."

She hurried along the path, glancing behind to see him tap a fist against his forehead, as if banging sense into himself. She swallowed a laugh and quickened her pace, listening for the sound of footsteps behind her, relieved when he caught up. They walked in silence along the trail now barely visible in the darkness, the crunch of their shoes on pine needles broken by an owl's hoot. They shimmied again under the barbed wire, strolled to her house and paused by the front porch.

"I had a wonderful evening, Annie."

"Yes," she said quickly. "Me, too."

They whispered goodnights and she breathed heavily as she mounted the first step.

"Goodnight," he said again.

She spun to him, saying in a rush, "The café's closed tomorrow. The weatherman says it'll be the last day of the heat wave, and who in the world knows what will happen then. I mean, we could end up right back in the cold rain, which will be so disappointing. But what do weathermen know, huh?" She stopped to breathe, heaved a sigh at the sight of his dimple-cheeked grin illuminated by the porch light. She almost held back what she wanted to say, then summoned courage and blurted, "I know a special place in the mountains. About an hour's drive from here. We could take a picnic lunch."

"I have an appointment first thing in the morning."

"Oh, of course." Her heart thumped and she felt her face redden with embarrassment.

"Shall we leave at ten?"

"Fine." She exhaled and rushed up the remaining steps to yank open the front door and hurry inside.

CHAPTER 12

Mornings in the canyon had become so familiar: a sun halo rising above the crags, his breath billowing white until the pine-scented air warmed. He'd swear the same hawk circled overhead, the same lizard skittered at his approach. In only three days, he'd become entranced with the canyon.

But, this morning, he would not jog. He would fish.

Rory's slouch and blank stare were meant to signal indifference, as if he hadn't been fidgeting and anxiously scanning the road. He acknowledged Zack's approach down the creek bank with a shuffle and wary eyes, on guard against letdown by an adult with more important things to do than fish with a stupid kid.

Zack blew warm breath on his hands and rubbed them together, nodded to the gear piled at Rory's feet. "Looks like you've got us covered."

The kid's shoulders relaxed and he handed a rod to Zack. "You can use this one."

Zack tipped the rod to test the weight and spring. "Cool."

Rory showed Zack how to prepare the line, demonstrated the arm action and flick of the wrist necessary to whip the fly. "The fish have to see the fly, not the line. 'Course, no guarantees they'll bite."

"No problem." Zack practiced casting perpendicular to his body, wrist locked, elbow tucked by his side.

"I mean, you might not catch anything."

"No problem."

Rory pointed to a deep pocket of water swirling behind a boulder. "Put the fly there."

Zack zipped the line over his shoulder, sucked a breath and whisked the fly toward the desired spot.

"Close."

Zack grunted and tried again.

"Better the first time. Here, watch me."

Rory was as good a fisherman as he'd claimed and an equally good teacher. But, after more than an hour of casting and unsnarling and mending line, Zack's concentration floated away like the leaves carried downstream by his feet. He reeled in and splashed out of the creek, tennis shoes soaked and ankles numb.

"You're getting the hang of it," Rory called over his shoulder.

"Takes practice."

"That's why I come out here. Not much action, but I'm ready for better holes."

"You caught two."

"Not keepers."

Zack laughed and plopped down on the gravel, face lifted to the aqua sky. "More than I caught."

Rory reeled in and picked his way over rocks in whirling knee-deep water. "You need waders. I should've told you."

"I'll pick some up."

They hadn't spoken much as they fished, Zack focused on learning the technique, Rory perhaps still nervous about his impulsive agreement to meet. Now, the boy climbed out of thick neoprene waders, carefully packed away gear and sat down a few feet from Zack. "I guess writing takes practice, too, huh?"

Zack took a moment to understand the reference to his cover story, which he didn't recall mentioning in their brief conversations. The Hope rumor mill again. "Sure. Do you write?"

"Sometimes."

"Like what?"

A classic Rory shrug. "Science fiction, I guess."

"You plan to be a writer some day?"

"Dad says it's stupid."

"All due respect to your father," Zack said, "but that's a bunch of bull. There's nothing wrong with being a writer. It may be a long, hard road, but the same is true for most things you want in life. You've just got to buckle down."

Rory shifted his eyes Zack's direction, then stared again at the creek. "We could swap."

"Huh?"

"Fishing lessons for writing ones."

Great.

He'd not figured on anyone giving a hoot about his so-called profession as a writer. Now, he either had to brush Rory off or promise what he could not deliver.

"The danger of going undercover," he'd once been told by a retired detective, "is losing perspective, letting the cover take control. Like ol' Freddy Mancuso. Spent two years undercover on a gambling sting. Became a damned gambler. Lost his job and wife because he lost himself. Remember," he'd warned with a wag of his gnarly finger, "don't forget who you are."

To which his captain had added, "But don't blow your fucking cover."

"Sure," Zack replied to Rory, "sounds like a fair exchange. Why don't you bring me something you've written and I'll take a look?"

Rory scrambled up from the gravel and began to gather gear. "Not tomorrow. Gotta help my grandma move some junk at her house and she's making me stay tonight so we can get an early start. Day after?"

Zack stood and grabbed one of the tackle boxes. "Deal."

***

Rory refused a ride to town, saying he was in no hurry to return home where his kid sister would be waiting to pester him. He ambled off, fishing gear banging against his skinny legs, as Zack pulled out his cell phone and dialed Stella.

Her voice was thick, the ending of each word slurred into the beginning of the next. "Yvonne is here. She makes a fine Bloody Mary. Oh, but not as delicious as yours, my love."

"What's her secret ingredient?" he asked.

"Wouldn't be a secret if she told."

"No, I suppose not."

Clattering exploded in his ear and he held the phone away until he heard her voice again. "Dropped the stupid phone. I mean, really, darling, you'd think they'd build these damn things so a person could hold on to them."

"Why don't you design a new phone? You'd make a fortune."

"I already have a fortune. As if you've forgotten. Say, I've got an idea—come home and join us for brunch."

"I'm a long drive away, Stella. Besides, I'm not finished with my investigation."

"Fine," she muttered and hung up.

Zack pocketed the phone with a shaky hand, the call shattering the calmness he'd enjoyed while focused on the fly rod and the rushing Cutwater Creek.

At first, he'd given Stella all the credit for controlling his actions. She's an expert, he reasoned, with persuasive skills honed by years in the courtroom. A hint here, an insinuation there, playing off doubts and weaknesses. But, after a while, he begrudgingly admitted that his decisions, and the guilt that guided them, were his to own. Perhaps Stella knew how to prod, but his sense of duty had been with him long before she came into his life.

"You spend too much time coloring between the lines," Terry told him one night as they downed beer in their college apartment. "Let that crayon streak right off the damn paper, man."

"You're full of it," he'd retorted.

"Full of life." Terry grabbed a blue marker and scribbled curlicues across scrap paper. "Go wild, man. Life is a canvas."

"You're practicing philosophy bullshit on me again," Zack grumbled and drained the last of his Budweiser.

"You've got too many *shoulds* in your head, man. Get them out before they strangle you."

He'd tried. Skipped classes and joined Terry in Santa Barbara, jumping from party to party, the days and evenings a blur of alcohol and girls. Yes, he'd enjoyed the carefree partying and, especially, the girls.

But, one afternoon, Terry pointed to the phone receiver in Zack's hand. "Who're you calling?"

"It's Sunday," Zack replied. "I always call my folks on Sunday."

To which Terry grunted in disgust. "You're hopeless."

Maybe, Zack thought now as he glanced at his watch, started the engine and headed to town. Lonnie told him his balls were shriveled from an oversized sense of duty, always trying to do the right thing, whatever the hell that was. Stella played that sense of duty for all it was worth.

Zack entered the graveled driveway to the Bluebell as Annie hefted a basket into the bed of her Chevy truck, ponytail swinging, ball cap shading her face. She lifted a hand for a hesitant wave.

He should be working on the investigation.

True, he was in a holding pattern: waiting on results from the lab, waiting on Isley to return. True, he had no idea what to do next, besides talking with people, hoping to pick up new information. A shot in the dark, yes, but he should be doing something, anything, on the case.

He should tell Norton about the bullet casing.

He should go to Stella.

He returned Annie's wave with a smile, held up a finger to indicate he'd be just a minute, hurried to his cabin and took the steps two at a time.

***

Zack tossed soggy athletic socks on the floor, rubbed his cold, white feet and wriggled into clean socks and a newer pair of Adidas. He shoved a windbreaker into a small daypack, slung it over his shoulder and started for the door, only to pause and chew the inside of his cheek. On impulse, he left his cell phone on the dresser before hurrying out of the cabin.

As he locked the door, he noticed Sarah standing on her porch, mouth drawn tight, brows knit, fingers busily twirling locks of hair. Zack waved and she threw him a quick glance before focusing again on the parking lot. Zack frowned and turned.

Annie stood beside her Chevy, head lowered, face hidden beneath the baseball cap, arms hugging her chest. Troy Isley leaned against the truck, cowboy hat tipped back, one knee bent, boot pressed on the vehicle. His mouth moved but Zack could not hear his words.

Whatever he said amused him, a grin spreading beneath his dark moustache. The grin faded as Annie turned on her heel and stepped away. Troy caught her arm and brought his face close to hers.

Zack clomped down the steps and scuffed across the gravel, yelling, "Sorry it took me so long."

Troy still held Annie's arm but she shook him off and moved away, face flushed and eyes averted. Troy's upper lip curled as he regarded Zack. "Well, if it ain't the writer."

Annie's chin rose and she hurried around the front of the truck. "C'mon, Zack. Let's go." She climbed in and sat with hands gripping the steering wheel.

"Seems someone forgot his manners," Troy said. "You interrupted a conversation between me and the lady."

"Looks to me like the lady's done talking."

Zack stood several inches taller and probably outweighed him by twenty pounds of solid muscle, a size advantage Troy apparently noted because he scowled and kicked the Chevy with a boot heel before stalking off to climb into his truck. He gunned the engine, threw the transmission into gear and spewed gravel as he sped from the parking lot, face contorted in anger, middle finger of his left hand extended skyward.

Zack watched him disappear from sight, tossed his daypack into the truck bed and climbed into the passenger seat. "You okay?"

"He's annoying and persistent, but I've handled everything by myself, including the constant badgering of Troy Isley, for three years now and I'm not looking for any help." She shuddered and fingered the ignition key, then closed her eyes as her tensed shoulders sank and she turned a rueful smile to Zack. "Sorry. Overreacted."

He wanted to reach across the bench seat and stroke the roses in her cheeks.

***

They rode west on the main highway and talked about the ranchlands they passed: cattle lazing beneath the shade of oak trees, irrigation systems shooting water jets. Pastures sprawled between rounded foothills, in turn flanked by rugged peaks.

After an hour, Annie slowed and eased the truck up a dirt road heading northwest into the mountains. The aging Chevy bounced along in creaks and groans, Annie gripping the steering wheel with both hands, intent on avoiding the worst ruts ahead of the pockmarked grill. Zack clutched the grip bar and winced when they hit a pothole dead on, bench springs jabbing from beneath the cracked vinyl. "I'm thinking this must be some special place we're going."

She laughed. "To be worth the ride? Well, I think so."

After twenty bone-jarring minutes, they reached a wide turnaround. Annie positioned the Chevy to face away from afternoon sun, killed the engine and removed the key. "C'mon," she said and jumped from the cab.

He gathered his daypack as Annie heaved a wicker picnic basket from the truck bed and walked ten steps, listing to one side as the awkward burden banged against her calf. She stopped and turned to find him grinning at her. "What?"

"How far do we have to walk?"

"Little over a mile."

"Then, you'd better let me take this." He reached for the handles, their fingers touching.

She started to protest, regarded their hands a moment and slowly released her grip. She headed to a trail leading through the trees as Zack secured the long leather straps on his shoulder and followed. "Who owns this land?" he asked.

"Ulster McGovern. Comes into the café most weeks. Black coffee and a piece of pie. Sits by the window. Main road cuts his land in two. He lives over on the other side." Her words exploded between quick breaths as her stride lengthened. "Most of the land's not very productive, but I guess he gets by. No wife or children. For some reason, he took a liking to Mark. I don't know, perhaps the son he never had. Anyway, he showed us this place, told me I can come whenever I want."

"He's very protective."

She glanced over her shoulder. "You mean all the No Trespassing signs? Whole lot of good those probably do."

"So, the place is not a secret?"

"Nothing remains a secret for long in Hope. People know about this trail, but not about where we're going."

They wound between trees and scrubby bushes, the leather straps chafing Zack's shoulder. However, any discomfort was minimized by the refreshing, fragrant air, the softness of pine needles beneath his feet, and Annie's strong, shapely legs and firm rear end swaying before him, a sight he enjoyed immensely. He boosted the basket with his hand, was about to shift it to his other shoulder, when she halted and pointed into the woods.

"Through here." She swept aside branches to slip off-trail, soon hidden by willow leaves.

He grunted and pushed forward in the spot where she'd disappeared, snagged the basket and struggled to pull free, muttering oaths under his breath.

"Come this way," she called and he followed her voice, arms protecting his face from scratches, eyes shifting from her form trudging ahead to the ground at his feet. After ten minutes that seemed like fifty, he emerged in a clearing, sucked in a deep breath of rich, moisture-pregnant air and whistled.

A sparkling pond, probably fed by an underground spring, was fringed with thick reeds. Lavender irises peeked between clumps of grass. Moisture dripped from a mossy jumble of volcano-spewed rock, silver-green ferns rested beneath gangly wild rose bushes. Scattered boulders cordoned a flat, graveled area to the left where she watched him with expectant blue eyes as deep and dark as the water.

"The most beautiful thing I've ever seen," he said.

She flung her arms wide and spun a circle, face uplifted to the sky.

***

Zack lay back on the red-striped blanket Annie had spread on a smooth spot by the pond, hooked his hands behind his head and gazed through pine boughs to the brilliant blue above, belly comfortably full of a delicious lunch, eyelids heavy. A bird darted overhead. A robin. Or, a thrush. Couldn't tell. His eyes closed, jaw slackened, the weight of his torso sinking into the cradle of earth.

He woke with a start, jolted up to survey the area, confused at first as to where he was.

"You're a hard sleeper." She sat to his left, knees drawn to her chest, toes wriggling into blanket folds.

"Whew," he said as he groggily ran a hand along his shorn hair. "How long was I out?"

"Almost an hour."

"Shows what great company I am."

"My talking put you straight to sleep."

"No, of course not." He focused on the fine lines forming at the corners of her crescent eyes as she smiled, cheekbones prominent and radiant, lips spread wide to disclose a small gap beside an upper tooth.

"It's like a fairytale world here. Any minute now all the four-legged creatures will come to drink from the pond and the elves will emerge from behind tree trunks and the fairies will sprinkle dust as they fly by." She peeked at him to judge his response to her flight of fancy.

"You forgot the unicorn." Zack reclined on his side, cocked an elbow and rested his head on his hand. "Do villains live in your fairyland?"

She squinted and drew a finger to her lips. "I suppose so. Seems there's always an ogre or wolf up to no good."

"All the noble creatures will form a coalition to defeat him."

"To turn him away from the dark side."

"Using magic?"

"Of course."

"A bewitched sword?"

"No," she said with a firm shake of her head. "No bloodshed in this fairyland. Besides, the heroes don't need weapons. Cunning wins the day, don't you think?"

"The virtuous are so much smarter than the bad guys."

"And braver."

"Stronger."

"Kinder."

"And," he lost his train of thought as he fell into her twinkling eyes, "shorter."

She laughed and pushed him gently on the shoulder so that he collapsed on his back. "See what you've done? You've ruined a perfect world. It's a punishable offense, you know."

"You'll set the dragons upon me."

"Oh, you'll be banished, for sure."

He sat up and leaned in until his face was only inches from hers. "That would be the worst punishment of all. Is there nothing this lowly servant can do to regain your good graces?"

Annie's lips parted but no sound emerged. Their eyes locked as they drew closer.

She jerked away. "What am I doing? I'm so sorry."

He blew out the breath he'd been holding. "Sorry?"

She brushed a palm along her forehead and squeezed her eyes shut. "You must think I'm horrible. You probably think I brought you out here to seduce you."

"What's wrong with that?" he asked with a grin and ran a finger along her cheek.

She opened her eyes to stare at him. "You're married."

Zack turned away, stood and walked to the edge of the pond, head bowed as he breathed deep to slow his heart rate. Annie shifted on the blanket and he looked over his shoulder at her. "Yes," he said finally, "I am."

They remained where they were for several minutes, thoughts to themselves, until Annie came to stand a few feet from him. "You don't wear a ring."

He shrugged and ran a hand over his mouth. "Used to."

She started to speak, stopped as if thinking better of it, then plowed ahead. "You said your wife isn't well."

"She's not. I mean, she's not ill. But she's not doing well, either. Her work meant everything to her. But, she got caught in a scandal and lost it all." His face flushed with a surge of anger. At Stella. At himself. He tried to summon pity, but it had burrowed beneath impatience. "Then, she had a botched medical procedure and she's not adapting. Too much pride, I guess. She won't work or socialize. Hardly leaves the condo."

He bent to scoop small stones from the bank, skipped one across the glassy pond. "Beat that."

Annie selected her own stash of flat stones. She flipped the rocks in her fingers, selected one to her liking and side-armed.

They took turns tossing, egging each other on until Zack managed five skips and the competition had served its purpose, which was to give him time to organize his thoughts. He declared himself the winner and brushed dirt from his hands as he faced her. "I took off my ring a year and a half ago when I moved out."

The first year of marriage to Stella was a whirlwind through a social life he'd never imagined: parties, openings, exclusive dinner invitations. The opulence made his head spin as he indulged himself with every exquisite luxury she was willing to buy. But, his excitement waned as he recognized, too late, that no Armani suit would help him fit into Stella's social circles, no Rolex would speed tedious hours of idle chatter with people he didn't really like. Stella was dispassionate, seemingly proud to enter a gathering on his arm, but soon in animated discussion with famous judges or wealthy entrepreneurs, unmindful as Zack was ignored and pushed beyond their circle. He was never alone for long, fending off numerous advances from bejeweled, middle-aged women with tight, surgeon-sculpted faces.

Little by little, he realized the marriage was a big mistake, a sham. He admired Stella's spunk and the ease with which she soared in her world, he enjoyed her wit and animation. But he doubted whether he'd ever loved her.

As soon as he expressed his thoughts, she tightened her grip, swore to pay attention to him but never did, offered extravagant gifts that no longer appealed. For a year, he tried to adjust, to convince himself he was acting like the spoiled gigolo her crowd considered him. You chose your bed, his father would have said, now you know what you must do. But lying beside Stella, spent and ill at ease, disgusted with himself for falling victim to greed, unable to conjure love or recognize the man he'd become, frustration grew until he finally slipped out of bed one night and packed a suitcase.

"It's very difficult to divorce an attorney who doesn't want to let go," he said to Annie as they resettled on the blanket. "One year later and she was still stalling. Yelling one day, sweetness the next. Her tenacity was one of the things I'd admired, until turned against me." He toyed with loose blanket fibers. "About the time I figured she'd finally given in, her legal troubles began. And, then the surgeries. She needed my help. I moved back."

"You did what you thought necessary."

He shrugged. "Despite her wealth, she has few people to call on. A girlfriend or two. Her parents are dead. Most of her former colleagues can't stay far enough away. I couldn't leave her so alone. Now, I don't know how to get out." Zack drew his lips tight, angry at his circumstances, but even more so at his poor judgment and rash decision-making.

Enough.

He straightened his back and turned to Annie. "What about you?"

"Me?"

"Were you happy in your marriage?"

She hugged her knees again and smiled. "I guess any marriage has ups and downs. Ours was mostly ups, until the end."

Zack leaned back on his elbows, glad to spin the conversation away from his troubles. She sat still so long, head bowed, face hidden between slender arms, he thought she would brush the subject aside.

"Things started falling apart when Scooter died." At his questioning look, she added, "Our son."

He'd been a miniature Mark, with the same dimpled chin and intense brown eyes, the unmanageable curly auburn hair and unbounded energy. "You could not keep that boy still," she told Zack. "One evening, before he'd learned to crawl, we set him on a blanket in the living room and dashed out to the car to unload groceries. When we came back inside, no baby. Oh my stars, did we panic! Found him in the spare bedroom. How in the world? we asked. Then, he took off right before our eyes, tucking one leg underneath and scooting down the hall. That's it, Mark said, I'm calling him Scooter."

"What was his given name?"

Annie tilted her head to one side. "Toby. I told Mark, you can't call him Scooter. He'll hate the name in school." She removed her cap and tossed it by the picnic basket. "Never got to find out if he would or wouldn't. He was only three when he died."

At first, they thought he just had a cold. They cooled his fever, snuggled him, fed him chicken soup from her mother's recipe. Their normally rambunctious son remained listless and withdrawn. The next morning, they rushed him to the hospital.

Too late.

"The doctor diagnosed a form of meningitis. Said there wasn't anything we could've done, the disease takes children fast sometimes." Her eyes brimmed and voice thickened. "Nothing can be worse than burying your baby."

Zack threw caution aside, sat up and drew her into his arms, rocking gently, holding her close as she wept.

She finally pulled away and hid swollen eyes behind her palms before heaving a big sigh. "Life goes on. At least, that's what everybody said. I hardly remember the first months. I guess we got by. Closed the café for awhile, but we needed money. Seemed I could forget when I worked, so I spent more and more hours in the kitchen. Just numb, I suppose." She shook her head and smoothed the blanket at her feet. "Mark never did get over Toby's death. He blamed himself for not calling the doctor sooner. I certainly felt that way, too, but he clung to guilt for comfort more than he clung to me. He was never the same and I was too hurt myself to do much for him. One day, he disappeared, just as he'd done before we came to Hope. I didn't see him for a week."

She'd thought getting away might restore some of the old Mark, but the only thing that changed was the booze.

"Sometimes he helped, but more often he'd be drunk by afternoon, sitting in the porch swing, staring off into a world of his own. He left me so alone. I needed the Mark I married, but he was buried beneath this new man I didn't like. I got angry. It's not all about you, I'd scream at him. I'm hurting, too." She grimaced as if reliving their arguments. "He'd leave again after our fights, come back in a few days and promise to do better. But it never lasted. He'd drink, we'd fight, and off he'd go."

Something had changed when Mark returned home from his longest absence. He seemed shell-shocked and scared, jumping at the slightest sound, rejecting her embraces, withdrawing deeper into a solitary world. Whatever haunted him was a millstone she had no strength to carry.

"He was drinking even more than before. One night, I found him kneeling on the floor of Toby's bedroom. We'd never seen our way to getting rid of anything. There Mark was, surrounded by toys he dragged out of the chest. I knelt and tried to hug him, but he jumped up and ran out the front door and I heard the truck engine. I should've chased him and got the keys, but I was too upset, what with all Toby's toys spread before me. I just let Mark go."

The police said he'd taken the corner too fast. Death was instantaneous.

A chill had descended on her fairyland, although Zack couldn't say if it spread from the unburdening of their souls or because shadows had lengthened and retreated as the sun slipped behind tall Lodgepole and Ponderosa pines. She shivered and pulled the blanket over her shoulders.

"I never did find out what happened on that final trip to make him worse," she whispered as she clutched the roughly-woven wool. Her lips parted to say more; she hesitated, then widened her eyes. "But, a strange thing happened a few weeks after he died. I've never told anybody."

He remained silent as she balanced the relief of unburdening against the hazards of sharing a secret with a man she barely knew. He found himself caring little about the details of whatever secret she considered revealing; only that she feel comfortable doing so.

She studied him a minute longer before making her decision. "I guess I was trying to purge bad memories. I went out to the shed, vowing to get rid of all the junk, but I didn't accomplish much because when I opened up this old trunk, I found a briefcase full of money. Lots of money."

Zack turned abruptly from her and peered into the shadows edging across the pond. "He never mentioned it?"

She shook her head. "I assume Mark put it there. Who else? But, why'd he hide it when we were so behind on our bills?"

"Maybe he intended to give you the money, but ran out of time."

"Maybe. But, you know the biggest question? Where'd he get it in the first place?"

Listen to your gut, Lonnie would say.

"What do you think?"

"Must have been something he knew I wouldn't like, otherwise why hide? Heaven help me, I've tried to imagine. Did he borrow from somebody? But, no one's come by to get paid. Gambling? He'd never been a gambler. I suppose that could have changed, like the drinking." She shivered, either from the chill trickling into the glen or the horror of her own imaginings. "I worry the money came from something illegal."

Hey, it's your gut talking, Lonnie would urge. Pay attention.

"When did you say he was gone the last time?"

"Three years ago. July."

The timing fit. "Any idea where he went?"

Her shoulders rose in a dejected shrug. "Not exactly. But, one night when he got really drunk and I was helping him to bed, he kept mumbling about evil in San Francisco."

Damn.

The last thing Zack wanted was to investigate Annie's late husband for the kidnapping. If Mark was involved, the knowledge would add to her sorrows and Zack would be the one to heap that upon her.

But the Lonnie in his head roared against coincidence.

"What happened to the money?"

"I paid off the mortgage on the Bluebell."

"I'm sure Mark would have been pleased."

"I suppose."

Their faces were masked now in the waning light. He hoped the subtle shadows veiled the conflict in his eyes. "The briefcase might hold a clue. I can look, if you want." She threw him an abrupt glance he judged as suspicion, knew he'd treaded as far as he should. For now. "It's getting dark. We'd better go."

She stared at him a long moment before rising and reaching for a corner of the blanket. He gathered corners, too, and they folded the fabric in fourths. Her expression was hidden from him as she jammed the blanket into the picnic basket. "I threw it in the trash. The briefcase. It wasn't Mark's. He wouldn't be caught dead with one." She gasped as she realized what she'd said, shivered and scrounged in the basket for a sweatshirt.

Zack slung on his daypack, grabbed the picnic basket and followed Annie through the undergrowth guarding her fairyland.

****

They rode along the dirt road in silence, Annie intent on potholes flickering into view beneath the bouncing Chevy headlights, the steering wheel jerking in her grip as they bumped and jolted. The pavement seemed smooth and serene when she turned toward Hope.

Their silence continued back to town. He stole sideways glances at her, trying to gauge her emotions. They'd bared so much that afternoon, yet he was certain there was more to learn and wished he could spend endless lazy afternoons exploring every corner of her heart and mind.

And body.

He speculated on her thoughts. Maybe sorry she'd shared her special place with him? Sorry she'd been so open? Perhaps she'd remembered how much she still loved Mark.

He was jealous of a dead man.

Annie stopped the truck near the café, killed the engine and sat with her face averted. "I guess it's past dinner time."

"I'm not hungry," he said.

"Me, neither."

His right hand squeezed the armrest with the force of the conflicts marauding through his mind. Finally, he unclenched his hand and pushed open the door. "I'll help you put this stuff away."

His action broke her spell and she hurried around the truck bed. "You don't have to," she said, but he waved her off and retrieved his pack and the wicker basket. "All right. It goes in the café kitchen."

He tried for levity. "You'd think this thing would be lighter now."

She laughed as she slipped the key into the lock. "Guess I overdid. Taking after my mother. She never liked running out of food for company. We ate lots of leftovers." She swung wide the café door and held it open for him to edge by. "Just put everything on the work table." She flicked on the lights and her smile widened. "Pie?"

He'd eat slugs and earthworms if only she'd keep smiling that way.

As she cut two pieces of pie and heated them in the microwave, filling the kitchen with the aroma of spicy peaches, Zack lingered by the sturdy shelves housing her baking ingredients. He lifted jars to read the labels, unscrewed lids for whiffs of Saigon cinnamon and smoked paprika. His gaze traveled to the messy desk shoved between the shelves and he smiled that her sense of order with all things culinary apparently did not extend to paperwork. He supposed she knew the location of invoices and correspondence, but the tumbled, uneven stacks would befuddle anyone else. Somehow, this made him happy, just recognizing her humanness laid bare on the desk.

"Ice cream?" she asked from the other side of the kitchen.

"Sure, why not?" He spied a cooking magazine sticking out from one of the haphazard stacks and pulled it out, several pieces of paper tagging along. He started to return them to the stack, but stopped as a glossy photograph slipped onto the desk.

She was pregnant. Her face was fuller and hair shorter than now, breasts swollen beneath maternity-blouse smocking. A man stood beside her, arm across her shoulders, pride evident in his smile as he pointed at her belly. He was a head taller, curly hair wild around a narrow face and high forehead.

Must be Mark.

"Ready," she called as she returned a carton of vanilla ice cream to the freezer.

Zack peeked over his shoulder. Her back was turned to him.

He slipped the photo into his pocket.

***

He couldn't sleep. He tossed and turned beneath the quilts, his mind a jumble of rapid-fire images and recycled worries, body aching for the one thing he could not have.

He'd come so close to kissing her. He'd tarried as they stacked plates in the sink, arm brushing against hers, an explosion of desire he wanted to believe she shared. He knew he should feel guilty about Stella, but struggled to dredge that emotion through the bad feelings piled up over the years.

No. Thinking of his wife was not what stopped him.

It was the photograph.

I only did what needed to be done, he told himself. Probably nothing will come of it. Mark is dead, the money gone. What difference could any of it make?

He kicked the quilts aside and bounded from the bed to grunt through pushups and crunches and squats, trying to sweat desire and conflict out his pores. He breathed heavily through his mouth and paced, hands on hips, head hung. On his fifth lap around the small room, he noticed the cell phone upside down on the dresser. He'd put the damn thing from his mind during his time with Annie. He puffed a disgruntled breath and grabbed the phone. The display indicated five new messages.

He dialed voicemail and skipped the first four messages, all from Stella. He recognized Lonnie's number and thought for the first time that day about the bullet casing.

Lonnie's messages sometimes droned past the allotted time.

This one was short.

"Bingo."

CHAPTER 13

"Thought maybe you'd left town."

Norton stood by the stained Mr. Coffee gurgling at the rear of the office, watching Zack's approach and greeting to Penny Chester. He offered a large ceramic mug with a faded Wells Fargo bank logo.

Zack shook his head, bitter Folgers a poor encore to the delicious brew he'd savored at the Bluebell. "Haven't given up yet," he replied as he observed the chief's slumped shoulders and drawn, tired face, worries sculpted into knit brows, sleepless nights weighing his ruddy skin. The man was going through hell. Zack opened his mouth to offer words of comfort, but changed his mind. If Norton wanted to talk about his wife's illness, he'd bring it up.

Norton gulped coffee, topped off his mug and nodded for Zack to follow. He plopped into his office chair and swiveled as he sipped, eyes intent on Zack, who slouched in the threadbare chair opposite. They sat in silence until Norton grunted and asked, "Well?"

The perfect time to tell about the bullet casing.

"Nothing new."

He'd yet to fully understand why he wanted to keep secret the most important evidence in the case. Did he trust Norton? Yes, as much as you can trust someone you've known only four days. Besides, what harm could the man do with the knowledge? Who would he run to? What next step would he take to inhibit Zack's investigation?

No one and no next step. So, why hide the evidence from him?

It wasn't like Zack had solved the murder. The lab results proved the same weapon had been fired at the ransom drop and by Cutwater Creek. Not proven was if the casing belonged with the bullet fragments lodged in Riordan's chest. The casing could have lain in the creek gravel for months, with no connection to the murder.

Possible, but not likely.

Zack felt in his gut that the two crimes were related. But, gut feel was a far cry from proof.

Withholding evidence from Norton hadn't seemed strange to Lonnie. "You hand over a complete package," he replied when Zack called. "Otherwise he might say thank you ma'am and boot your sorry ass. Next thing you know, he'll drop kick the damn case through the hoop and all your hard work will be out the window."

Whatever conclusion the chief drew about what Zack had or hadn't learned, was or wasn't saying, he apparently decided not to pursue the issue. He brushed papers aside to unbury a clay coaster and glanced at his watch. "Mr. Ray Isley returned my call yesterday evening. He prefers to meet here. Should arrive in fifteen minutes or so." He paused at the sound of knuckles rapping on the doorframe.

"Heading to the courthouse, Chief."

"Okay. I'm expecting someone soon, Penny. Please forward the nonemergency numbers to voicemail."

"Will do." She nodded to Zack and hurried away.

Zack waited for Norton to continue what he'd been saying, but the man sat staring at the doorway, Penny's interruption perhaps allowing troubles at home to overcome the business at hand. After a couple of minutes, Zack lightly tapped the toe of his shoe against the back of Norton's desk. "What do you intend to ask Isley?"

Norton blinked and sucked in a long breath. "Just clarifying if he was acquainted with Edward Riordan." Steely blue eyes dared Zack to suggest he question Isley about the kidnapping three years earlier, too.

Zack got the message and held his tongue.

The chief grunted and rubbed a roughened hand across his cheek. "Like I said, Isley's no dummy. I don't think he'd appreciate you taking part in this conversation." Zack started to object but Norton waved him off. "That is my considered judgment and you know I'm right. Trust this old man to handle the situation."

Nothing would be gained in battling Norton on the point, so Zack held up both arms in surrender.

With a satisfied nod, Norton grabbed his coffee mug and rose from the chair. "Doesn't mean you can't listen to what he has to say." He beckoned for Zack to follow and headed for the coffeemaker, pointing an index finger at the small supply room adjoining his office.

The room housed the office printer, copier and fax machine. One wall was lined with shelves of neatly stacked reams of paper, cartons of pencils, carefully labeled cardboard file boxes.

"Quite obvious Penny's in charge of this room and not yours truly," Norton chuckled behind Zack. He slurped and nodded at the squat Xerox copier. "Damn thing drives me crazy when I'm in my office trying to concentrate." Another slurp as he cast Zack a meaningful glance. "Movable wall. Very thin."

Zack motioned to the fax machine. "Okay if I make a few copies and send a fax?"

"Instructions on the bulletin board." He turned toward his office.

"Chief?" Zack called and Norton stopped with a wary squint of his eyes. "Ask Isley if he owns a nine millimeter."

A penetrating stare and a slurp before Norton grunted and disappeared around the corner.

Zack lifted the copier cover and pulled the snapshot of Annie and Mark from his back pocket. At least, he assumed the tall, curly-haired man was Mark. No way to find out for sure without asking and he did not want to explain why he took the photograph.

Most witnesses are unreliable even shortly after a crime, let alone three years later. But, the bartender at Jonathan's Bar & Grill, Ed Riordan's favorite San Francisco haunt, had a razor-sharp memory for faces.

There'd been at least three kidnappers: the two who'd exchanged gunfire and the driver. Was Mark one of them? Evidence tying him to the kidnapping was circumstantial, at best: the timing of his absence, his demeanor upon return, the briefcase full of money.

Zack punched the button to copy the photograph and the machine whined and groaned. No wonder it annoyed Norton in the adjoining room. Zack pulled the copy from the stacker, located scissors in a supply box and carefully cut away Annie's image. He slipped Mark's picture back on the plate and made another copy, wrote a quick note across the top and faxed the sheet to Lonnie. He pocketed the original photograph and ran the copies through the shredder.

He heard Norton clear his throat. Listening in on a conversation with Ray Isley should be easy. Zack noted a metal chair shoved against the far wall, brushed away paper fragments before squirming to find some comfort on the hard surface.

He didn't have long to wait. The front door creaked open and shut and Isley called out hello.

"In here, Ray," came Norton's voice through the wall.

Boots clomped across the vinyl floor.

"Thanks for coming in. Got some coffee in back."

"No thanks, John. Gave up caffeine. Doc says it was bothering my heart."

"I sometimes think it's the only thing keeping mine going."

Chair legs scraped along the floor and Zack imagined Isley lounging in the side chair. "How is Amelia, John?"

"About as well as can be. She's a mighty strong woman. Says that comes from putting up with me all these years."

The men were silent a moment, perhaps uncomfortable in their conversation, Isley wondering how much to ask about Amelia Norton's illness, the chief lost in his thoughts. Finally, Isley asked, "What did you want to talk about, John?"

Norton cleared his throat again. "This business of the murder down at Cutwater Creek."

Isley's voice contained puzzlement and impatience. "What's that got to do with me?"

"Just tying up loose ends. You know these bureaucrats. Got to dot the i's and cross the t's or they're breathing down your neck. I aim to keep them away from mine, so I'm making sure my reports are complete. In that regard, I'm wondering if you were acquainted with the dead man, Mr. Edward Riordan."

"I heard he was a stranger to town."

"Appears so, yes. But, I've been puzzling why he showed up in Hope. Thought maybe he had business with you out at the ranch."

"No, he did not. And, to my knowledge, I've never met this Riordan."

Chief Norton's chair squeaked. "You might know him by another name. Edward Freeman ring a bell?"

"What's this about, John? You aren't calling every able-bodied citizen of Hope to your office to inquire if they were acquainted with a dead man."

"Here's the thing, Ray. I got a report of Riordan being out at the Rockin' I Ranch in a heated conversation with you."

Chair legs scraped again. "Who the hell fed you that crap?"

"You know I'm not at liberty to tell. Suffice it to say, this is a point I must clarify."

"It's a damned lie."

"Very well, I will note your response in the file."

"You damned well better."

"No offense intended, Ray. Just dotting and crossing."

"When did this murder take place?"

"Doc Foster puts the deed before dawn on June the tenth."

"Before you ask, I'll tell you. I was attending a cattle auction." Zack listened to the scratch of pencil on paper. "Here's the contact information. Check, if you must. I assume that's all?"

"Yes, and I thank you for taking time out of your busy schedule to set the record straight."

Isley took two thundering steps.

"Oh, one more question." A pause, as Isley likely spun in the doorway and leveled an angry sneer at his inquisitor. "You own a nine millimeter?"

"Now, what the hell?"

"Just routine, Ray. Perhaps the guilty party followed Riordan to Hope and brought the murder weapon along. Helps support that theory if I know the whereabouts of similar guns in town. I can check registrations, but it's much quicker to ask."

Isley's response was curt. "I own two, John. Locked away at the ranch."

"Okay, then. No more questions from me. I appreciate you coming in."

Footsteps thudded across the office floor and the front door slammed.

Zack rose from the folding chair and walked around the corner to lean against the doorframe. "Defensive."

"Not unexpected. The man felt his integrity called to question."

"He could have been lying."

"I don't think so, which means Driscoll lied to you." Norton reached for a stack of papers. "I suggest you find out why." He leveled a penetrating stare at Zack. "And, I assume you'll be telling me how you zeroed in on a nine millimeter for the murder weapon."

***

Zack called the auction house to verify Isley's alibi, but struck out as a clerk growled that he weren't no babysitter and couldn't remember who the hell was at every damn auction. Another roadblock. He'd have to leave the task to Norton for an official request.

No answer when he called Clyde Driscoll's number.

He swung by the Ace Hardware, which doubled as the town's sporting goods mecca, and inquired casually if the clerk had met Riordan. He left with waders, rod and reel, a tackle box and selection of flies, but nothing new on the case.

The phone rang as he stored his new gear in the Fiesta.

"Who is he?"

Zack used his shoulder to anchor the cell phone against his ear. "Who is whom, Lonnie?"

"Don't give me that 'whom' crap. The guy in the photograph. Whom the hell else would I be asking about?"

Zack slammed close the trunk. "Did you talk to the bartender?"

"Best barkeep in the city. Pretty damned sure the guy spent time in the company of Mr. Edward Riordan."

The odds had been against Mark as one of the kidnappers, the odds still longer the bartender would remember him with Riordan. In a way, Zack had hoped he wouldn't.

"Pick the guy up. We'll squeeze a confession from him."

"He's dead."

"Shit." Silence as Lonnie absorbed the information. "How'd you get on to him?"

Zack shrugged as if Lonnie could see him. "Desperation, I guess. Nothing else to go on, so I scraped bottom."

"And came up with gold."

"Still doesn't prove he took part in the kidnapping."

"You think he did or you wouldn't have faxed the damn photo. You holding out on me, partner?"

Zack rubbed a hand across his forehead. "No."

"Then, who the hell is the guy?"

He told Lonnie most of the story: how Mark had been missing from home at the time of the kidnapping, his despondency and death in a car accident, the briefcase of money. He glossed over any details about Annie, but Lonnie was not to be deterred.

"She spent every dime?"

"Yep."

"The briefcase?"

"Gone."

"Shit, again. At least, I hope you got a description matching the bag we saw at the payoff."

"It was a painful time for her, Lonnie. She doesn't remember the details."

"She finds a shitload of cash but can't remember the details? Well, I got a bridge for sale. Maybe she has reason to lie to you."

"What's that supposed to mean?"

"Nothing says the driver wasn't a woman."

"You're barking up the wrong tree."

"Riordan and this O'Connor character hatch the plot and recruit the wife for the getaway. Or, hell, she may be the mastermind behind the whole enchilada."

Zack shifted the phone to his left hand. "Then, why tell me about the briefcase? If she was involved, she'd keep the secret to herself."

"She couldn't resist your cunning interrogation."

"Give it up, Lonnie."

"Okay, she slipped up. The words came out of her mouth before she could stop them, so she tries to throw you off by saying the evidence is gone. For all we know, the loot is still buried somewhere. In either case, Riordan shows up to get a bigger piece of the pie. She panics and whacks him."

"You're wrong."

Lonnie hesitated before chuckling. "Don't tell me you've got something going with the widow." When Zack didn't answer, Lonnie laughed. "Shit, Sherlock, that's one hell of an investigative technique."

Zack hung up and paced beside the car, angry breaths exploding as if he'd just run ten miles flat out.

The phone rang again and he heaved a long sigh before answering. "Sorry. No more comments."

Zack squeezed his eyes shut and swallowed anger. "Yeah."

"But, stay objective on this, okay?"

He was right, of course. Even as Zack rejected the idea of Annie's involvement in the kidnapping or the murder, he recognized how the possibility would strike Lonnie. "No problem."

"Two of the kidnappers are dead, but there's at least one still around and I intend to find the sonofabitch."

"Don't worry. We're close."

"Damn right we are. How are things going with the police chief?"

"The office is short-staffed and he's preoccupied with his wife's illness. He'd love to wipe the investigation from his hands, but seems reluctant to deal with state investigators. I might be able to stall, but we're definitely on a short timeline."

"Then, I guess we'd better grab us a helluva damn big shovel and keep digging."

***

Clyde Driscoll lived on Talmadge Road, about a half-mile from Gene Harris' tack repair shop. Zack eased the Ford up a long drive to a modest ranch-style house with peeling forest-green paint. Light-green shutters hung crookedly alongside a large picture window. Three rusted Chevy trucks flanked the house to the west, together with an off-kilter barbecue grill and two bent bicycles, former color no longer discernible.

The record-breaking early summer heat wave had ended in cloudy skies, which would be refreshing and welcomed if not for the chilled wind sweeping in from the north. Zack drew his jacket close as he approached Driscoll's house with a sideways glance at a listing detached garage, apparently not used for parking vehicles, at least none to be driven, because the warped door was blocked by stacks of brick and jumbled wood scraps. The porch steps creaked under Zack's weight and the railing wobbled at his touch as he wondered why anyone would hire a handyman whose own home was such a dilapidated, neglected mess.

No one answered when Zack knocked, although he banged several times and uselessly pushed the doorbell, which was most likely broken, as no chime rang in the house. He pounded the door one last time before returning to his car.

Why must everything in this damn case come hard?

He headed toward the Rockin' I Ranch, his thoughts swirling like hay in a dust devil.

Should he tell Annie about Mark's possible involvement in the kidnapping?

No. No need to hurt her.

He didn't buy Lonnie's theory of Annie's role, but his training and experience forced him to recognize the logic. Under other circumstances, he'd pursue the angle. But, not with her. She was not involved in the kidnapping or the murder. She couldn't be. Lonnie hadn't watched the pain in her eyes when she whispered of Toby's death, Mark's drinking and disappearances. Zack doubted she could manufacture such a haunted stare even if spinning tales to conceal her own criminal involvement.

No way. Not Annie.

He eased the car beneath the thick timbers heralding the Rockin' I Ranch and considered what excuse he'd give if he encountered Ray Isley. He could think of no good reason for a freelance writer to show up and doubted Isley would welcome idle bullshit. Best to stick to the truth and say he was looking for Clyde Driscoll.

He saw no one as he drove past the house to the barn, thinking he might inquire of Driscoll with Kent Baker. He walked to the huge doors standing ajar, stepped inside to the smell of manure and hay and waited as his eyes adjusted to the dim light. A horse whinnied in a middle stall and a high-pitched female voice cooed.

She walked around the horse's flanks and yelped at the sight of Zack silhouetted in the doorway.

"Sorry," he said and approached the stall. "I didn't mean to scare you."

She was a petite woman, perhaps sixty years of age, with dyed platinum blonde hair in a whirl around her heart-shaped face. Her tan riding breeches and high-necked, ruffled shirt had been crisply laundered, her black paddock boots polished to a waxy shine. "Oh, my. You gave me a start." The horse snorted and eyed Zack. "Easy, Tara. What has gotten into you today?"

"A mind of her own?"

"Yes, I'm afraid so." She stepped away from the stall and regarded Zack. "Should I know you? My husband has so many business acquaintances, I simply cannot keep them straight. But then, perhaps you're here to see Troy? I am Elyse Isley, his mother."

"Pleased to meet you, ma'am. My name is Zack Dalton."

"Such fine manners, young man. Your mother would be pleased. You did learn at her side, did you not?"

"Oh, yes, ma'am."

"Well, I wish you'd rub a little sophistication onto my Troy." Not a wisp of hair-sprayed platinum flew out of place as she shook her head. "I'm afraid I have yet to impress upon him the importance of good manners. Living out here in the wilds is the problem, I do believe. Brings out the beast in a man rather than a gentle nature. I've said as much to Mr. Isley. Of course, my husband has finer points, but even those fail to influence our roughneck son." She paused and her eyes brightened. "Tell me, do you live in a city?"

"Several years now in San Francisco."

She clasped tiny hands to her chest. "Oh, my, how wonderful. Such a vibrancy to the city by the bay. I recall a delightful restaurant. Completely booked every night. Took a hearty tip to the maître d' to secure the best table."

She stared past Zack and he twisted to check if someone had entered the barn, but memories were all that transfixed her. He was impatient to find Driscoll and considered cutting short their conversation, but knew that evidence is often gathered from the least likely sources. If time allows, better to listen.

With so little to investigate, he definitely had the time.

Her reverie ended in a slight shiver and her gaze wandered the barn, finally resting on Zack. "It's been years since my last visit to San Francisco."

"You should come. You'd probably notice big changes, but the heart of the city is the same."

"Yes, I should. Perhaps Mr. Isley will accompany me, if I can pull him away from business. He's a dedicated rancher, you know, with little time for frivolity." She sighed and walked past Zack toward the rail where the saddles were stored and fingered tooling on the show saddle with the missing concho. "Do you ride, Zack?"

"I'm afraid I've never mastered it."

"You should try. Such a wonderful synergy between man and beast. I used to ride in New York, all the while romanticizing about the wild west. I suppose that's what drew me to my husband. To the complete disapproval of my parents, I might add." She caressed the saddle's smooth leather. "Threatened to cut me off without a penny, although they came around in the end. We used my inheritance to purchase this ranch."

"Where did you live before the Rockin' I?"

"Here and there. Do not be fooled by our current fine standard of living. We have suffered financial ups and downs as any businessman does, but my husband is resilient and determined, if not downright stubborn."

"It appears all is well now. That's a beautiful saddle."

"A bit of vanity, I confess. I seldom use it."

"I see a concho is missing." He pointed to the empty space.

"Really? Oh, bother. It's not the first one to dislodge."

"Shall we search?" Zack toed the dirt below the saddle.

"How nice of you to offer, but I can't ask you to waste your time on the fancies of an old woman."

"I have the time and you're not that old," Zack replied with a wink as he continued to walk the area by the saddles.

A flush crept beneath the foundation and powder masking her papery skin. "Ah, silver-tongued you are. Still, I do not wish to detain you with a fruitless search for this trinket."

Zack shrugged and raised his eyes from the mock searching of the ground. "Maybe somebody already found it."

"Perhaps, although I'd think they would have told me. I shall ask Mr. Baker, our stableman. Not many people venture into this barn, only Mr. Baker, Troy and myself."

"Your husband?"

"Seldom has time to ride." She returned to the stalls, motioning for Zack to follow. She gave Tara a final caress, moved her back in the stall and closed the gate. "I'm sorry. I've forgotten why you're here."

"Well, actually, Mrs. Isley, I'm not a business associate of your husband's or a friend of Troy's, although I've met them both. I'm a freelance writer doing a story on law enforcement. I've been working with Chief Norton."

"The poor man."

"Yes," Zack replied with a solemn frown. "He has a lot on his mind."

"I dare say."

"Not only his wife, but he's got the investigation into the murder by the creek."

She wrinkled her nose. "A nasty business. I do so despise the idea of violence in our little town. Perhaps we are unjustly secure here so far from the big cities. I suppose murders happen almost anywhere."

"Unfortunately true. By chance, did you know the man who was killed?"

Startled blue eyes widened. "What a horrid thought, to know a murdered man. Why would you ask such a thing?"

They walked out of the barn. "I'm sorry. I didn't mean to offend. I thought perhaps he was one of Mr. Isley's business associates who'd been here at the ranch."

"Goodness me. Well, I suppose it's a logical question. Still, it gives a person pause." She pursed rose-painted lips before continuing. "I saw his photograph in the newspaper. So little of interest occurs in sleepy Hope, a murder captures the front page. I did not recognize him, but I don't meet everyone who visits my husband."

He'd hoped she would corroborate Driscoll's account of Riordan at the ranch, proof of Isley lying to Norton. A long shot that did not pay off. "I understand. I'm sorry to raise such a distasteful subject."

She smiled blandly. "No offense taken. But tell me, was inquiring about the dead man your purpose in visiting?"

"Actually, I was hoping to speak with Clyde Driscoll."

"Clyde? Why, I don't believe I've seen him here today. Come to think of it, Mr. Isley did say something about Clyde taking a few days off."

Zack bit back an expletive and smiled. "Well, then, I'd best be on my way."

Her brows knit. "Oh, won't you stay and take some refreshment?"

She was not at all like his strong-willed, outgoing mother—a sharp contrast between the delicate features and refined manners of Mrs. Isley and the down-to-earth robustness of Elizabeth Dalton. Yet, he enjoyed listening to her and it occurred to him that he'd had little contact with older women since his mother died. There was something vaguely comforting about this conversation, even though he'd failed to gather additional evidence.

However, prolonging the conversation increased the odds of running into Ray or Troy Isley. "I should be going," he said. "I do hope you come to San Francisco one day. I know a fantastic bistro I'm sure you'd enjoy and I'd be happy to show you around."

She clasped her hands and smiled at him. "Such a lovely invitation. Perhaps I can persuade my husband to take me there. I'm afraid I've never conquered the art of driving."

No wonder she appeared so lonely. She was probably stuck at the ranch while the men in her family attended their own affairs. "Perhaps your son can bring you."

She waved a dainty hand as if swatting a fly. "Not likely he'd take the time. Oh, he has visited San Francisco, although not so much in the last few years. But, I dare say his choice of dining establishments would leave something to be desired."

Zack extended his right hand, which she clasped between chilled, bony fingers. "It's been a pleasure to meet you, Mrs. Isley."

"A pleasure, indeed, Zack. Your mother must be proud of you."

He smiled and bowed, climbed into the Ford and rolled down the window. "I certainly hope so."

***

"He's on a call." Penny Chester glanced up from the stack of manila folders she was sorting.

"Nothing too bad, I hope," Zack replied, noting Norton's darkened office and the absence of his Stetson on the hat rack.

"Mrs. Jarvas again. Claims someone broke into her garage and stole a bicycle." A grin sneaked across her thin lips. "Things aren't clicking so well for the poor dear. I doubt she's owned a bicycle in fifty or sixty years. Chief Norton is patient with her. More than I would be, for sure."

"Patience is a good trait for a police chief."

She stacked the manila folders on the corner of her tidy desk, slouched in her maroon secretarial chair and folded her arms beneath small breasts. "Anything I can help you with?"

"No, thanks."

"Chief ought to be back in a half-hour or so. Takes him that long to calm Mrs. Jarvas."

"Sounds like she's a character."

"Nothing in this town but characters. Yours truly an exception, you understand."

He returned her grin. "Of course."

She released her arms and rolled her eyes theatrically. "You'd exclude yourself, too, if you stayed here long. Take Mr. Pendergast, for example. Walks around with a pet cockatoo on his shoulder."

"I don't think I've run into him."

"You'd know. The bird swears. Nonstop. Reverend had to ask Mr. Pendergast to leave the cockatoo at home or stop coming to church because the darn bird interrupted the service and offended the old ladies. Mr. Pendergast's not been in church since."

"Guess he chose his pet over the sermon."

Penny swiveled the chair and drummed a pencil on the desktop. "Oh, I could tell you stories. You can't live here and work in this office without having stories to tell."

Up until now, Penny had offered him only polite greetings and a nod. Zack wasn't sure why the change, but the time seemed right to explore what she might add to the case. "You know everyone in town?"

"Some just to say hello to, but, yeah, pretty much."

"How about the murder victim?"

She shook her head. "Wasn't from around here." She lowered her voice and leaned in. "The strange thing is that he must've come to Hope for some reason. It's not a place you accidently happen by. But no one seems to know. So, that leaves only one possibility, in my humble opinion."

Zack raised his eyebrows in question.

"Why, he came to meet with whoever murdered him, who surely isn't saying so now."

"Could be. But if there's proof, Chief Norton's missed it."

She tapped a skinny finger against her cheek. "Me, too. And, believe me, I've tried. I suppose I should mind my own business. Working here, you just get caught up, you know?"

"You might have resources not available to Chief Norton."

"Or, to you." She regarded him with a smirk. "You're no reporter. I smell law enforcement." She nodded in satisfaction when he opened his mouth to reply, closed it again with a quick lift of his shoulders. "None of my business, I'm sure. Just happy you're here to lend a hand. Turning the case over to the state police would mean a whole lot of paperwork and interference. Been there. Don't want to do it again and neither does the chief. The last time was not pleasant. So, I'm glad you're pursuing suspects."

Zack furrowed his brows. "What do you mean?"

Penny lifted reading glasses from the desk and twirled a stem between two fingers. "Well, I assume that's why the chief pulled in Ray Isley for a chat." She'd left the office before Isley appeared, a fact she expected Zack to recognize, because she hurried to explain. "Saw his car parked out front."

Zack's eyes flicked to her gold wedding band as he thought that poor Mr. Chester and any Chester children probably didn't get away with much under Penny's watchful eye. "Why would you think Isley a suspect?"

She regarded him as if his fall from the turnip truck must've been very far, indeed. "Most murders are about sex or money, right? That's what they say on television. Well, calling Mr. Isley in here certainly cannot be about sex." She exaggerated a shudder.

"Hard to imagine money being a motive for Ray Isley."

"Can't always tell a book by the cover."

"Are you saying he's not as flush as he appears?"

"All I know is he was in the bank a few days before the murder. My cousin works as a teller and she heard him talking to the loan officer. Ain't that the way, she said to me, snooty land-rich and pocketbook poor."

Maybe the Rockin' I Ranch was not as prosperous as it appeared. If Isley's coffers were empty, he might seek a working capital loan.

Or, maybe he needed cash to pay off Riordan.

"Did he get the loan?"

The telephone rang on Penny's desk and broke her confiding mood. She reached for the receiver with a dismissive shrug of her bony shoulders.

Zack raised a hand in a quick wave and headed for the door.

***

Still no sign of anyone at Driscoll's house, no answer when Zack knocked. The phone had gone unanswered, too, but he'd driven out, more for something to do than with any real thought of confronting the man.

He called Lonnie about Ray Isley's possible financial woes. "May be nothing."

"May be something. I'll start with the auction houses. Got a buddy who can help. A rancher most likely owes money for equipment, livestock or land. Or, maybe the man's got bad habits he can't afford."

"Gambling?"

"Wouldn't be the first."

"Might connect him to Riordan."

"Far as I can tell, Riordan was a loner when gambling. Preferred to swindle innocents rather than swim with the sharks."

"Sharks bite."

"So can innocents, if you rile them up enough. Let's summarize. So far, you've dug up one positive and three possible Riordan accomplices."

Zack frowned. "Mark O'Connor's the positive, but how do you count the possibles?"

"One, this Isley guy. Two, the guy you first fingered, Leroy Montrose. Three, Mrs. Mark O'Connor."

"I told you she's not involved."

"Just keeping it real. We already eliminated Montrose with an airtight alibi. You describe Isley as a large man in his sixties. Not a match to the shooters, right? That means he'd have to be the driver. You figure this so-called big-shot rancher as the wheelman?"

"No," Zack admitted. "But, he could've been the brains behind the whole thing."

"Yes, he could. Which means someone else drove the van and the only suspect left is Mrs. O'Connor. I say we pursue who we've got until you dig up additional suspects."

"Just get the dope on Isley."

Lonnie grunted and Zack could hear computer keys clacking in the background. "She told the truth about the money, you know."

"What do you mean?"

"The mortgage on the O'Connor property was paid off a couple years ago. Prior to the big bonanza? Late payments. Hefty interest charges. Suddenly, all debt wiped out. Pretty damn good motive for kidnapping."

"For him. That doesn't point a finger at her, too."

"Beware of femme fatales, m'boy. Keep your fly zipped and your mind open."

Zack hung up and slumped against Lonnie's Ford.

There had to be someone else.

If Riordan came to Hope seeking Mark O'Connor and learned he was dead, what would he have done? Squeezed the widow, Lonnie'd say. But how? With what leverage? Threaten to ruin Mark's reputation? Not much of a threat. Besides, he couldn't expose Mark without highlighting his own complicity. He might threaten bodily harm, but Riordan was more of a conniver than a fighter.

If Mark was the only accomplice in Hope, Riordan would've left in a huff. Instead, he hung around, most likely turning to his other partner or partners in crime. Threatening exposure might be a more effective blackmail tactic against a living accomplice than a dead one.

Zack kicked at rocks by his feet, climbed into the Ford and drove downtown. He meandered side streets, past giggling preteens lounging in front of the county library, a harried mother toting a squirming toddler into the Rexall, a delivery truck pulling into the Ace Hardware.

Just driving.

He wasn't due at Annie's for dinner until six o'clock. More than an hour to kill.

He thought about going to the Roadside, see if Wendell and Gaylord were perched on their designated bar stools. He'd probably learned all he could from them, but their good-hearted banter was entertaining. He could picture Kitty waving a plump arm as if wiping Gaylord from her bar, Gaylord tipping a beer mug with a wink and sly grin when he managed to get her goat.

Wait.

There were two taverns in town and he'd not been to the Woodsman. Riordan had. How'd he miss such an obvious connection? He'd not given the place a single thought since reading Norton's police report. Riordan had left the Woodsman Tavern around eleven o'clock the night before he was killed. Nothing had come of Norton's inquiries, but Zack chided himself for neglecting any potential lead in the case.

He turned in the grocery store parking lot and headed west.

***

Rough-hewn wood planks, darkened to the color of overbrewed coffee, were brightened only by the Bud Lite neon sign hanging in a small, high window. The plywood door required a hard yank to creak open from its warped frame. The stale smell of cigarettes assaulted Zack as he stepped inside and glanced at a No Smoking sign. Apparently, patrons of the Woodsman were not big on obeying signs.

Norton had described the Roadside Tavern as the hangout for good ol' boys, road construction workers, rain-soaked hunters, victorious softball teams, City Councilmen after meetings.

The Woodsman got the roughnecks.

The place was smaller than the Roadside, floored with chipped linoleum, furnished with mismatched tables and chairs, a twenty-foot bar straight ahead. Two bikers lounged at a table; passing through Hope, Zack thought. He'd noted their motorcycles in the parking lot, travel gear strapped on back. They eyed him as he walked across the room, then returned their attention to a map spread on the uneven table, the guy with the red do-rag and bulging beer gut stabbing a thick finger at the paper.

The only other patron was Leroy.

Zack had recognized Leroy's truck parked at the far end of the Woodsman's lot. You're a burden Annie and Sarah don't need, he thought as he slid onto a stool. "Hey, Leroy."

Leroy squinted bloodshot eyes, bushy salt-and-pepper brows drawn together before he relaxed with a lopsided smile. "Well, now, if it ain't…"

"Zack."

"I knew I'd remember. Hey, Roland, get my friend here a drink, will ya?"

The burly bartender had a shaved bowling-ball head and eyebrows so black and thin they appeared painted on above skeptical eyes. He probably doubled as the bouncer, his biceps the size of a small man's thighs, neck short and thick, torso bulging beneath the T-shirt stretched to bursting. Many hours in the gym, Zack figured, but enhanced with steroids. Everything about the man was meant to intimidate, to show who was boss and who'd do better to stay out of the way. Everything was powerful, dominating.

Except his voice.

"What can I get you?" he asked in a high-pitched purr.

"Beer, thanks," Zack replied, thinking maybe Roland's lack of masculine vocal cords was the impetus for bulking up. He'd probably taken one too many lickings in grade school.

"On me." Leroy fumbled in the back pocket of his loose-fitting jeans, pulled out a worn leather wallet and slapped a twenty on the bar.

"No need," Zack said.

Leroy waved him off. "I said, my treat. What, you don't think I'm good for it?"

Roland slid a mug of beer in front of Zack and snatched the twenty.

Zack lifted the mug. "I guess I'll just say thank you."

"That's right." Leroy rested his elbow on the bar and scratched at the back of his head. "Wouldn't have offered if I didn't mean it." He picked up the glass before him, ice tinkling as he sipped. "I see you're a beer man. I used to be, but any more I do better with a little whiskey. All those beer calories go right to my gut, know what I mean?"

"Yes, sir, I do."

Leroy paused with the glass to his lips, a startled expression turned toward Zack. "Sir? Been a long time since anybody called me that. You wouldn't be makin' fun of old Leroy, would you?"

"No, sir."

He harrumphed and took a sip, wiped his mouth with the back of his hand. "Man comes into a bit of money, he likes to pay his debts, right down to the bar tab."

"Well, you don't owe me a dime."

"Huh?" Leroy scrunched his weathered face as he tried to puzzle through Zack's words. "You tellin' me you ain't never bought me a drink?"

"No, sir, I haven't."

"Hmm," he frowned at his glass before slugging the last ounce and beckoning to Roland. "Well, no need to start now. I can pay my way." He licked his lips as the bartender poured a stream of whiskey into a clean glass, added ice and placed the drink on the bar. Leroy's gaze wandered the tavern a moment before settling on the glass. "Payin' my own way."

"No reason to spit at good fortune."

"Huh? Oh, yeah. That's the thing right there. What you said. A man's got every right to take advantage. God moves in mysterious ways."

"I didn't realize that you're a religious man, Leroy."

He rocked on his stool, hand unsteady as he raised the glass, eyes flitting between Zack and the television behind the bar soundlessly tuned to a baseball game. "Ain't so much, now. Wife had me at church years ago, before she passed on. I remember some of the messages." He leaned toward Zack and whispered, "The ones I want to remember." He laughed loudly at his joke, rested the highball glass on the bar and drifted off into his thoughts.

Zack sipped the beer and tried to nudge Leroy back to his previous train of thought. "So, you've come into good fortune, huh?"

Leroy focused watery eyes on Zack. "What's that they say about possession?"

"It's nine points in the law?"

"Ain't so much about where you find somethin' as that you got it."

"You found a lot of money?"

"Wait a minute. Who said I found money?"

"You did."

He scrunched his face again. "I did?"

"Yes, sir."

"Guess I did. Well, finders, keepers. I got a right."

"Makes sense to me. I'd keep money if I found it fair and square. I'd sure like some of the luck you've got. So, where'd you find the money?"

Leroy slid shakily from his stool and drained the remaining whiskey. "Gotta get on home. She'll be waitin' for me." He twisted awkwardly and would have fallen if Zack had not caught him.

"Hey, I'm going that way, too. Maybe I can pay you back for the drink by giving you a ride home."

"Nah, I got my truck," Leroy slurred.

"We can come back for it later. C'mon, my friend, it's the least I can do."

Leroy tried to steady his gaze on Zack, rocked on his heels before shrugging. "Got to hit the head first." He pushed away and hobbled toward the restrooms.

Roland had maintained his distance, seemingly focused on the ballgame, but he nodded as Zack approached. "I usually call a cab. We got two part-timers in town."

"It's okay. I'm staying at the Bluebell."

"Yep."

Apparently the long tendrils of the Hope rumor mill even reached the Woodsman Tavern.

Zack eyed Roland, figured he probably noticed everything happening in the tavern, even as he feigned indifference. "I heard the murdered man was here the night before he was killed. You serve him?"

Roland's head swiveled on his thick neck. "Already told the police."

Zack nodded and shrugged. "Tell me, too?"

The bartender refocused on the television. "Gin and tonic."

"He with anybody?"

A one-shoulder shrug. "Short conversations with a couple different guys at the bar. Nothing much. Weather and stuff. No one seemed to know him." He looked at Zack. "No one seemed to care."

A door slammed and Zack watched Leroy exit the men's room, take unsteady steps in the direction of the two bikers. "Over this way, Leroy," he called and hurried to clap an arm across the man's shoulders as the do-rag biker's chin rose and eyes narrowed. Zack steered Leroy to the tavern door with an apologetic nod. "Let's head for home, huh?"

"Got my truck."

"It's not working right now, Leroy. Better come in my car."

Leroy shuffled beside Zack to the door, was silent as Zack helped him into the Ford. Zack climbed in and rolled down his window, hoping fresh air would help sober Leroy and carry away the stench of booze and sweat.

Leroy pointed an arthritic finger at his truck as they drove past. "Piece of crap."

CHAPTER 14

Gardenia-scented steam floated above the bath water as Annie eased her foot into the tub, sucked a breath and quickly withdrew at the sting. She swished the water before gritting her teeth and stepping into the foam, submersing to the chin.

A long soak was a luxury foregone in her busy life of running the business and caring for Toby and Mark. After Toby died, the unopened jar of foaming bath salts had seemed a self-indulgence she did not deserve. When Mark followed their son to heaven, she shoved the mauve-colored jar deep in the bathroom vanity behind shampoos and cleansers and hairdryer attachments.

But tonight she'd remembered the salts as she brushed her teeth, avoiding her reflection in the mirror, unwilling to glimpse the flush along her cheeks. A hot bath might relax her, might boil away images of the dimple in Zack's square jaw, the bulge of biceps, the rise and fall of his chest as he lingered at her front door.

***

She had debated and fretted all afternoon, one minute scolding herself for being childish, the next scribbling excuses on notepaper with every intention of marching to his cabin and taping the note to his door. She'd torn the note into tiny pieces she threw resolutely into the trash, only to pace the house, eyeing the wastebasket and envisioning the note whole again in her hands.

The weather was the cause of her dilemma, the chilled wind blowing aside any thought of dining on the patio as they had the previous nights.

Which meant inviting him into her house.

She'd finally steeled her nerves with vigorous housecleaning: rearranging pillows on the couch, vacuuming up cat hair, dusting shelves. She pounded chicken breast fillets, rolled them around wine-infused spinach and mushrooms, coated them with Panko bread crumbs and reduced drippings to an aromatic sauce. The activity calmed her and she scoffed at how she'd come to such a state of juvenile indecision and temerity.

Despite hours of worrying and waiting, his knock startled her.

He stood on her threshold, customary lopsided grin dimpling his cheek, green eyes boring into hers, chest muscles defined beneath the sleek shirt he wore.

All confidence fled.

"So, this is the infamous Buffy?" he asked as he entered.

The tabby mewed and slinked away from Zack before circling to sniff and crane her neck, peering at him with iris-filled eyes.

"You're not allergic to cats, are you?" Annie bent to scoop up Buffy, who skirted her reach with a sideways dart and haughty pink-nosed snub.

"Only if I touch them."

"How thoughtless of me not to ask," she said as Buffy squished behind the couch. "Come out from there, you bad kitty."

"No problem, really, Annie. I'll be fine."

She held up a finger to beg a minute and hurried into the kitchen, nosily opened a cupboard and shook the box of cat treats. Buffy sprinted across the living room to sit in full attention at Annie's feet. "You think you deserve this?" She waved her hand above the focused cat, snatched her before surrendering the treat.

Zack deposited a bottle of red wine on the round oak table. "Smells wonderful in here."

She caught her breath and forced a smile, tried to blink away the sight of his large frame in her small kitchen.

Buffy squirmed and mewed. "I'll just put her in the back," she said and hurried down the hall, practically tossing the cat into a spare bedroom to disgruntled meows.

Get hold of yourself, she admonished for the hundredth time.

She ought not to trust anyone. She should maintain a careful, measured distance physically and emotionally; keep her guard securely up.

Usually quite expert at boundaries, she'd been unable to erect them with Zack, relaxing into his company with ease she thought never to experience again after Toby died and Mark was all but gone to her.

She'd not felt this giddy since her teens.

If the door knob could make a sound, it would have screamed in her death grip, which she finally released and managed a casual gait to the kitchen. "There, she won't bother us now."

His easy smile relaxed her. A little.

She enjoyed the evening more than she would have imagined, sighing in relief when he declared the meal delicious. They talked about favorite movies and recipes and funny childhood escapades, lingering until she noticed him shift on the uncomfortable oak chair and suggested they have dessert in the living room. He insisted on helping clear the table, seemed unperturbed that the kitchen lacked an automatic dishwasher. He declared himself an expert at clean-up and placed strong hands on her arms to ease her aside and position himself at the sink.

It was the first time he'd touched her that evening, the warmth of his hands unhinging her fragile shield of indifference, threatening to tumble her topsy-turvy to the skittish emotions of earlier in the day. She pulled away, busily spooned leftovers into containers and snapped shut lids, dried the dishes and put them away, leaving behind those belonging in the cupboards closest to him.

She insisted he sit in the recliner, the most comfortable chair, she said, far better than the lumpy old couch upon which she perched. He ate coconut cake, sipped herbal tea, made her laugh with amusing stories of the parents he so obviously loved and missed.

He did not touch her again.

He did not try to kiss her.

***

Of course, the decision to honor the dinner invitation had been hers alone, but she supposed she could place some of the blame on Kitty. Without her friend's goading, she'd most likely have folded herself in a favorite afghan and ignored his knock.

The café had been empty of patrons shortly before closing. Annie wrapped the remaining baked goods, getting a jump on the afternoon cleanup so she could scurry to her house and prepare dinner.

Or, write a note to Zack and bow out.

She cringed when the bell tinkled at the café door, expelled a loud breath as Kitty lumbered in, her scarlet muumuu like a gaudy, billowing sail. "Oh, it's just you," Annie said.

"Well, if that ain't a gracious greeting to a friend."

Annie leaned both elbows on the counter and hung her head before glancing up with a sheepish grin. "Sorry. I meant I was glad it was you and not some customer I'd have to be nice to. No, wait. That didn't come out right, either."

"You keep digging and you'll end up in China," Kitty said as she plopped her oversized red leather purse on the counter and regarded Annie.

"Sorry. Again. I'm a little out of sorts today."

"So it appears. What in hell has you bent like a pretzel?"

Annie rose and swiped a damp cloth across the laminate. "Nothing."

Kitty snickered, blue eyes bright with mischief. "Nothing, my butt. Only a few things get a woman so twisted in her pantyhose. Lemme see. About six-two? Handsome as a movie star?"

"I have no idea what you mean."

"Don't kid a kidder, girlfriend."

Annie blushed and backed away from the counter, the cleaning cloth knotted in her hands. "Do you want something to eat or drink, Kitty?"

Kitty's rosy cheeks puffed with her grin. "In other words, mind my own business, huh? All right then, heat me one of those oatmeal cookies and I'll change the subject." She watched Annie unwrap a large, moist cookie, slide it on a green ceramic plate and heat it in the microwave a few seconds. Vanilla steam rose as Annie removed the plate and set it on the counter. Kitty licked crimson lips, tore off a morsel and stuffed it in her mouth, eyes closed in rapture, neck flesh wobbling as she chewed. "You sure can bake." She opened her eyes and broke off another hunk of cookie, raised it to her lips before saying, "So, about Zack."

"You said you would change the subject," Annie admonished with hands on hips and a mock frown of annoyance.

"Well, I did change it. I was speaking before in general terms, no names mentioned. Different subject, you ask me." The remaining cookie disappeared. "I guess while I was talking in generalities, you were focused on Zack."

Annie waved her off with both hands, grabbed a cloth to scrub the microwave. "You're getting on my nerves today, Kitty."

She chuckled and dabbed with a paper napkin. "Okay, I get it. Enough teasing. But, seriously, dear, it's about time you had yourself some fun, know what I mean? Heck, if I were you, I'd be staking my claim to the best-looking man this town's seen since my Joe."

"Well, what's stopping you?"

Kitty spread her arms. "Too many years and way too many pounds. Question is, what's stopping you?"

Annie tossed the cloth on the counter and faced her friend. "He's married."

Kitty pursed her lips and raised her eyebrows. "That does present some difficulties, to be sure. Happily married?" Kitty asked as she waddled to one of the café tables and pulled out a chair, tested its ability to support her weight, kicked the chair aside and tested another before she sat, muumuu-ensconced flesh spilling around the small seat.

Apparently, there was no moving Kitty off the subject of Zack, so Annie relented with a sigh. Perhaps unburdening would steel her resolve, help relegate Zack to a darkened corner of her mind— forgotten, unimportant, harmless. She abandoned the cleaning cloth on the counter and sat in the chair Kitty had discarded. "I don't think so, but what difference does that make? Married is married."

Kitty shrugged rounded shoulders. "I used to think in black and white like that, but the older I get, the greyer everything seems." She held up a finger to stop Annie's protest. "Now, I don't go along with these so-called open marriages, sleeping with anybody you damned-well please and expecting your spouse will do the same. They're fooling themselves, if you ask me, pretending nothing matters, which is a bunch of bull. And, I'd be the first to tan the hide of any man who's unfaithful to a good, faithful wife. Or, vice versa. But, sometimes life happens out of order, know what I mean, hon?"

"No, I don't," Annie whispered as she pulled a paper napkin from the holder and tore strips along the edges.

"Maybe he's married to the woman he met first, not the one he'd love the most."

Annie shook her head as she folded and unfolded the napkin. "You can't change the past."

Kitty reached across the table to grip Annie's hand. "That's right, hon. You can't. But, you can change the future."

"It's more complicated than that. His wife needs him."

"From the look in your eyes, I'd say you need him, too."

Annie smiled and squeezed Kitty's hand. "You worry too much about me."

The older woman smirked. "Somebody's got to." She withdrew her hand and pushed up from the chair. "Don't throw the future away like day-old donuts."

"That's what I'm saying, Kitty. There is no future to this."

Kitty shouldered her bulky purse. "Fine. Then, just have some fun while you can. I'm telling you, girlfriend, you need romance to break out of your humdrum life in this dreary town."

"I don't fool around with married men."

"You don't fool around period, darlin'. You ask me, it's about time you did."

"I could tell you to mind your own business," Annie said as Kitty crossed the café, stopped and turned with her hand poised by the door handle.

"You are my business, darlin'."

***

With eyes closed, Annie swished water over her shoulders and refastened the pins holding tangled blonde hair. She sank lower in the bath.

Kitty meant well, she supposed, even if her advice was unconventional; but then, the woman was unconventional in many ways, the contrast to Annie's own primness an endearing quality.

Annie raised a leg above the water, ran a dripping loofah along her calf. Her life really had become humdrum, hadn't it? She'd not thought it so as she and Mark settled into Hope, nor during her too-brief time with Toby. Life after Toby had been tumultuous and emotional, daily chores a respite from second-guessing and rehashing failures, Mark's breakdown a distraction from her own needs. His death fractured the façade she'd created, remnants of her soul scattered like brittle leaves along the paths they'd walked together, across the rooms where she'd chased her giggling son. Now, the Bluebell no longer felt like home; she had no home, only the dwellings where she slogged through the hours, the woods where she cried.

Yet, she stayed.

At first, she'd been incapable of breaking away, in part because she couldn't bear to leave the small, simple granite tombstones in the Hope cemetery. She also had nowhere else to go, nobody who'd welcome and comfort her. She'd severed all ties with her dogmatic parents years before, had no connection with girls from her Tennessee school days, developed no lasting friendships in her vagabond life with Mark. Fine, she'd thought, as she moved like a robot through chores, pasted on a false smile for customers, sat countless hours staring at nothing, thinking nothing, Buffy purring in her lap.

Eventually, loneliness mocked aloofness, tantalizing her with stray thoughts of camaraderie, even of love.

That's when Leroy had shown up on her doorstep seeking work, shy Sarah hidden behind him. The girl's innocence and gratitude for simple pleasures had captured Annie's heart, not filling the void Toby left behind, but at least restraining her from sinking irretrievably into a black hole of sadness. She'd taken them in as much for her own sake as theirs, happy in their undemanding companionship, inching open her heart like one cracked a door, peering beyond with a hand poised to slam shut the barrier if threatened. It had been enough to sustain her.

Until Zack came along.

She shivered in the tepid bath water, moving her arms in small circles to keep warm, reluctant to end the comforting soak, finally sighing and dislodging the plug with her toe. She stood and wrapped a fluffy terry towel around wrinkled pink skin, squeezed water from her hair and pulled a brush through tangles. She wiped clear a small circle in the steam-frosted mirror, leaned in to apply nighttime lotion across cheeks and neck, into the fine lines around her eyes, a ritual she usually performed absentmindedly.

Tonight, she stood motionless, breathing shallow and quick, mirrored eyes startled by the longing reflected back. She rubbed her arms and remembered the heat of Zack's touch.

A flush bloomed on her cheeks as she dropped the towel to the floor and hurried to the bedroom, flung open the closet door and yanked a long cotton dress from its hanger, slipping into sandals as the thin fabric cascaded around her ankles. She rushed to the hall closet and grabbed a sweater, wrapped it over her shoulders as she fled out the front door, crossed the graveled lot and hurried up the cabin steps.

Zack opened the door, brows knit with worry as he started to ask if something was wrong.

His eyes bored into hers as he understood and drew her into the room.

CHAPTER 15

A sliver of moonlight filtered between the drapery panels to illuminate the rise and fall of her chest as she slept. He eased the quilt over her bared shoulder, lingered with the temptation to draw the covering down instead, to expose breasts and hips, run his hand down her thighs.

They lay facing on their sides, close enough for gentle puffs of air to tickle his face. He breathed in her sweet smell, fingered a hank of blonde tumbled on his pillow. Her hair had been cool and damp against his chest as she embraced him last night, soft in his hands as he lifted her face to his, spread like a halo as he lowered her onto her back.

He'd never made love as he had with Annie.

There'd been no first-time awkwardness, no fumbling or insecurity. She returned his kisses with passion, groaned softly as he explored her body, fit herself to him as two halves of a mold. Afterward, she curled beside him, snuggled on his chest as he lay on his back, one silky leg wrapped around his.

She stirred and sighed, eyelids flickering open to find him staring at her. "I should go," she whispered.

"Stay."

She smiled and he pulled her close for a long kiss. When they parted, she lightly traced his jaw with her palm. The thump of his heart amplified as he braced on his forearms and watched desire awaken in her eyes.

They made love again.

Sleep enveloped him as a womb until she pulled away. "Don't go," he said.

She leaned across to place a finger on his lips. "I have to."

He frowned and twisted to the nightstand, pressed the button to light the alarm clock and flopped back on the bed. She was right. "I'll come help you."

"No." She tugged on her dress and fingered mussed hair. "I need this morning to myself."

He watched her search the floor for the sandals she'd kicked off the night before, slip into the sweater he'd tossed across the dresser. "Annie," he began as she crossed to the door, but she silenced him with wave.

"We'll talk later. Right now, we both have work to do."

It took him a moment to realize she referred to his cover as a journalist. The thought insinuated the real world into the dream of their lovemaking and he glanced again at the clock. "First, I'm going fishing."

"You're a fisherman?"

He rose to his elbows, the sheet cascading to his waist. "Not really, but I promised this kid we'd fish and I can't disappoint him."

She stood frozen by the door, emotions flickering across her face until she smiled and fled from the room.

***

He fell back asleep, limbs like dead weights. If not for Lonnie's call, he'd have missed his fishing date with Rory.

He fumbled groggily for the cell phone. "Yeah."

"There you go again. The morning grouch. Thought we talked about this, Susie Sunshine."

He blinked at sunlight slipping between the drapes where moonlight had danced as he embraced Annie. He ran a hand over his forehead and stared at the alarm clock. "Damn!" He threw off the covers and bolted from the bed.

"Well, that's better."

"I'm late," Zack mumbled as he tried to dress one-handed. He hastily pressed a button to put Lonnie on speaker and dropped the phone on the bed.

"Working on the case, I hope."

"What else?"

"Seems to me you're getting pretty comfortable in that hick town."

Zack scowled as he laced his shoes. "You got something to report?"

"Remind me to get a new partner."

"We aren't partners any more, Lonnie."

"Good. Mission accomplished." He left a silence Zack did not fill. "Okay, okay. Mr. Ray Isley. Big ranch. Big ego. Big time money troubles."

Zack grabbed his billfold off the dresser and snatched up the phone. "How big?"

"Send-you-to-the-bottle big. Sounds to me like the man doesn't have much time left to make good on his debts or he'll lose the ranch. And get this—his present difficulties are but a continuation of financial troubles that began more than three years ago."

"Three years, huh?"

"Seems he came up with enough to fend off the vultures, but got further into debt since."

"Where'd he get the money back then?"

"Out of nowhere, my sources say."

Zack slipped the daypack over his shoulder and reached for the door handle. "His share of the ransom?"

"Makes sense to me."

"I'll see what I can find out."

"You do that, partner."

***

Rory lounged by the side of Canyon Road, hangdog expression betraying his fear of being stood up. Zack eased the car off the road and leaped out, hurried to the trunk and pulled out his new gear, turning the boy's scowl into an uneven smile and nod of approval.

The waders sure made fishing more comfortable than his first attempt two days before, insulating against the cold, allowing him to wade farther into the icy Cutwater Creek. Zack worried his attention would wander; instead, he found himself focused and serene as he gently landed the fly in white-rimmed ripples. He thought of nothing but the water, the fish, and the rod as an extension of his arm. There was no need to push aside thoughts of Annie; rather, she seemed omnipresent, a gardenia-scented aura enveloping him every second, specific remembrances unnecessary because he'd absorbed her so completely.

He did impatiently shove away intruding thoughts of Stella and Lonnie and the murder investigation.

He caught two trout big enough to keep.

When they'd reeled in and secured their gear, tugged off soaking waders and donned jackets to combat the chill, Rory offered a slice of beef jerky. "You got better."

Zack pointed with his sliver of jerky. "Thanks to you."

"Nah. You'd get the hang of it without my help."

"It's good to have a teacher."

Rory shuffled his feet, then bent to extract a lime green folder from his daypack. He tapped it against his leg, head bowed and nose wrinkled in thought, before extending the folder to Zack.

"What's this?"

Rory shrugged and looked away, a flush coloring his baby-faced cheeks. "You don't have to read it."

Zack inwardly groaned. He'd hoped the kid would forgot their deal, or be too shy to follow through. "Your writing, huh?"

Another shrug.

Zack noted the header with title, author and date. "Very professional. Looks like you know what you're doing."

"They got books in the library that show how."

He'd made the effort to find out, which spoke volumes about how important writing was to him. Zack tested excuses in his mind, knowing none would do. He could not let the boy down. "I'll take a look tonight."

"Really?"

"So long as you're ready to hear what I've got to say, good or bad."

Rory tried unsuccessfully to cover puppy-dog eagerness. "I want the truth."

Which was the one thing Zack couldn't give him. "You bet." He tucked the folder under his arm and bent to retrieve his gear.

Rory gathered his rod and daypack and pointed to the creel at his feet. "You can take the catch."

"One of them is yours."

"The little one. My mom gets tired of cooking trout but you said you like them."

He'd coat them lightly in flour and pan fry them golden, served with a slice of lemon. Annie would be pleased, for sure. "Okay, thanks."

"So," Rory began as they walked up the creek bank to the road.

"Tomorrow?" Zack jumped in to ease the boy's shyness. He'd much rather sleep late with Annie, hours of kisses and gentle exploration, but knew she'd have to leave his bed early to work in the café. He might as well go fishing.

He realized with a start that he assumed she'd be in his bed again. He could not imagine the night without her.

"McPherson River's about an hour away but has way better fishing."

Zack tossed his gear into the trunk. "Meet me at the Bluebell Café at six o'clock?"

This time, Rory didn't even try to hide his excitement.

***

Penny Chester theatrically rolled her eyes, pointed to the phone she held, said "Uh huh," and nodded toward Norton's office. Zack chuckled and saluted her, walked to the chief's open door and rapped his knuckles on the frame. "Got a minute?"

Norton sat at his computer, staring over the top of his readers at the screen. He twisted to regard Zack. "You expert at these things?"

"I get by."

"Years ago, Al Gore talked about the information superhighway. I'm still on a wagon road." He rolled the chair to his desk.

Zack eyed the side chair with the scratchy fabric, decided to lean against the wall. "What would you say if I told you Isley's got money troubles?"

"Still on that, are you?"

"What would you say if I told you he had similar trouble three years ago?"

Bushy eyebrows rose as Norton rested his hands across his belly. "I'd say things aren't always what they appear. I'd say it's not unusual to have financial problems in the ranching business."

"Interesting timing."

"Pretty general. You're not exactly matching specific dates."

"Maybe I will."

"Maybe you won't. But, let me give you the benefit of the doubt for a minute. Your theory is Riordan came here to find Ray Isley and demand more of the ransom money."

No, Zack thought, my theory is Riordan came seeking two fellow kidnappers, learned Mark O'Connor was dead, so focused on Isley. "Isley couldn't pay. Riordan wouldn't back off, so Isley shot him."

"We verified his alibi."

"He's smart. Might have created a false alibi and was here at the time of the shooting."

"You ever confirm the account of him arguing with Riordan?"

Zack frowned and knocked his fist against the wall. "Driscoll's still not around."

Norton unclasped his hands, removed his reading glasses and tossed them on the desk. "What is it you want from me?"

"More time."

Flesh wobbled as the chief shook his head. "I'm pushing the limit as it is. District attorney's getting impatient."

"Five more days. I either nail the perp or write you the best damned report to let you close the case with assailant unknown. Or, you can pass it along to the state investigators. Your choice." Zack pushed away from the wall and slumped into the uncomfortable chair.

Norton tapped a finger on the desk. "Should have turned the case over days ago."

"But, you didn't."

"I'll be dang-blasted if I can figure out why."

"Because you know I'm right about what happened."

"Being right and proving it are two different animals."

Zack grimaced and sank lower in the chair. "I'm close."

"This isn't horseshoes, son." Norton spread his arms wide. "Okay. Five more days. But, you go carefully on Ray Isley. I've got too much worry as it is without fending off an irate rancher and his attorneys."

Zack hesitated, then decided he'd avoided the topic for too long. "How is your wife?"

He half-expected Norton to end their conversation abruptly, but instead he heaved a sigh and stared at the desk. "Slipping. Not much the doctors can do except keep the pain at bay."

Having broached the subject, Zack now found himself bereft of words, not knowing whether to extend condolences or inquire as to details or back off and leave the man alone to his anguish. After a silent, searching moment, he spoke softly. "Lost my mother to cancer. Not how you want to see someone you care about."

"No," Norton whispered. "Rips your heart out." A quick, wry smile appeared below his bushy mustache. "She's one tough woman. Handling this better than me."

"Yeah, that's how Mom was, too. Stronger than my dad and me."

"She's always been sensible, Amelia has; able to face the darnedest circumstances. Never ceases to amaze me. Not sure I understood this about her when we married, but then, you don't know much of each other when you marry young, do you? All these years later, I'm still learning, and every damn thing I learn makes me love her more."

Zack leaned forward to rest his forearms on his thighs and stared at the mottled blue and brown linoleum at his feet.

Norton heaved another sigh and lifted his reading glasses from the desk, slipped them on his nose and rolled back to the computer station. "Five days." Norton's hands were poised above the keyboard, his eyes fixed on the screen. "Thanks for asking about Amelia."

Zack nodded and walked out of the office.

***

Still no sign of life at Driscoll's house. As he had the day before, Zack drove by the place not really expecting to encounter the handyman.

What else did he have to do? Lonnie was busy digging dirt on Isley, trying to connect him to Riordan. They had no other suspects, unless you considered Lonnie's off-kilter suspicions of Annie, which Zack discarded like the trash they were.

Although he'd coerced five days leeway from Norton, there was little he could do to solve the case.

But, he'd gained five more days to be with Annie.

It had been so tempting to hustle to the café after fishing with Rory. He wanted to be with her, to watch a smile light her face, happiness twinkle in those blue eyes.

No, he wanted to touch her, too. Slip up from behind and wrap his arms around her, kiss her long, smooth neck, blow aside silky blonde strands to nuzzle an ear.

Reluctantly, he stayed away, knowing she'd worry about embarrassing Sarah and customers, and about her reputation and the Hope rumor mill. He didn't want to push her. Maybe she regretted last night.

He stopped at a few businesses he'd yet to visit, half-heartedly probing for information about Riordan, learning nothing new.

He should be more frustrated by the lack of progress in the case, should be chomping at the bit, retracing every lead no matter how seemingly insignificant. Something was bound to pop open if he did. Yet, he couldn't summon his old fire, couldn't reignite the anger that had driven him to hunt for the kidnappers the past three years.

With nothing better to do, he drove. Out to Driscoll's uninhabited house. Back to Main Street. Down the road to the Rockin' I Ranch, where he considered visiting Elyse Isley, but turned around, wary of encountering Ray without a plan or additional evidence.

Finally, he headed back to the Bluebell, strode to his cabin with a quick glance at the café, changed into his running clothes and Nikes, jogged out of the parking lot and down Canyon Road.

Yesterday's wind had left behind cloudy skies and moderate temperatures, perfect for an early afternoon run. The canyon seemed to be napping at this hour, colors bleached as sunrays tried vainly to beam through clouds, the air flat and limp. The animals must be hunkered beneath low-hanging branches or dug into loose soil. Even the hawk that circled and dipped each morning was nowhere to be seen.

He'd have lazed away the afternoon, too, if Annie were by his side.

He'd never felt this way before, didn't have the vaguest idea how to handle the emotions flushing through him. He'd enjoyed some wild flings with beautiful, sexy women, but any attraction faded quickly after physical needs were met. He'd found it far too easy to walk away without a twinge of regret, disgusted that he'd again failed to find the love he'd once thought possible.

Despite his parents' marriage as evidence to the contrary, he finally decided that love is a fiction, a charade. Best to give and take what comfort possible, lay aside hope for an unbreakable bond because it was never going to happen.

He hit that low right before he met Stella. He chose money and the high life over the fruitless search for love.

Now, perhaps he'd found what he'd abandoned hope of ever finding. But impediments stretched like hurdles on the road before him, not the least of which was the unthinkable possibility that Annie did not feel the same way about him.

And, there was Stella.

He'd never been unfaithful, not even after he moved out of her condo. She didn't believe this, flinging sharp accusations like a circus performer whose knives landed inches from his sympathy and compassion. Of course, if she accused him now, it would be a different story. He should feel guilty, but that emotion was lost in the absolute joy of embracing Annie.

Zack made a wide turn in the road, breathed hard through his mouth and lengthened his stride, unable to stay away from the Bluebell any longer.

***

The T-shirt was plastered against his chest and sweat dripped from his forehead as he slowed into the Bluebell's parking lot, gulping air, calf muscles burning. He reached the steps to his cabin before looking up to see Sarah standing on the porch clutching a coffeemaker, eyes wide at his approach. "Hi, Sarah," he said.

She started to speak, caught a breath and turned her side to him, swiveled to peek over her shoulder.

"It's a nice day, huh?" He remained at the bottom of the steps.

"Did you run?"

Zack wiped upper lip sweat across the shoulder of his T-shirt. "Yes, I did."

"It's good for you?"

"Well, that's what they tell me."

She smiled and turned to face him. "Annie says it's important to do what's good for me. Maybe I should run, like you."

"You could give it a try."

"Would I get sweaty like you?"

He chuckled and spread his arms wide. "I certainly hope not." He pointed to the appliance she carried. "That for my cabin?"

She glanced down as if startled to find herself carrying the coffeemaker. "Annie told me to put it on the dresser after I cleaned."

"Sounds good," he said as he mounted the steps to the porch, thinking that the new coffeemaker would go unused because he planned to sip coffee in the café with Annie. "I guess the old one wasn't working, huh?"

Her nose wrinkled. "It got broke. I'm not supposed to talk about it. Annie says sometimes things happen even if you don't mean them to." Sarah stared the direction of the café. "I never seen her so mad."

"Annie? Why was she mad?"

"The man," she whispered, then caught her breath and focused frightened eyes on him.

"What man, Sarah?"

She shook her head and backed away.

"The man who was here before me?"

"I'm not supposed to talk about him." She scrambled down the steps, stopped when he called her name.

"Don't be frightened, Sarah. I won't hurt you." Zack hurried to stand before her, bending over to peer into her eyes. "I'm your friend, remember? You can trust me. Did the pot break during a fight?"

Sarah's brows knit and eyes filled with worry.

"It's okay. You don't have to talk if you don't want to." He waggled his eyebrows until he coerced a smile. "Hey, you know what I think?" When Sarah shook her head, he leaned in to whisper, "I think you should give me the coffeemaker and I'll put it in the room." He straightened and smiled, held out his arms and waited as Sarah slowly extended the appliance to him and loosened her grip. He tucked it under one arm and waved as he backed toward the porch. "Thanks, Sarah."

She followed his example, walking backward ten strides before running to the café and up the steps. She leaned over the railing to wave, flung open the door and disappeared into the kitchen.

Zack entered the cabin, set the coffeemaker on the dresser and paced the small room before pulling the sweaty shirt over his head.

Something wasn't adding up.

Annie told him she never really talked with Riordan. Yet, Wendell witnessed them in fierce argument and now Sarah let slip enough to indicate the coffeepot had been broken during a confrontation.

Ain't no such thing as coincidence, Lonnie would say.

She's lying to you, Lonnie would say.

So what? I'm lying to her, too.

Not the same thing.

You're off base, Zack argued with himself as he pulled off shoes and shorts and underwear, heaped the grimy clothes in the closet and cranked on the shower. Steam billowed from the hot water he let pound his neck and shoulders as he tried to drown out the Lonnie screaming in his mind.

CHAPTER 16

Such a long morning and afternoon—the black hands of the wall clock barely inching past the numerals, customers leaning against the counter with gossip and opinions that careened off her masked indifference. She caught her breath each time the bell above the front door jangled, blew air across her upper lip when it wasn't Zack walking through the doorway.

Don't make too much of this, she told herself. You took Kitty's advice and satisfied a craving, that's all. A fling. A lighthearted affair with a man who'll soon be gone from Hope. No strings. No binds. No expectations.

And then, at closing, he was there in the kitchen, arms sunk in sudsy water, pans and utensils dripping in the dish rack, Sarah smiling beside him as she wiped a baking tray. "Thought I'd help you get out of here early," he said with a grin.

They walked a long ways that afternoon, their footprints disappearing in fine dust beneath swaying pines, as if removing all trace of where they'd been, leaving only what lay ahead.

"Do you like living in Hope?" Zack asked as they plopped onto a grassy hillside.

"Mostly. Sometimes I think about leaving."

"Where would you go?"

She shrugged.

"There must be some place you've always dreamed of going."

She smiled as she remembered. "Florence. In fifth grade, we each selected a European city to study. I don't remember how I ended up with Florence. We wrote to government agencies for information and

I was so entranced by the beautiful brochures. I kept them in a box by my bed and sorted through them a million times."

"But you never went?" He added at her headshake, "You could go now."

"I suppose, if I saved for a trip. Have you been there?"

"No, but friends say it's wonderful. Incredible art. So much history."

"Yummy food," she said, licking her lips.

"How about culinary classes? Rent a Tuscan villa. Shop the markets in the morning, learn the art of Northern Italian sauces in the afternoon."

"Attention must be given to wines."

"Most definitely."

"A busy schedule."

"Italians don't rush the way we do. Five hours to prepare one's meal? No problem. Leaves plenty of time to relax or explore the countryside." He drew closer. "To make love."

"I suppose lovers are in abundant supply in Italy."

"It's much nicer to bring your own."

"Did you just invite yourself on my fantasy vacation?"

He cupped his hand gently under her chin. "You can't leave me behind."

***

Moonlight slid into the cabin as it had the previous night. She inhaled aftershave and perspiration and felt his chest rise and fall. The strong arms that had crushed her to him were now relaxed atop the quilt.

Zack shifted beside her, his movement both calming and arousing. His eyelids flickered open and he rolled to face her. "What spell have you cast on me, fairy queen?"

"Even we fairy queens cannot force you mortals against your will."

"Then, it must be my will to be completely bewitched." He rested on an elbow so his face was above hers and bent for a kiss. As they parted, he inhaled deeply and fell back on the bed. "My God, Annie, I am so..."

"Shh." As she had the morning before, she silenced him with a finger to his lips. Right now, she had no need for words that could never describe her feelings. The thrill of his touch. The deep longing he satisfied.

Nor could words describe the hurt certain to overwhelm her when he left Hope and she was once again alone.

CHAPTER 17

He'd have kept her by his side all day, if he could; nuzzling beneath honeyed blonde hair, pulling her on top to blanket his torso with velvety breasts, firm navel welded to his. He'd have held her captive, broken her will to leave with the press of lips and the tingle of an exploring touch.

But, Annie woke early and slipped away as she had the morning before, chuckling softly at his sleepy-tongued attempts to persuade her back to bed.

"Hush, now," she said. "You tempt me to misbehave."

"Don't resist." He sighed as she leaned in for a quick kiss and squirmed from his embrace. "Okay, but I'm going with you to the café."

It was amazing how well they worked together. She directed their efforts, but he often knew what she wanted before she asked. He took every opportunity to touch her—covered her hand with his own as she stirred and scraped, wrapped himself around her curves to present a muffin tin just as she lifted a batter-filled bowl, decorated her skin with floury caresses.

Sarah entered, curiosity tingeing her bright smile upon seeing him again in the kitchen, and he reluctantly moved beyond tempting reach of Annie, who shot him a conspiratorial smile. He lingered, singing in passable tune to a country radio station, snitching from the cookie trays, making Sarah giggle with his inexpert attempts to juggle lemons. Finally, he glanced at the wall clock, pecked Annie's cheek when Sarah was occupied, and hurried to the cabin to grab his fishing gear.

Rory trudged into the Bluebell parking lot as Zack stored waders and rod in the trunk of his car. "Good day for it," he said and reached for Rory's tackle boxes. "Fish don't stand a chance."

"Maybe."

Zack laughed at the typical, noncommittal Rory answer, but he truly believed he could conquer trout this morning, could conquer about anything. "Sounds like you need a challenge. Bet I catch more fish than you."

"What'll we bet?"

Zack slammed close the trunk lid. "You win, I spring for breakfast. I win, you tie me three flies."

A grin tugged the corners of Rory's mouth as he considered the deal. "You're on."

***

The count was even. Four fish each. Caught, displayed with glee, released back into the McPherson River. Zack winced from a strain in his casting arm, noticed Rory's casts had grown shorter and less precise. If not for the bet, they'd probably both call it quits.

Rory was right—fishing was much better here than in Cutwater Creek, the trout more abundant but elusive, forcing the angler to read the river, select deep holes and land the fly precisely. The process was consuming, meditative. As he had the previous morning, Zack relaxed into the moment, all thoughts of Riordan and Lonnie and Stella banished. The only realities were the flowing green water, the slippery rocks beneath his rubber boots, the flittering willows lining the river bank.

And the memory of Annie's curves molded to his body.

Rory shouted and Zack pivoted gratefully to the proud display of a wriggling rainbow trout. He raised his arm to salute an end to their competition, reeled in and waded to shore. "I give," he shouted as Rory slogged up the bank to stand before him with a triumphant, freckle-faced grin. "Best fisherman won."

Rory twisted his baseball cap around backwards and disassembled his rod and reel. "Just lucky."

"More than luck, that's for sure. But, you know what? I'm glad you won." Zack waited for Rory's squint of disbelief before shouldering his gear. "I'm starved."

Unlike their silent early morning drive to the river, when Zack had been immersed in thought and Rory too shy to interrupt, the hour back to Hope was filled with conversation. Rory offered little information about his home life, only saying he was the oldest of four kids and his parents worked a lot, but he became animated when describing his offbeat grandmother who raised Australian Shepherds and filled her house with five hundred Santa Clauses at Christmas.

They slid into a booth at the Downtown Diner, Zack scanning the room but concluding it must be Gladys' day off. They ordered morning specials from a chubby young waitress who apparently had yet to master the coffee-from-on-high trick. As they waited for their food, Zack reached into his daypack and handed Rory's folder across the table.

"You read it?"

"Yep. I wrote comments in the margins. You can read those later. For now, just read the part at the end." Zack watched as Rory squirmed and flushed. He sipped coffee and waited.

"You liked it," Rory said in a low, incredulous voice.

"Very much." Which had surprised the heck out of him. He'd not expected much when he began to read the previous afternoon, when guilt at misleading the kid had compelled him to follow through. Given Rory's tendency to sparse verbal communication, Zack expected the same in writing and figured a few grammatical corrections and general comments would get him off the hook. He could keep a promise and still maintain his cover. Instead, he'd been captured by the mature prose and the story of a young man watching the world beyond his window. "You're darn near as good at writing as you are at fishing. Do you take writing classes?"

"They don't have them at our school. Not enough teachers or something."

"When you go to college, then."

Rory fingered the pages and shrugged. "Dad says college costs a lot."

The chubby waitress arrived with their food and they put aside serious talk, Zack amused by Rory devouring his breakfast. When they finished, Zack paid the bill and they sauntered out to the car.

"What do you do all day after fishing?" he asked as they climbed in.

"Nothing."

Zack cast a glance at Rory. "Doing nothing is a surefire way to find trouble. You could get a job. Put money in your pockets to buy more gear." He peered over his shoulder and eased the Ford into the street. "Or, save for college."

Rory seemed to consider the idea, then grimaced and drummed his fingers against the passenger door. "Places won't hire unless you're sixteen."

"You asked around?"

A one-shouldered shrug. "It's what I've heard."

Zack shook his head. "Can't always trust what you hear. Better to find out for yourself. Where would you like to work, if you could?"

A two-shouldered shrug. "The gas station?"

The Texaco was up ahead on the right. "Well, I need gas, anyway. You go talk to the owner."

"Now?"

"No time like the present."

"I'm all like dirty and stuff."

Zack pulled into the station and eased up to a pump. "Got a comb? No? Well, put on your cap and tuck in your shirt. Hey, the worst that can happen is he says no." He got out of the car as Rory stared at the station building with a frown. "Think of it like casting a line. Put the right fly in the right hole and the fish'll bite. This might be the right hole and you the right fly."

Rory rolled his eyes, but shuffled toward the building.

"Stand tall," Zack hollered, grinning as he unscrewed the gas cap and nodded to the elderly attendant who hobbled over to lift a nozzle.

The roar of an engine made him glance up as a jacked-up white Chevy Silverado pulled to the pump on the other side of the island. Troy Isley leaned his arm out the open window and scowled at Zack. He killed the engine and stepped to the ground, leaned against the truck with his cowboy hat pulled low.

The attendant jammed a nozzle into the Silverado's tank, shifted a toothpick in his mouth and left to help a young woman struggling with the air pump.

Zack grabbed a squeegee from a white bucket of soapy water, raised a windshield wiper and concentrated on dislodging plastered insect remains.

"Thought you'd have left town."

Yellow and red streaks smeared and disappeared as Zack scrubbed.

"Well, now, the polite thing to do is acknowledge when you're spoken to. Guess you're too damned high and mighty."

"Got nothing to say."

Troy snorted and walked the length of the island to stand opposite Zack. "Hell you don't. City boys are nothing but talk. All talk, no balls. Ain't that right?"

Zack shoved the squeegee into the bucket, waved off the attendant and replaced the nozzle, punched a button to print his receipt.

"I said, ain't that right?"

The machine whirred and spit out a white slip of paper.

"Apparently, you got bad hearing, too."

Zack spun to face Troy. "What's your problem?"

Troy recoiled a step before he narrowed his eyes and balled his fists. "I don't like your looks. I don't like your smell."

"Hey, Zack, I'm ready to go."

Zack broke the staredown with Troy long enough to spy Rory hurrying along the passenger side of the car, eyes flitting between the squared-off men. Zack jingled his keys and tried to calm himself, finally nodding to Rory, who yanked open the car door and climbed in. Zack followed him, started the engine and eased past Troy. He squeezed the steering wheel hard when Troy landed a kick at the departing bumper.

Rory swiveled to stare out the back window.

"What'd he say?" Zack asked as he stifled the impulse to throw the car into reverse and finish what Troy had started.

"Huh?"

"About the job. What'd the guy say?"

Rory twisted back around, glanced at Zack, then shrugged. "Said to come in tomorrow. A guy just quit, so I can start right away. Nothing exciting. Just cleaning up and stuff."

"It's a start. What'd I tell you?" Zack raised a hand for a high-five. "Right fly at the right hole."

"Gotta get my mom's permission."

"That a problem?"

A typical Rory shrug.

"Well, let me know if I can help. In the meantime, direct me to your house. I'll drop you off."

Rory pointed for him to turn left down a side street. "You got trouble with that guy?"

"Nothing I can't handle."

"What's he got against you, anyway?"

"No idea."

"I live in the yellow house on the right."

Zack pulled into the driveway of a 1950's boxy house, built for a millworker's family, now sporting wavy clapboard siding and a roof of composite shingles curling at the edges. Bikes and skateboards littered the sparse lawn. A rosy-cheeked face beneath tousled red hair appeared at the living room window to watch as Zack rounded the car, lifted the trunk lid and handed Rory his gear.

"Thanks for taking me today. And for, you know, reading my story."

"Hey, it's me who thanks you for letting me read it. And, for knowing the best fishing holes."

Rory slung a creel strap over his narrow shoulder. "Guess I can't go fishing tomorrow morning."

"Nope."

"Guess that's good."

Zack laughed and closed the trunk lid. "You won't be working every day. There'll still be time for fishing."

"Yeah." Rory frowned, perhaps lamenting the end of carefree summer days, wondering if earning money was worth the sacrifice. He finally looked up and cocked his head. "You asked me once if I saw the guy who got killed."

Zack leaned against the car. "You said no."

"I didn't. See him, I mean. I didn't hear gunshots, either. But maybe I did see something that day."

"Well, you did or you didn't," Zack said in a low voice.

Rory squared his shoulders. "That guy at the gas station. I saw him in his truck. I was walking along the shoulder of Canyon Road and he drove past me headed into town. Thought he was going to knock me over the side. Grandma would say he was driving like the devil was chewing his butt."

"What time was that?"

"About seven o'clock, seven-thirty."

"How come you never mentioned this before?"

"Only thing you or the police asked about was the man who got murdered and the gunshot. I never thought about this other guy until today."

"Fair enough." Zack pushed away from the car. "Anything else?"

Rory shook his head.

"You did right to tell me. I'll make sure the information is passed on." He rounded the car and climbed in behind the wheel. "Thanks again for the great morning. Maybe we'll go on your day off work? Seems I must redeem myself by winning a bet."

Rory's shrug was topped with a lopsided, toothy grin.

**

Five minutes remained for the rinse and spin cycles, so Zack wandered around Bubbles Laundromat, pausing at a bulletin board slathered with advertisements and business cards. He hurried to the front-loader when it clicked and beeped and ground to a violent halt. He shuffled wet clothes into a dryer and shoved in two quarters.

He'd returned to the cabin after leaving Rory, realized he had few clean clothes remaining, so stashed everything in a canvas bag and drove to the laundromat. Half a dozen times he reached for his phone but stopped short, replaying the gas station encounter with Troy and Rory's revelation about seeing him the morning of the murder. It could mean nothing. Or, something. Possibilities spun like his clean clothes in the washer.

Rory might have witnessed Troy fleeing the murder scene, although the timing didn't fit Dr. Foster's estimate. Perhaps Troy being in the canyon had nothing to do with Riordan.

Maybe Ray Isley wasn't involved in the kidnapping at all. Or, he called the shots and Troy supplied the muscle.

When it came to Troy, Zack didn't trust his gut.

"Gut feelings are like a damned radio station," Lonnie once said. "If there's interference on the airwaves, a fine Randy Travis tune will be drowned out by some weirdo punk rock and you'll be slamming your fist against the dashboard. Same goes for your instincts. Got personal feelings for or against somebody? You've got interference. You might end up at the wrong damned station."

Typical Lonnie armchair wisdom, but Zack figured he was mostly right, which was why he hesitated to jump on Rory's information. He didn't like the man any more than Troy apparently liked him, interference enough to throw off his instincts, even without the added annoyance of Troy bothering Annie. He finally decided to learn more of Troy's activities before calling Lonnie.

He waited for the dryer to halt, opened the door and grumbled at the heavy, wet denim. He reached into a pocket, withdrew only dimes, frowned at the change machine with duct tape across the bill slot.

"Been busted for six months," came a voice behind him and he spun to find a woman with salt-and-pepper hair in a tight bun, deep wrinkles cornering her eyes. She reached into a pocket of her gingham apron and brought out a fistful of silver. "I keep telling the boss and he keeps saying he'll fix it. In the meantime, you come to me for change."

Zack pulled out two bills. "Think this'll do it?"

"Should, even though these machines ain't what they used to be." She handed him quarters and slipped the bills into a separate apron pocket. "Guess you could say that about most things in this town. Me included."

Zack fed in coins and pushed the button to start his clothes tumbling. "Might say it about most things, period." He smiled broadly and leaned against a large wooden table bolted to the center of the concrete floor.

The woman eyed him head to toe before returning a rueful smile. "Time has a way of moving on. Before you know it, everything's different and you never even saw the changes coming."

"Some changes are for the better, aren't they?"

"I suppose." She brushed a stray wisp of hair from her forehead, sunk her hands into the apron pockets. "You should've seen this town when the mills operated. Lots of money then. Everybody working good jobs, buying nice cars and gussying up for charity dances. Kids obeyed their parents. Folks had self-respect." She stared past Zack into memories before jingling the change in her apron and nodding at him. "You're not from around here."

"Shows, huh?"

"We mostly get regulars. Strangers stand out."

He waited for her to ask if he was the writer-fella she'd heard about, but apparently the Hope rumor mill hadn't reached into the laundromat. He decided to waylay questions. "My name's Zack Dalton. I'm here for a week or so. Staying over at the Bluebell Inn."

"A mighty decent place. You tell Annie that Geraldine says hello." She indicated the dryer. "You might want to check. These machines run hot sometimes."

Zack pushed away from the table and opened the glass door. His jeans weren't dry but he took out T-shirts and boxers.

"Annie's a good woman."

He paused with a blue shirt in hand, checked for insinuation or gossip-mongering in her tone, but found only neighborly goodwill.

"The café was a dump before she and her late husband bought it. An example of change for the better, I guess. You tried her cinnamon rolls yet?"

"Loved every bite."

The woman snorted and shook her head. "I tried to make them as good, but never came close. Finally, Fred, he's my husband, he told me to quit wasting my time and buy the darn things. I suppose I could've been real mad at him, but he was right. So, I buy two rolls every Saturday and we gobble them down in no time." She touched her chin with her index fingers. "See what we've done? I'm hungry for a cinnamon roll right now."

Zack laughed and nodded. "Me, too."

"Can't beat them," she said as she grabbed a broom leaning against the concrete block wall. "Except that one day. They just weren't up to par."

"I can't imagine them less than wonderful."

She bent to swipe the broom far under the table. "I know. We couldn't believe it, either. Are these as tough as I think? I asked Fred. Tougher, he told me, and the icing ain't right, neither. We were so disappointed, thought she'd changed recipes or something and we'd never buy them again. But, this past Saturday come around and I couldn't stay away. Sure enough, the rolls were as delicious as ever. I guess it was just a bad batch."

The dryer buzzed. Zack swung open the door and decided his jeans were dry enough.

"That was a strange day in this town all around."

Something in her tone made Zack pause. "What do you mean?"

"Why, that was the day those boys and their dog found the body down by the creek. Fred said maybe Annie was so upset that her rolls didn't come out right, but I told him those rolls are baked early in the morning and no one knew about the body until the afternoon."

Zack turned from her and placed his clean clothes in the canvas sack. "I guess a person would remember such a day."

Geraldine stopped sweeping and regarded him with wide eyes. "Not every day we got a murder around here."

"Thank goodness."

"You got that right. Hope may not be half the town it once was, but at least a person's usually safe here. Which is why having a murderer amongst us is so disturbing."

Zack shouldered the sack. "I wouldn't worry too much. Probably somebody passing through and long gone by now."

"Would be a comfort."

He waved a distracted goodbye and hurried out the door.

Geraldine was correct that Annie's cinnamon rolls would have been baked long before news of the dead man spread like wildfire. Being upset about the murder could not have affected her baking.

Unless she knew about Riordan before everyone else.

No, he thought, you're letting Lonnie's harebrained ideas sneak into your mind.

He tossed the canvas bag into the car and climbed in, hand poised by the ignition. There must be a simple explanation.

He started the engine and headed down Main Street. As he passed Mitchell's Barber Shop, he hit the brakes and swung into an empty parking space.

Annie had nothing to do with the kidnapping or the murder. Period. He needed to focus on learning more about Troy Isley and he couldn't think of a better place to start than with the talkative barber.

***

Jim Mitchell was seated in one of his swivel chairs, head tilted back to peer through bifocals at a newspaper. He folded the paper and leapt to his feet when Zack entered. "Good afternoon to you."

No one else was in the shop. Perfect. "Afternoon," he replied.

Mitchell's eyes twinkled, perhaps at the prospect of earning a dollar or two, but more likely in anticipation of a captive audience. "What can I do for you?"

Zack ran a hand over his short hair. "Don't need a haircut."

"No, wouldn't appear so."

"But a professional shave sounds good."

The barber swiveled a chair, motioned for Zack to sit and lifted a cape off the counter. "I use the finest cream and a choice of three aftershaves. None of those cheap drugstore lathers in my shop." He waited while Zack settled into the chair, snapped open the cape and fastened it loosely around Zack's neck.

He hadn't expected much from the small-town barber, was surprised to recognize the same brand of products Pierre used in his swanky San Francisco salon. Mitchell applied warm towels and babbled as he wielded a lathering brush. Zack let him talk. He waited until Mitchell had examined his handiwork and cranked the chair upright before broaching the topic that brought him into the shop. "My good luck you had time to squeeze me in."

"I was real busy earlier."

"Like you were the day I came in for a haircut. You were finishing up two other customers. Let me see, father and son, I think."

"The Isleys," Mitchell said as he tidied the work area. "Ray and his son, Troy."

"Yeah, I remember now. The older guy seemed all right, but his son was another story."

"Between you and me," Mitchell leaned against the counter, arms crossed over his chest, "Troy's too full of hisself. Had his nose in the air ever since they moved here. He's got no reason to think he's better than the rest of us. His father's the brains, for sure. Name one thing Troy's ever done except cause trouble."

"Trouble, huh?"

Mitchell released his arms and dunked a comb in cleaning solution. "Well, nothing illegal I can recall, but he makes people miserable. Like my brother, Steve. Now, I'm the first to admit Steve's no prize himself. Got a gambling problem, for sure. He was bumming around with Troy at Indian casinos and borrowed money with the understanding he'd have a month to repay. What's Troy do? Shows up two weeks later demanding his money and a whole lot of interest. Got pretty nasty, from what I hear."

Zack rose from the chair and pulled out his wallet. "Not exactly friendly."

"Like I said, Troy's not the friendly type."

"Did your brother pay him?"

Mitchell observed closely as Zack selected bills and laid them on the counter, his eyes lighting at the healthy tip included. "Came to me for help. Gave him what I could. Guess it was enough, 'cause Troy backed off." He gathered the bills with a sad shake of his head. "Gambling's a sickness, but what can I do? He's my brother."

Zack walked to the door and paused with his hand on the knob. "When did you say this happened?"

The barber was balling up the cape, his brows knit and shoulders slumped. "Huh? Oh. About a week before you ran into the Isleys here." He tossed the cape into a wicker basket. "Had to cut Troy's hair like nothing had happened. Still sticks in my craw."

Zack nodded sympathetically and left the barber pacing the floor and muttering to himself.

***

The timing fit. Troy Isley had squeezed Steve Mitchell for money about the time Ed Riordan showed up in Hope. Another coincidence? No. Add up a whole bunch of supposed coincidences and you often get the truth.

He still needed to straighten out the discrepancy with Clyde Driscoll. Ray Isley claimed he'd never met Riordan. Driscoll put the two of them together. Zack cursed as he dialed Driscoll's home number and listened to endless ringing. With nothing better to do, he followed the familiar route to Driscoll's rundown house and hustled up the porch steps to pound uselessly on the door.

Damn it. Still no Driscoll. Zack stood with hands on hips as he surveyed the place.

Wait a minute.

He tromped down the steps and over to the junk pile blocking the lopsided garage, stood before an upside-down metal Coleman ice chest. The chest hadn't been there before. He expelled a sharp breath when he spied a utility trailer parked behind the rusted hulk of a truck on blocks. The trailer hadn't been there, either.

"Driscoll!" Zack shouted as he picked his way between cast-off appliances and uneven stacks of lumber to circle the garage and house. No Driscoll. Still, he was confident the man had returned to Hope.

His cell phone rang and he noted Stella's number in the display. A guilty shiver worked up his spine. He closed his eyes a moment and answered, "Hello."

"You haven't called."

"Sorry. Been busy." He grimaced at the ensuing silence, toed dirt at his feet. "How are you?"

Stella's voice sounded weak and lifeless. "Fine."

"You sure?"

Her sigh whispered through the airways. "Yes, of course."

Silence hung again.

"Has Yvonne been over?"

"Last night. She brought dinner."

"Pad Thai?"

"Sure."

This time, Zack let Stella break the stalemate.

"When are you coming home?"

That's not my home, he wanted to say. Not your condo, not San Francisco. He gripped the phone tighter. "I've got loose ends to tie up here."

"Fine," Stella said with a hint of her typical fiery sarcasm and he imagined the effort it took to moderate her tone. "I need you, Zack."

"You're fine without me, Stella."

"You know that's not true."

"No, I don't. You're a strong woman, Stella. Smart and educated. Maybe it's time to move on."

Her laugh was mirthless. "Would that please you? Your wife as the inspirational example of triumph over hardship?"

"What's wrong with respect?"

"Not respect, Zack. Pity."

He kicked viciously at a rock and shook his head, weary of familiar arguments. "I've got to go, Stella."

She must have sensed his temper. "Oh, let's not argue, darling. I miss you so. Can you blame me? You're the best thing that ever happened to me."

He watched a grey jay swoop between the branches of a sprawling oak.

Stella's voice hardened. "I can read you like a book, Zack. I know."

"You know what?"

"Come home." She hung up.

Zack fought the urge to hurl the damn phone across the yard. The jay squawked and bounced along a branch as Zack stomped to his car and climbed in, rested his forehead against the steering wheel.

He recognized her tone; she'd accused him of infidelity many times before. He was certain she accused him now in general and had no way to learn about Annie, but it didn't matter what she knew or guessed. This time, she was right.

And he really didn't care.

He started the engine and headed for town. As he passed the police station, he thought of stopping in, but he had nothing new to report and no questions to ask Norton. He was not in the mood to chat. Besides, the man probably had more important things to do.

What must it be like, watching your life companion slip away? The woman you've loved for so long?

He'd helped his father as best he could when his mother died, but he watched Walter Dalton sink into himself. Tell me what you're feeling, Dad, he'd asked. The only response had been a dazed expression and a sigh.

When Walter died, Zack understood that the separation had been too much to bear. He realized he'd yet to experience such a profound love, a hole that was not filled when he married Stella.

Now, it had taken less than a week to find the love his parents had cherished, the kind Chief Norton shared with his wife. He could not walk away. He needed Annie with him always, to build a life together.

There was no room in that life for Stella.

***

Exercise always helped clear his head, so he drove to the Bluebell, donned his running clothes and headed out at a quick jog. He tried to focus on his breath and put his mind in neutral.

It didn't work, snippets from his life with Stella darting beyond his reach like mischievous imps playing an annoying game of tag. He panted through his mouth and quickened his stride, but finally gave in and allowed himself to think about his marriage.

The whole mess was his fault. He'd been greedy and weak when he married her, regretful but strong when he moved out, weak again when he moved back in. She was right—it was pity many people tried to hide from her, pity that compelled him to her wishes and returned him to the condo. He'd known he didn't love her and probably never had. He should have stood firm.

He would stand firm now.

He had to.

It was almost three o'clock as Zack toweled himself and pawed through clothes fresh with the smell of laundry detergent. He hurriedly dressed, anxious to be waiting in the kitchen when Annie closed the café, to sweep her into his arms, no matter who might see.

Anxious and apprehensive. He needed to clear up the discrepancies in her stories, needed reassurance that she had nothing to do with Ed Riordan's death. He had to ask.

It was the possible responses that made him nervous.

He yanked open the kitchen door and hustled in, startling Sarah as she set a large stainless steel bowl on the preparation table. "Oh, sorry. I didn't mean to scare you."

"It's okay," she giggled.

"Can I help put those things away?" He pointed to platters and pans stacked on the drain board.

"I guess so," Sarah said and selected a baking tray. "This one goes up high. Over there."

"You bet." He stood on tiptoes to slide the tray along a top shelf where she directed. "Guess you can't reach, huh?"

"I use the stepstool."

"Give me another high one."

He made a game of it, pretending to misunderstand her directions and place an empty bowl in the refrigerator, a ceramic plate with the coffee cups and a cast iron pan on the floor.

Sarah laughed and shook her finger at him. "You're being silly."

"Who, me?"

"Yes." She snatched a bag of graham flour from the counter. "This goes in a special place."

Zack nodded and eased open the swinging door to peek into the café. Annie was standing near the front window, clutching dirty dishes, her smile tight as a stout woman babbled and two screeching children chased each other despite admonitions to stop. Zack waited until Annie glanced his way, flashed a grin and turned back into the kitchen.

He froze.

Sarah stood on the other side of the table, frightened brown eyes wide, fingers rapidly twirling hanks of hair.

"Sarah?" He eased toward her.

She stared at a bin on a low shelf, a moan escaping her opened mouth.

"Hey, what's wrong?"

She pulled away when he reached for her, banged into a collection of pans and jumped at the clatter.

Zack knelt by the bin and looked inside.

Oh, God, no.

"It's okay, Sarah, I won't let it hurt you." He gave her a bright smile. "I think we're done working. Why don't you go on home?"

She stared at him a long moment, released her twisted hair and inched past, finally breaking into a run, the door slamming behind her.

Zack stood and walked to the desk, selected a pen from the holder. He returned to the bin and used the pen to hook the floury trigger guard of a nine millimeter Beretta.

CHAPTER 18

The door to the kitchen swung open and Annie backed in, balancing a grey tub. "Oh, am I ever glad…" she began, her voice fading as she focused on Zack's forlorn expression and the gun on the stainless steel table. She lowered the tub to a counter and forced an innocent smile. "What's all this?"

Zack bowed his head and leaned against the table. "Don't, Annie." His eyes met hers. "Don't pretend."

"What are you talking about?"

"C'mon, Annie. I know about Riordan."

Tears welled as she fumbled with the ties of her apron. She started to speak; stopped and stared at the apron as if the words she needed were printed there. Finally, she whispered, "How did you find it?"

He reared back, eyes raised to the ceiling.

"Zack, please."

"I'm trying to sort this out, Annie." He exhaled sharply and pointed at the Beretta. "Why the hell did you keep it?"

She looked around the kitchen as if now seeking answers written on the walls. "I was going to get rid of it, but then they found the body and I was worried they could find a gun, too." She tossed the apron on the counter. "I didn't know what to do, Zack. I don't face this every day."

He nodded and paced the linoleum floor. "Sorry. Of course not." As his pacing took him past the gun, he ran a hand along the table. "He demanded money."

She gasped and drew a hand to her mouth.

"Did he tell you why?"

"Something about Mark owing him, that he'd make trouble if I didn't pay. Big deal, I said, how much trouble can you make for a dead man? I figured it had to do with the briefcase of money I found."

"You didn't pay him?"

"With what? The money's gone. Besides, I wouldn't, even if I could. He was a creep, Zack."

"He wouldn't let up."

"Not at first." She shuddered and rubbed her arms. "After a couple of days, he pretty much left me alone."

Zack frowned. "He stopped asking for money?"

"I guess he believed me."

"But, you had a big argument later in the week."

Annie returned his frown. "How do you know all this?"

He held his hands up to stop her. "It's important that I understand what happened so I can help you."

"I don't need your help."

"Yes, you do." He hurried over to grasp her shoulders. "You do need me, Annie."

She stiffened and seemed ready to flee, but finally hung her head and stepped into his embrace.

He stroked her hair and breathed in her familiar sugary smell, his heart thumping and mind racing. He kissed her lightly, broke away and walked around the table to pause again by the gun. "It must have been self-defense."

Annie slumped onto a stool. "You think I shot him."

"I'm just saying maybe you didn't have a choice."

"Oh, my God." She closed her eyes and rocked on the stool.

The outside door banged open.

Sarah rushed in, tears streaming, her fingers busily twisting hair. "No!" she screamed and raced to Annie. "You can't!"

Annie reached for her. "Sarah!"

"You can't lie!"

"Sarah, listen to me…"

"No! I know what you're doing. I'm not dumb."

Annie rose from the stool and managed to catch one of Sarah's hands in her own. "Of course, you're not dumb. But you should let me handle this, okay?"

Sarah's heavy brows knit and her lower lip protruded as she shook her head. "You'll get in trouble."

Zack watched the interchange until anxiety and curiosity forced him to speak. "Annie, what's going on?"

As she shook her head, the sound of boots clomping on the steps preceded Leroy's hurried entrance. He pulled up, eyes widening as he took in the scene. "I told you he was trouble," he shouted, drew back a fist and rushed at Zack.

"Leroy, no!" Annie yelled.

Zack blocked the punch and twisted Leroy's arm securely behind his back.

"Sonofabitch!" Leroy tried vainly to strike with his free hand as his feet slipped on the linoleum floor.

"Stop! Stop! Stop!" Sarah screamed and drew her hands up to cover her ears.

Her screams finally reached beneath Leroy's fury and he froze, upper lip curled in a scowl.

Zack released Leroy and pushed him away.

"It's all my fault," Sarah said between gape-mouthed sobs.

"Hush," Annie said. "You don't have anything to worry about."

"No!" Sarah wriggled from Annie's grasp. "I heard you. I know what you're doing." She swung her head viciously, turned imploring eyes to Zack as her fingers found frazzled prey.

With a glance at Leroy slumped against the table, Zack inched toward Sarah and ducked his head to stare into her eyes. "It's okay, Sarah. I can help you."

"Zack, please," Annie tried to insert herself between them.

He blocked her with a gentle but firm arm. "Do you have something to tell me, Sarah?"

A slow nod. She gulped and her chest heaved with a final sob. "Annie didn't shoot the gun."

Zack glanced at Annie, who had retreated to lean against the counter, beautiful blue eyes glistening. "Who did, Sarah?"

"I did," she whispered. "I killed Eddie."

***

She'd woken to the sound of a door closing and rose from her bed, tiptoed to a window and drew back the drape.

He was getting into his car. Where was he going so early in the morning? As she watched, he suddenly climbed back out of the Buick, walked with long strides to his cabin and disappeared inside, leaving the car door open wide, the overhead light like a beacon in the darkness.

Later, she'd not been able to explain her thoughts or actions, why she scrambled out of her nightgown and into jeans and a sweatshirt, slipped on sandals and hurried out the front door. She could not recall if she hoped to speak to him, implore him to stay, or simply stand on the porch and wave as he drove away. She could not recall thinking anything at all.

As she scampered down the porch steps, she watched a light flick off in his cabin. She rushed to the car, climbed in and clamored over the seat to crouch on the rear floor.

Maybe she planned to surprise him. Maybe she sensed adventure. Maybe she feared him leaving and wished to go, too. After all, he'd told her she was pretty. He'd told her she was smart. He'd put his arm around her shoulder and she hadn't minded that his breath smelled of onions, that his calloused hands were rough as he stroked her neck. He'd said she was special and, if she let him, he could teach her things Annie never would. He treated her like in the movies she'd seen.

He treated her like a normal girl.

She peeked over the top of the car seat to watch him exit the cabin, ducked before he swung his legs beneath the steering wheel. The engine roared and she suppressed a giggle. She always tried to be such a good girl. Now, she was being bad and excitement made her heart beat fast as she huddled and swayed.

Only a few minutes later, the car slowed and stopped. The overhead light brightened as he exited the car, blackness returning as he slammed shut the door.

He had not seen her.

She crouched very still, unsure when to reveal her presence, a niggle of doubt penetrating her excitement. If he was going away, why did he stop so soon?

A second vehicle roared up behind the Buick and she curled into a tighter ball so the headlights wouldn't illuminate her hiding place. She heard a car door slam and then two male voices arguing. Curiosity compelled her to rise to her knees, inch upward to peer through the side window. It was too dark to see much, only the dim outline of two men.

Suddenly, the man she thought sure was Eddie jumped back a step and raised his hands above his head. The other man pointed toward the creek and poked Eddie before following him along the road to disappear over the edge.

Something was wrong. She didn't know what it was, but she could feel it. Like how she could feel a storm coming long before her grandfather or Annie seemed to know. A tingle up her spine. Heaviness in her chest.

She eased open the back door and slipped out of the car, tiptoed down the road and searched through the darkness, listening to the snap of twigs and crunch of rock below. She followed the men down the path. When they reached the bottom, they trudged beside the creek until the man behind shouted something drowned out by the creek burbling over rocks.

Yes, something definitely was wrong. Her fingers found hanks of hair as she turned from the creek, scurried to a copse of willows and shoved between them to hide.

She breathed hard through her mouth. She heard shouting, but could not understand the words. Just as she was thinking maybe she ought to return to the car, Eddie sprang. She held her breath as the men struggled. Eddie laughed when the second man backed away with his arms raised. More loud, wordless talk and the man turned and ran back the direction they'd come.

Everything was all right, then. The second man was gone. Only Eddie remained. He'd probably be happy to see her.

She emerged from behind the willows and ran toward him, crying out as she stubbed her toe against a rock.

"Hey! Stop!" he yelled.

"It's me!"

"Shit," he said when she came within arm's length, a broad smile on her face. "What the fuck are you doing here?"

His angry tone frightened her, but she figured he was actually mad at the other man. How could he be mad at her? Hadn't he told her how special she was? "I came in the car," she said.

"Fuck." He paced and rubbed his forehead before turning to her. "What did you hear?"

"Nothing," she said in a quiet voice. "The creek is loud."

He grunted and waved his arm.

That's when she saw the gun in his hand.

"You stupid bitch. Were you spying on me?" A sneer contorted one side of his face.

"No," she whispered.

Suddenly, his expression changed as he laughed and pointed at her. "What the fuck? You believed me, didn't you?"

Her chin quivered and mist formed in her eyes. "Stop talking like that."

"You fell for me, didn't you?" He stepped toward her, used the gun to knock her feverish fingers from snarled strands of hair. "Quit with the compulsion, for crap's sake. You're getting on my nerves." He spit a wad of saliva that landed in the rocks by her feet. "Nah, not interested. I got no use for a half-wit." He threw his head back to laugh, then focused on her again. "Now, you're mad, aren't you? I burst your half-wit bubble. I'll bet you'd like to kill me right now, wouldn't you?"

She shook her head and started to reach for her hair, remembered at the last moment and clasped her hands together.

"Sure you would. You'd like to take this gun and shoot me. Like you've got the brains to do it. Here," he shoved the gun at her, "go ahead."

She hid her hands behind her back, but he grasped her right arm and pulled, snugged the gun into her hand, his face contorted with a bully's cruelty.

"You wouldn't even know how to fire the damn thing." He kept laughing, a penetrating, raucous sound, brutish eyes boring into hers. "It was a joke, hear me? I got no use for you. Go home and play with your dolls or whatever a retard like you does."

"I'm not a retard!"

The gunshot was so loud.

His eyes so wide and shocked.

So much blood gushed through his fingers to splatter on the gravel below.

CHAPTER 19

S he ran home," Annie whispered as she clasped an arm around Sarah's shoulder. "Woke Leroy."

The old man cast a wary glance at Zack before grunting and continuing the story. "Couldn't make out heads or tails at first. Finally figured I'd better take a look."

"Was he dead?" Zack asked.

Leroy nodded.

"You buried him."

"Didn't know what else to do." He waved an arm in circles as if corralling possibilities. "Didn't know how the police would handle it." His arm circles became pointed-finger jabs. "No way they're gonna take my granddaughter. I may be a worthless old man, but I'll do whatever's necessary to protect the only good thing ever come to me in this wretched life." Deep lines crinkled as he squinted at Sarah resting in Annie's arms. "Did what I had to do."

Zack leaned both hands on the table and stared at scratches in the stainless steel as he gathered his thoughts. "You went through his pockets before you buried him."

Leroy winced and brought a hand up to scratch his neck.

Annie's eyebrows rose in surprise. "What?"

"That's where you got the money, isn't it?"

Leroy waved a hand as if to whisk away the unimportant. "He didn't need it no more."

"Oh, Leroy," Annie whispered.

"How much?"

"Couple thousand. Thought I could use it to protect her." Sarah squirmed from Annie's hold and inched toward her grandfather, who kept his face turned away. When she reached for his hand, the stalwart bravado crumbled like a tear-soaked ancient ruin. "She's all I got," he mumbled.

"Sarah," Zack asked quietly, "did you recognize the second man?"

She peeked at him from behind drapes of tortured hair and shook her head.

"Do you think you'd know if you saw him again?"

"It was dark."

Zack nodded and stared at the ceiling a moment before facing Annie. "How'd you get the gun?"

She sighed and her shoulders slumped. "I noticed Leroy's truck was gone, which wasn't normal so early in the morning. Then, I saw Riordan's car was gone, too. I don't know, this feeling came over me that something bad had happened. I was so worried. When Leroy drove into the parking lot, I went out to question him."

"You drove him out to retrieve Riordan's car?"

Annie nodded. "There was no time to think. I just reacted." She turned toward the table and jerked as if the gun sprang for her. "We were afraid someone would see us, so I hid the gun in the bin."

"Don't you realize they can charge you both as accessories?"

She blinked, folded and unfolded her arms. "Not at first, I didn't. Later, I figured something like that. But, don't you see? I had to protect Sarah." Her eyes searched his face. "I told Leroy to keep quiet; that the only way we're in trouble is if someone finds out and reports what happened."

He hung his head.

"What are you going to do, Zack?"

He sighed before locking with the desperation in Annie's eyes. "I don't know." He tucked the gun into the back of his jeans and whirled toward the door. "I just don't know."

***

The canyon drew him to the promised peace of cocooning walls and the steady, soothing cadence of rushing water.

But he found only turmoil.

What are you going to do? Annie had asked him.

He had no answer.

Of course, the situation was more complicated than she knew. He had a sworn duty to uphold the law, which he could not do without endangering Annie and the happiness he'd only just begun to envision.

Ain't no such thing as black or white, Lonnie once said, only shades of grey. Pick the shade you can live with and be done.

You're wrong, he'd replied to Lonnie.

Zack had been a rookie detective then. Certainly, his experiences as a street cop had colored his black and white view of the world, but he clung to his convictions of right and wrong, rejecting shades of grey.

He was no longer so sure.

He'd compromised many times over the last three years, cringing as he dipped a brush in platinum or slate and painted over regulations, just as Lonnie had suggested. Sidestepping rules. Sneaking beyond protocol. As they had with their clandestine investigation into the kidnapping.

Peanuts, Lonnie said. Ain't nothing we've done amounts to a hill of beans.

Yes, Zack agreed, comforted that none of the greys he'd painted hid significant wrongs. He'd done nothing illegal or immoral. He'd even come to rely on grey-shading, to embrace the freedom of bypassing bureaucratic minutiae in favor of getting the job done.

What shade of grey must he paint now?

His duty was clear—tell Norton what he knew.

Perhaps Norton would select his own color of grey, decide that more harm than good would come from pursuing charges against Sarah, Annie and Leroy.

Perhaps not.

Could he take that chance?

If he didn't go to Norton, then he must give up capturing the third kidnapper. Continue his investigation and the whole story was likely to come out.

Yet, the unknown spelled potential trouble, too. Surely the man suspicioned his gun was used to kill Riordan. He may choose to keep his mouth shut and hope the entire incident fades away. But, what if he gets curious, starts putting pieces together? He might seize a perfect blackmail opportunity, with Annie as his target.

Zack hooked his thumbs in front pockets and scuffed through gravel on the creek bank, head bowed, focused on nothing but the rumbling of possible actions and consequences.

Suddenly, conviction stopped him.

For the past two years, he'd been going through the motions, not only in his marriage but in his career, too. No dedication. No focus. No heart.

Time for a change.

Zack turned on his heel and quickened his pace toward the car, jaw clenched with determination.

***

After so many visits to Clyde Driscoll's ramshackle property, the Ford practically drove there by itself. This time, the trip was not in vain. Zack spied the grizzled handyman slouched in a high-backed cane chair on the porch.

"Well, now. You best be delivering my reward money," Driscoll called out as Zack slammed the car door and hurried to the house.

"I've been looking for you," Zack said and marched up the steps.

Driscoll pulled hard on a cigarette pinched between two knobby fingers. "Always nice to be wanted." He dropped the butt on the warped wood planks at his feet, crushed it with the heel of a worn work boot. "Nicer still when backed with green."

Zack shook his head. "Rewards are paid for solid information, not false leads."

Driscoll glanced up sharply. "Hell, you say. You didn't get no false lead from me."

"I've got evidence to the contrary."

The man snorted and leaned forward in the chair. "Hell, you say. I know what happened and that's what I told you. You got so-called evidence to the contrary, well then, you got somebody jerking your chain."

"I don't think so," Zack replied.

"Then, why the hell come bothering me if you're so all-fired set on disbelieving?"

"Thought I'd give you one more chance to clear things up. You claim you saw and heard the murdered man in an argument with Ray Isley. He claims he never met the man and has an airtight alibi for the time you said they were together."

Driscoll reached into a pocket for a pack of cigarettes, shook one free and stuck it unlit between his lips. "Well, now. You see, there's your problem."

Loose, splintered boards creaked as Zack shifted his position, arms folded across his chest. "What do you mean?"

The handyman shook his shaggy mane. "Uh-uh. Lemme see that reward money first."

Zack hesitated, then pulled out his wallet and extracted several bills, waved them out of the man's reach.

"Sure is a puny reward."

"Far more than the bull you fed me as evidence. You've got to do better, Driscoll, or you won't get a dime."

Driscoll gurgled with a smoker's laugh, lifted an arm and wriggled his fingers until Zack stepped closer and let him grab the money, but kept his own hold on the bills. "I never said nothing about Ray Isley."

"You said you heard him argue with Ed Riordan two days before the man died."

"Nope. You see, you weren't listening proper. Wasn't talking about Ray. It was Troy Isley arguing with that fella."

Zack held Driscoll's gaze a long moment before releasing his grip on the money. This was one possibility he'd considered, was the main reason he'd been so anxious to speak again with Driscoll. Even with this tidbit, all he had was circumstantial evidence, but every bit of it pointed to Troy Isley as the third kidnapper and the man Sarah had seen with Riordan.

Zack watched Driscoll shove the money in a ragged pocket of his stained jeans. "Seems like you've got a good memory," Zack said as he withdrew two more bills from his wallet.

Driscoll's eyes flit from Zack's face to the money he held. He removed the unlit cigarette from his lips. "Folks see a man who's comfortable in modest surroundings and they figure he's not got much upstairs." He tapped the cigarette against his head. "My upstairs works just fine. Ex-wife used to say I got the memory of an elephant. Told her she had the ass of one, so didn't we make a good pair." He pulled a lighter from his pocket, cupped and lit the cigarette, regarding Zack with narrowed eyes.

Zack leaned in to hold the bills within tempting reach. "This time, I'm not paying you to remember. I'm paying you to forget."

One thick eyebrow rose as a smirk built in deep lines around Driscoll's mouth and he snatched the bills.

Zack backed away and leveled a stern glare on the grinning man before him. "You were mistaken. You never heard or saw anything. We never talked."

A raspy gurgle slipped between Driscoll's weathered lips as he tucked the money into the same worn pocket where he'd stashed the first payoff.

"I hear you say otherwise, I'll be back." Zack let the implied threat hang a moment and tromped down the steps.

"Won't hear nothing from me," Driscoll called out with a laugh. "I got nothing to say."

Zack yanked open the car door and climbed inside.

***

He needed to sort his thoughts after leaving Driscoll, so he swung the car through the streets of town. He noted the closed sign hanging crookedly in the Bluebell's front window. Only Annie's truck was parked in the graveled lot. Leroy's was nowhere to be seen. Zack's grip tightened on the steering wheel as he resisted the urge to hurry to her.

Not now. He had to see this thing through.

Troy Isley's vehicle was parked in front of the Woodsman Tavern. Confronting Troy in the tavern, or even in the parking lot, would not do. Too many potential witnesses. But, it might be hours before Troy returned home.

Zack didn't care. He'd wait.

Which is what he'd been doing for more than an hour, pulled off the road near the ranch. He'd switched off his phone and allowed thoughts of Annie to drift across his awareness.

He did not rethink his plan.

Maybe there were alternatives, but he could not imagine them. Protecting Annie and Sarah was his prime objective. He could not trust their safety to chance. Mangy dogs may slink away, tail between their legs, but they'll turn and attack when your guard is down, unless you pen them tight. If Troy was the third kidnapper and met Riordan by the creek, Zack needed leverage to force his never-ending silence.

Although protecting Annie and Sarah was paramount, he finally admitted to himself that after the embarrassment of the botched ransom drop, his partner getting shot, and three years of fruitless investigation, he had a second motive for confronting Troy. He wanted to learn the truth.

Headlights approached. Zack fingered the gun on the seat beside him and waited for a white truck to speed past, heard brakes squeal as Troy turned into the ranch too quickly, probably spooked by Zack's car outlined in his headlights.

The Ford Fiesta roared to life and Zack sped to the ranch road, cranked the wheel for a sharp turn, gunned the engine and roared beneath the timbered crosspiece. Stop, you bastard, he thought. He needed to confront Troy here, not up by the house. No witnesses.

He slapped a palm against the steering wheel in triumph as twin red lights blinked before him. He watched the truck spin and angle to block the road. He roared up and caught Troy full on in his headlights, the man's left arm raised to block the brightness as he climbed out of his truck.

Perfect.

Zack threw the car into neutral and leapt out, the gun clasped in his right hand.

"Get your ass off my property," Troy managed to yell before realizing Zack's charge. He tried to sidestep but Zack lowered a shoulder and caught him full in the chest, drove him into the side panel of the truck. Troy doubled over, gasping for air, vainly struggling as Zack spun him, clenched a strong arm around his neck and held the gun barrel against his temple.

"Familiar?" Zack asked. "Cold metal. Could only be one thing, huh?"

Troy's muscles tensed and he twisted his neck to try and see the gun.

"Oh, it's what you think it is. No other feeling like a gun at your head, is there?" Zack sniffed the sourness of beer on the man's breath. Troy did not appear drunk, but the alcohol would slow his reactions, an advantage Zack intended to fully exploit. He jerked back on his captive's throat, the man grunting and clawing at the arm holding him immobile. "Don't think I won't use it." He shoved Troy again and stepped back, lowered the gun to aim dead center at Troy's chest.

Troy rubbed his neck and squinted against the lights trained on him.

Zack was on full alert, standing where he'd appear a black silhouette in a glaring halo.

"Get off my fucking property."

Zack waved the gun. "We've got business."

"I got no business with you."

"Not true. You've been in my face ever since I got to this town. I'm returning the favor."

Troy leaned against the truck and crouched as his eyes narrowed.

"Uh-uh," Zack warned. "Don't even think about rushing me. Don't take that chance. You know I can whip you even without the gun. But, you see, that's the thing. I'm the one with the gun."

Troy slunk back and scowled. "You want to do business? Put the gun away."

"No can do. Feel better holding it." He waved the Beretta. "Nice piece, wouldn't you say? Yes, you would, since it's your gun."

Muscles twitched as fear filtered through Troy's scowl.

"No use denying it. Serial numbers lead right to you." A bluff. He'd not checked the serial numbers, couldn't check them without bringing attention to the weapon and endangering Sarah and Annie. When Troy didn't deny the charge, Zack released the breath he'd been holding. "Not good when your gun's a murder weapon."

"I didn't kill nobody."

"Your gun did. Blasted a hole right through Ed Riordan."

"Wasn't me!"

"You and I know that, but how would you convince the police? Tell them the gun did the deed all by itself? That'll never work. No, if

Chief Norton comes by this gun, you're on your way to prison." Zack took two steps to his right, Troy's wary eyes following every movement. "So, now, you're asking yourself, where'd he get my gun? Not that hard to figure, is it, Troy?"

Comprehension spread like a wildfire across the man's pale face. "You!"

"That's right. Me."

"You killed Riordan."

A shrug and two steps back to the left.

"I'll turn you in. You'll be the one locked up."

"I don't think so. Why would anyone take your word over mine? After all, it's your gun. Maybe one day there'll be an anonymous tip to the police to search your truck and what will they find? Your gun. The murder weapon. All the evidence will point to you, especially after Norton has motive, too, when he finds out about the kidnapping."

Troy squinted hard as if wracking his memory. "Who the hell are you?"

"You shot a cop. Not something we forget." Zack watched as Troy understood and leaned heavily against the truck panel.

Troy seemed to weigh his options, finally turned his head from Zack and mumbled, "What do you want?"

Zack sighed inwardly in relief, confident he'd seen the confirmation he'd sought. He'd been banking on his quarry believing he was caught with more than circumstantial evidence tying him to the kidnapping and murder. "Answers, to start with."

"I got nothing to say to you."

"It's either me or the police. Your choice." Zack waited a moment before pressing his advantage. "And, then, there's the gun."

Troy shuffled his feet and banged a fist against the truck. "Okay, okay."

Zack reminded himself to keep up his guard. "Whose idea was the kidnapping?"

"Riordan. At least, that's what I thought at first."

"What do you mean?"

"Seemed too good to be true. Should've figured it was. No one will get hurt, he said, because it's all for show."

Zack frowned and tightened his grip on the gun as Troy again slammed his fist against the truck. "All for show?"

He wrinkled his nose as if against a stench. "Such a bigshot Riordan pretended to be. Should've seen through him right away. No way he'd come up with a plan so good."

"Who did?"

"You don't get it, do you?"

Zack cocked the trigger and widened his stance, causing Troy to jerk backwards and hold a hand in front of his face. "Enlighten me."

"It was the woman, for crap's sake. Her idea. Some harebrained scheme to get money from her husband. He'd cut her off or something. Guess she knew Ed before she got lucky with the rich guy. She come running with this whole plan for a fake kidnapping, how her husband would pay the ransom to keep the cops from digging into his life."

So much was explained: the wife stonewalling them, the fits and faints and doctor's interference, her frightened eyes when confronted in the department store, worried Zack had figured out her game. And, as they'd suspected, the husband had stopped their investigation to cover other illegalities. "So, Riordan recruited you and O'Connor."

Troy stared a moment, then shook his head. "Me."

"You brought O'Connor in?"

"Just to drive. He didn't know what the fuck we were doing until everything went to hell." He paused a moment before asking, "You one of the cops?"

"You shot my partner."

"Wasn't supposed to happen."

"But, it did."

Troy drew in a long breath. "Yeah."

Silence hung before Zack continued. "You split the ransom money. You and O'Connor returned to Hope."

"Mark didn't take it so well. I kept telling him, what's done is done. Just enjoy the fucking money and get on with whatever the hell you're doing. Bugged the hell out of me, always coming around wanting to talk things through. Ain't nothing to talk through, I told him. Keep your head low and your mouth shut. Bastard couldn't take it, I guess. Smashed himself to hell in a car wreck." He heaved a long sigh. "I don't care what the fuck you think of me, but I was truly sorry about that. Never should've involved him. If I'd known what was coming down, I'd have stayed away myself. Believe what you want, but I'm telling you I'd never done nothing illegal like that before."

"Why'd you get involved?"

"Money." He practically spat the word. "Money for my fucking father and this stupid ranch."

"You bailed him out."

"Damn right I did. You think he gave a shit? Never said a word." His anger had now traveled from Zack to Riordan to Ray Isley. "Big man. Big nothing man."

Zack let him stew before pressing on with the story. "You must have thought the whole thing was behind you. Until Riordan showed up."

"He was a fucking weasel. Like I was going to give up my share after the way he suckered me in the first place. No way."

"You gave him a few thousand." Another guess fired off to keep him talking.

"Not enough, the bastard said. I want your whole share or I go running to your old man."

"So, you convinced him to meet in the canyon."

He leaned his head against the truck as his features hardened and he glowered at Zack. "You must've been there and got the gun from him."

Zack shrugged again. "This gun gets around."

"You're the murderer."

"Like I said, your word against mine." Zack had learned what he needed to know. Time to end the encounter before something happened he couldn't control. "Which brings me to what happens next." He watched as curiosity and apprehension lifted Troy's eyebrows. "Nothing."

"Huh?"

"You keep your mouth shut and so will I." He waited as Troy turned possibilities in his mind. "I get one hint that you've opened your big mouth and I'll be back. Two perps are dead already. I can make it a clean sweep."

"You're bluffing. Why not kill me right now?"

"Nah, gives me great pleasure to know you'll always be looking over your shoulder for me."

Troy feigned bravado but Zack saw relief comingled with fear. "Why should I trust you?"

"You've got no choice."

He clasped his arms around his chest and stared at the ground before kicking at dirt. "Deal."

Zack kept the gun trained as he backed to the car. "If you slip up, I'll know. Our deal will be dead. Just like you." He carefully lowered himself into the car, threw the gears in reverse and backed at top speed for twenty yards before spewing gravel as he turned and sped away.

*****

If he gripped the steering wheel hard, it kept his hands from shaking. A guilty panic surged with the rapid thump of his heartbeat.

He'd hurled himself into the murky abyss somewhere beyond the law. No smattering of silvery hue could paint over his actions with an acceptable shade of grey. This was black and white.

He'd broken the law.

He'd do it again, if he had to. For Annie.

There was risk, of course. Troy Isley was a cocky, self-deceived, small-time bastard who might shore his nerve, wait for Zack to disappear, then creep out of his hole. If he had the nerve, he might try and find a way to reverse the blackmail. Hopefully, not. Zack was counting on fear to keep the man at bay; if necessary, that fear could be reinforced.

As his trembling subsided, shame was overtaken by resolution and determination, and a smattering of regret. Like Leroy, he'd simply done what had to be done. But, he regretted that he'd found his actions necessary in the first place. He was glad his father would never know.

There was no going back. Not to what had been before.

He could live with that.

He parked by his cabin and walked in long, anxious strides to Annie's house. He banged on the door and called her name, listened intently but heard only Buffy's meow. He slowly backed away.

Where could she be? He peered through the dark. Yes, her truck was parked by the side of the house. Leroy's truck was still missing. Probably at the tavern, vainly trying to overcome his own regrets. Zack thought maybe he should go find him, make sure he got safely home.

First, he wanted to see Annie, wanted reassurance that he hadn't lost her before they'd had a chance to begin.

Light shone through a front window in the cabin Leroy and Sarah shared. Zack approached the cabin slowly, unsure of the reception he'd get and not wanting to frighten Sarah. The front door was cracked open. A tingle of apprehension crept up his spine as he pushed the door wide.

A lamp on a pine end table lit the sparse living room, illuminating the hooked rug below a magazine-strewn coffee table, two flowery upholstered high-back chairs and a green couch.

She was slumped on the couch.

"Annie?"

She pushed herself to seated, sad blue eyes meeting his as she whispered, "They're gone."

CHAPTER 20

She'd been sure her life was under control. Predictable. Constant. A routine of work and occasional amusement. Unattached. Invulnerable.

Empty.

She'd been so worried about being hurt again that she'd shoved away all possibility for happiness, thinking sheltered meant serene, obstruction guaranteed peace.

Zack had penetrated her defenses and she was no longer content to hide.

He eased onto the couch beside her and whispered assurances that he would find Sarah and Leroy.

"No," she said. "Leroy's right to go. It's not safe here."

"I'm not going to tell anyone, Annie. You know that, don't you?"

She entwined her fingers with his. "Yes, I know. But, if you learned what happened, so might someone else."

He slouched and squeezed her hand. "No one's going to bother you or Sarah. I've taken care of it."

She bit her lip and ran a thumb along his palm. "I don't want you in trouble, too. You don't owe me that."

"You're wrong. I owe you everything."

Yes. She understood. What didn't you owe someone you loved so immediately and intensely? And, who loved you in return? Still, she was worried. "What have you done?"

He shook his head.

She withdrew her fingers and toyed with a loose thread in the upholstery. "No secrets, Zack."

He studied the ceiling a long moment before directing his eyes full into hers. "I'm not a journalist. I'm a cop."

***

They talked until hunger beckoned them to her kitchen, talked through preparation and cleanup, until desire overwhelmed the need for words and they tumbled into her bed. She did not sleep after their lovemaking, content to stare through filtered moonlight at Zack's lips moving with a dream, to study his square jaw and the small mole behind his ear. Her mind and heart were too full for sleep.

The most extraordinary revelation was Mark's involvement in the kidnapping. Zack insisted her husband had been an unknowing accomplice, but she understood how that hadn't helped Mark live with what he'd done. No wonder he'd been so distant after his return from San Francisco. She supposed not seeking her comfort had been a symptom of their fragile marriage. Maybe she'd been unavailable, physically and emotionally. She'd been preoccupied with running the business and fighting off her own despair. Now, she wished she'd done more to help Mark.

The money was another matter. She felt no guilt about using the money to pay off the mortgage. Yes, it was ill-gotten, just as she'd worried. But, the people who involved her bruised, innocent husband in their dirty scheme? They owed her. They might as well have been in the car with Mark, crammed the gas pedal to the floor and spun the wheel toward the tree.

Zack muttered in his sleep, eyelids flitting open, smiling as he found her awake.

"So many secrets," she whispered.

"Not anymore," he replied and ran a hand along her hip.

"Still a few."

"Yes?"

"You never said what you did with the gun."

"You don't need to know."

"Then, it remains a secret."

"Perhaps some secrets are necessary. Can you live with that?"

She did not answer, only rolled on top of him and pressed her lips to his.

CHAPTER 21

Penny Chester tossed a distracted wave as Zack smiled and hurried past to knock on the doorframe to Norton's office.

"Yep." Norton raised a hand and kept his eyes trained on the computer screen. Knobby fingers attacked the keyboard, a final thrust signaling the conclusion to a distasteful task. "Damned paperwork."

Zack chuckled and lowered himself into the side chair. "Eleanor again?"

"Pesky and demanding as always."

"That's her job."

Norton twirled his reading glasses between two fingers. "One hell of a job description, you ask me." He placed the glasses atop a ragged stack of papers and regarded Zack with a penetrating stare. "You got something to tell me?"

The question startled Zack. Had Troy Isley confessed all, including Zack's threats and harassment? Was Chief Norton even craftier than he appeared, somehow witnessing the scene at the Rockin' I Ranch and now believing Zack to be the murderer? Had he put two and two together to implicate Annie?

No. Zack searched the man's steely glare and concluded Norton was simply probing with his typical gruffness.

"Nothing," Zack finally replied, "and, that's the point. I've got nothing."

"No?"

"Never had much to go on and nothing's panned out."

"What about Driscoll?"

"A misunderstanding."

Norton's eyes narrowed as he leaned back in his chair. "That so?"

"Kills me to say this, but I've got nowhere to go with the case."

"Giving up, huh?"

"Just being realistic."

"Well, now, what a shame. You were so certain solving Riordan's murder would lead you to the kidnappers."

"Doesn't mean I'm wrong, but I can't prove I'm right."

Norton swiveled the chair and tented his hands.

Zack rose and tried to unclench abdominal muscles tight with guilt and fear. He hooked a thumb in a front pocket of his jeans and adopted what he hoped was an expression of professional detachment. "I'll be happy to write the report, sir. Case closed, murderer unknown."

"There you go with that 'sir' stuff again." The chief snatched a paperclip from his desk and bent it out of shape, as he had the day Zack arrived in Hope. He stared at the mangled clip before turning a questioning look to Zack. "You leaving town?"

"I thought I'd stick around a day or two. Do some fishing."

"For trout or clues?"

Zack smiled wryly. "No more clues to find, Chief."

"So you've said." He tossed the paperclip aside and leaned his elbows on the desk. "Although I complain about paperwork, it is part of my job. Much obliged for the offer to write the report, but I will handle the matter."

"Sorry I couldn't bring better results."

Norton shrugged. "Clues are there to find or they're not."

"Are you going to turn the case over to the state police?"

"If the district attorney insists. I'll follow procedure, but I doubt they'll spend much time on it. Got a spate of bank robberies and drug-related murders and who knows what else clogging their caseloads, and the legislature's threatening budget cuts. They won't much care about a two-bit criminal murdered out here in the boonies."

Zack stepped forward to reach across the desk. "Was a pleasure working with you, Chief. Thanks for letting me in." They shook hands and Zack moved toward the door, paused and again faced Norton. "How's Mrs. Norton?"

The chief ran a hand along his neck. "Stable. For now. One hell of a woman. Told her the other day I'd trade places with her, if I could. I wouldn't want you to, she said. Guess that's how love is. You'd do almost anything for each other." He fixed sharp blue eyes on Zack. "Yep, almost anything." Norton pushed back in the chair and scooted to the computer. "Perhaps you know about that."

***

He must be a horrible liar. His early morning phone call with Lonnie had gone much the same as the conversation with Norton. Both men sensed something was up. Both let him off the hook.

"What're you saying, Zack?" Lonnie had groused when told the investigation was at a dead end. "You quitting?"

"Nowhere to go. No witnesses, no clues."

"That only means you haven't looked in the right place. Keep looking."

"There's no place else to look, Lonnie."

A long static-filled moment before Lonnie asked, "What about the wife?"

Zack had anticipated the question and predetermined his reply. "She has an air-tight alibi for the kidnapping and the murder."

"You checked."

"Of course, I checked."

Lonnie grunted. "Guess that's it, huh? Three years of work up in smoke?"

"Guess so."

"Let sleeping dogs lie with the fleas, huh?"

"Time to move on."

"Yeah. Move on." A clattering as Lonnie cursed and muttered. "Damned slippery phones."

Zack clutched his own phone tightly.

"All right, then. When you coming back, partner?"

"We're not partners anymore, Lonnie."

"We could fix that."

"I don't think so."

"You're getting out."

"Maybe."

"Figured." The sound of chewing and a swallow came through the phone line. "Best damned bagels money can buy, right here in my neighborhood."

"So you've always said."

"Well, I'm right, aren't I?"

"You usually are, Lonnie."

"Damned square. Well, never did figure you for a lifer. Took you long enough to recognize it yourself. Guess you were waiting for the right incentive."

Perhaps Lonnie hadn't pieced the entire story together, but his gut must be rumbling with theories and suspicions nibbling around the truth.

"I'll see you in a few days," Zack said.

"Hell, yes. You've got my damn car."

***

Lonnie was right—Zack wasn't a career cop. He didn't live and breathe police work the way lifers did, the way Lonnie did. As he thought about the past three years, and the most recent year in particular, he recognized how dissatisfaction had slithered beneath his careful disguise of professionalism; how the criminals seemed more inept and pathetic, the cases mundane. No excitement or challenge. For some time, he just hadn't cared.

He cared now. For Annie. He had no idea what direction he'd head after leaving the force, but he knew he wouldn't be going alone.

He'd probably never be comfortable with what he'd done. Covering up a crime was a far cry from simply bending rules. Maybe he'd forever be looking over his shoulder. Maybe a shiver of guilt would worm up his spine every time he saw someone resembling Ed Riordan or Troy Isley. So be it. He'd do it all again in a heartbeat to protect Annie.

Zack set his jaw. He was headed to the Bluebell. With any luck, the café would be empty. He'd flip the closed sign, turn off the lights, kidnap Annie and escape to Ulster McGovern's hidden spring, spend the afternoon in a cozy, fragrant cocoon with nothing more important than being together.

He was yanking impatiently on the Ford's door handle when his cell phone rang.

CHAPTER 22

I've told you before, don't kid a kidder," Kitty said as she forked a bite of pie.

Annie watched flaky crust and spiced apples disappear and lifted her hands in innocence. "I don't know what you're talking about."

"Hell you don't." Kitty scooped another bite. "You're fooling nobody, darling, least of all me. A woman in love always has the same glassy eyes and rosy cheeks you got."

"So, you're a love expert, are you?"

Kitty's expression registered genuine surprise. "I thought you knew that."

Annie stifled a giggle. Oh, what the heck. Why hide? She'd become too cynical, too fearful. Why not throw a little caution to the proverbial winds? A broad smile spread as she winked.

"There!" Kitty pointed the fork.

"And, so what, huh?"

Kitty examined the plate for remaining crumbs, shoved it aside when convinced she'd eaten every morsel. "So, nothing. I just like being right." She hefted from the stool and dabbed her lips with a paper napkin. "Truly, darling, I couldn't be happier for you. It's about time." She gathered a giant purse matching her lime-green kaftan. "I'd better get to the Roadside. Ten to one the dimwits got the lettuce on the stove and the chicken in the dishwasher."

Annie laughed and waved as Kitty walked to the café door, her kaftan like bright jungle foliage in a hurricane.

"Speaking of help," Kitty said as she reached for the doorknob, "where's Sarah? She usually comes out to say hello."

Annie hid her face as she cleared Kitty's empty plate. "Leroy got a call from a relative in Colorado. Offered him a job. Sarah went with him." It was the lie she and Zack had concocted the previous night.

"Too bad. I'll miss her."

"Me, too," Annie whispered as Kitty blew a kiss and waddled out the door.

Annie carried a tray of dirty dishes to the kitchen and set them in the sink. The day had felt so strange without Sarah. Yes, she would miss her young friend's lopsided smile and innocent chatter.

The outside door to the kitchen creaked open and she spun in expectation. Perhaps Leroy had learned Zack wasn't going to tell the police. Perhaps he and Sarah had decided to take their chances in Hope.

But, it wasn't Sarah's merry brown eyes meeting hers.

It was Zack's green ones.

Her heart jumped as she rinsed soap from her hands and reached for a towel.

Too many years alone.

Too many years lonely.

Now, she had Zack, with more than enough love to fill the hole Sarah left behind.

She turned to him, but stopped short, the pin-striped towel drooping from her fingers.

Not bad news, she thought. Not now. Not again.

She registered his slumped shoulders and downturned mouth, dropped the towel on the counter and drew herself up tall. "Tell me."

"It's Stella."

"Oh." It was all she could manage. Perhaps because she'd just been thinking of her, she'd anticipated bad news about Sarah. Injured in a car wreck. Captured by the police. Not for the briefest second had Zack's wife crossed her mind, which only proved how blissfully self-absorbed she'd become.

"Her doctor called. She's in the hospital." He shook his head and walked across the room to lean against the preparation table. "She swallowed half a bottle of sleeping pills."

So naively head-over-heels. So blind.

"Annie?"

"You must go to her." She retrieved the towel with trembling hands. She should have remained alert. Too late, the walls were breached and she was lost to a dream, only to tumble down now, fingers clawing puffs of nothingness.

"Yes." He inched her way.

She stepped out of reach, eyes averted, afraid to recognize a forever goodbye.

"She doesn't have anybody else."

"No. Of course."

"I have to make sure she gets help. I owe her that much. But I'm coming back, Annie. You believe me, don't you?"

He'd asked her a similar question the day before, about believing that he wouldn't turn Sarah in to the police. Yes, she had believed him. She'd felt safe and comforted in trusting him. She wanted so much to trust him now, too.

Zack crossed the vinyl floor and gently spun her around to face him. "I love you, Annie."

Maybe she'd always worry. Maybe she'd always be vulnerable.

She needed to take the chance.

"Yes," she whispered. "I know."

EPILOGUE

Dang-blasted hot," Art Bucknell griped as he removed his baseball cap.

"Always hot in August," Pete Morgan said.

"Not like this. Setting a record, believe me." Art leaned back in his chair as Annie approached. "Coffee's the best drink on hot days, you know. Cools you right down."

"So you've told me." Annie set mugs on the table, filled them to the brim, gave the two regulars a quick smile and hurried away, doing her best to tune out their chatter.

She supposed she should be grateful for their company, despite the repetitive dissecting of mundane topics. At least voices filled the silence that taunted her in the Bluebell these days.

Business always slowed in late summer; folks away on vacation or just not having much of an appetite for baked goods. The café barely broke even. Still, she was usually grateful for the slowdown and a little time to herself.

All to herself.

She'd not heard from Leroy or Sarah. Probably for the best, although she couldn't help but worry about them. Hard to imagine Leroy staying off the bottle. No, more likely, Sarah would have to take care of him. She'd be okay. In some ways, she was stronger than the rest of them.

Annie idled by the cash register and kept an eye on Art and Pete's coffee mugs.

Zack had not returned to Hope, but he called every night. She'd sit in the porch swing, one hand wrapped around a dewy glass of iced tea, the other cradling her cell phone, the brush of a warm breeze across her cheeks.

How she wished for Zack's touch instead.

They never lacked for conversation. Funny stories from the past, tidbits about their days. Sometimes, she had to hurry inside and switch to her landline, having run the battery dry on the cell phone.

They'd tell each other goodnight, I love you, and she'd replay those words all through the next day.

He hadn't called in two nights.

She tried not to worry. Of course, she could call him, but she knew he'd reached a particularly difficult juncture with Stella. Perhaps he needed time to sort things out.

Soon we'll be together, he kept saying.

She was growing fidgety and tired of waiting.

The bell above the café door jingled. Art and Pete broke their tirade against all things governmental as a brown-clad deliveryman hustled in.

"Annie O'Connor?"

"That's me." Her brows knit as she tried to recall ordering something for delivery.

"Got a package for you. Sign here." He waited as she penned her name on the receipt. He placed the envelope on the counter, tipped his cap and turned on his heel.

"Thank you," she said. "Can I get you anything? Pie? A soda? On the house."

He twisted around with a smile. "No, thanks, ma'am. I'm behind on my route. Trying to make it home for my kid's birthday party. Maybe next time."

The bell jingled again as the door closed behind him.

"On the house, huh?" Art harrumphed. "Shows how we rate, don't it?"

Annie stared at the return address on the envelope.

Pete waved a hand at Art. "Like she don't pour more coffee in your cup than you'd pay for in two lifetimes."

"Well, it weren't coffee what caught my attention. It was the pie."

"Here," Annie said and pulled a berry pie from the cooler and carried it to their table. She set down plates and forks and a server. "Please, help yourself."

"Oh, now, you know I was joshing, Annie."

"Please, both of you, have some pie." She clutched the envelope to her chest and hurried to the kitchen, ignoring Pete's hollered inquiry as to what she'd got. She held the envelope at arm's length, as if the paper might strangle her, and closed her eyes until she calmed her breathing.

When she opened her eyes, she focused on Zack's name in the upper left corner. He hadn't mentioned sending anything and she couldn't imagine what it was. Oh, please don't let this be bad, she whispered as she pulled a tab to open the envelope.

A white paper slid to the counter, scribbled writing upside down. She slowly rotated the paper and frowned in confusion.

"Please say yes," the words read.

She placed the remaining papers on the counter.

A glossy brochure with photographs of white-painted buildings, red tile roofs, lush green hills in the background.

A rental confirmation for a villa near Florence.

And a plane ticket to Rome.

ABOUT THE AUTHOR

Martha Sargent retired after an enjoyable career as a professor of accounting and entrepreneurship and is now pursuing her passions for writing, travel and the great outdoors. She and her husband, Dennis, own a training business and split their time between Central Oregon and Arizona. Her first novel, *Smokin' Joe*, is available in print and as an e-book.